Advance Praise for
Four Seasons at Angelino's

"Caroline McBride takes a fun-loving satiric bite out of New York's hyper charged restaurant world filled with over the top characters that those in the know may even recognize. It's both sharp and sweet, like any good meal!"

—Jennifer Gould Keil, *New York Post* Columnist

"An engaging, fast-paced journey with unexpected twists that will warm the hearts of hopeful romantics."

—Rebecca Bienstock, Penske Media

"Just like its heroine, this delightful read is timeless yet modern. You'll feel like you're listening to your most intriguing friend as her romantic tale unfolds."

—Celia Shatzman, Journalist

FOUR SEASONS AT ANGELINO'S

a year to find the one

CAROLINE McBRIDE

Post Hill
PRESS

A POST HILL PRESS BOOK
ISBN: 978-1-64293-563-9
ISBN (eBook): 978-1-64293-564-6

Post Hill Press
New York • Nashville
posthillpress.com

Published in the United States of America

Dedicated to Paul Allen
Thank you for accepting my quirkiness and
encouraging me to write this lighthearted tale of love.
Until our next milkshake, in Heaven...

Part 1

SPRING

Chapter 1

NEW YORK CITY

"You shouldn't have such high expectations in life. You're just setting yourself up for disappointment." Jorge's cruel words stung Charlotte McPherson. Moments earlier, she'd wrapped her leg around him, pulling him closer to savor their steamy romp, indifferent to the normally disconcerting spring hail pelting their hotel window. She'd blissfully purred into his ear the suggestion to visit his house in Atlanta.

Jorge sighed. "*Guapa*, you know that's impossible. My wife's there."

A wave of panic hit Charlotte. "We didn't talk much about her...but you're separated, right?"

"No. I'd never do that to my kids."

"So...you're not getting divorced?" Charlotte's body trembled.

"Don't pretend like you didn't know," he said with irritation.

Charlotte bolted up and glared at him. Her world crashed upon her as she stuttered, "But...I mean...I'm so confused."

"You're being dramatic, Char," Jorge said. "Don't make it a big deal. My wife's busy with the kids and we have a 'Don't Ask, Don't Tell' policy, so it's not like I'm doing anything wrong."

Charlotte struggled to catch her breath. "Oh really? Does she date other people? And what the hell is going on between us?"

"No, she doesn't. And we're just having fun." Jorge spoke with eerie calmness while nonchalantly adjusting his pillow. "Look, if I could be with you, I would. But that's not the situation."

Charlotte sat motionless, completely bewildered. Although they'd only dated for three months, Jorge led her on with hints of marriage: He'd repeatedly said their initials would be the same once they wed and she'd make the perfect wife. Their long-distance relationship between NYC and Atlanta was feasible due to his hedge fund job that brought him to the city often; he'd even whisked her away for a weeklong vacation in London. Suddenly, the infidelity signs became clear: He never called after work unless it was poker night, and his trip to Europe was the perfect opportunity to cheat while he was "traveling on business" away from his family. It all made sense.

"Don't stare at me like I killed your puppy. You're overreacting." Jorge rolled over, putting his back toward her as he shifted into his final sleep position before murmuring once more that she shouldn't have such high expectations...

In shock, she watched him as rage pulsated through her veins, his smugness too much to bear. She grabbed a pillow and whacked him on the back of his head before darting into the bathroom and frantically turning on the faucets to muffle her cries. Jorge was perfect on paper: Yale undergrad, Wharton MBA, athletic, fluent in a foreign language (his native Spanish), and tall with blue eyes. But married!

Charlotte balanced on the edge of the tub, absorbing the harsh reality. She hadn't been this upset since her sister informed her that their dad was killed. The memory of that horrific day three years earlier rushed back. She'd been running between restaurant locations, late for a meeting, when she answered that heart-wrenching call. Her sister tearfully blurted out the news just as Charlotte was passing Trump Tower: Dad was hit and killed by a drunk driver. Charlotte had leaned against the building for support while the sidewalk swayed back and forth.

Jorge reignited that agony in her fragile heart. Sadness gave way to rage and her redheaded feistiness took over as she threw everything within reach, cursing the evil bastard. Her head spun as she hurled towels, shampoo, soap, and a toothbrush against the wall.

When her anger finally succumbed to hurt, she slumped down in defeat. Her mind roamed as she stared into space for nearly an hour. Jorge was a ruthless liar, but she loved him and wanted to be next to him. Rather than run away to her empty studio apartment, she wiped her tears and quietly slipped back into bed next to the peacefully snoozing pompous jerk.

* * *

"You still spent the night with him?" Sofia was in disbelief. The curvy, olive-skinned brunette arrived late and heard the news about Jorge as she sat down at the nail station.

"Seriously, Char. He's another married loser. Complete waste of time." Tracy Zheng was direct as usual during their Sunday afternoon ritual at her trendy ViewPoint Nails salon on Madison Avenue. Tracy owned three additional outposts in the city, all located on top floors with incredible views of Manhattan, each offering a sleek lounge area to enjoy fresh juices and teas. Charlotte often brought brunch from a nearby Angelino's, the iconic Italian restaurant chain that employed her as public relations director.

"I really love him." Charlotte knew she sounded pathetic. "But when he said I 'shouldn't have such high expectations in life,' it felt like he stabbed me in the heart."

"Oh Char, he's such an asshole. I'm so sorry." Sofia hugged her tight and stroked her hair. As the general manager of Angelino's busiest location in Midtown, Sofia Longo dealt with different personality types and resolved customer complaints daily. If the pasta wasn't *al dente*, a busser refused to work overtime, or health inspectors dropped in for a surprise evaluation, she always provided a solution. Inherently eager to help, she was a lifeline when Charlotte first landed the job at Angelino's, especially when dealing with the temperamental Italian owners.

"Oh, please! Charlotte. Stop. You barely know Jorge. Wipe your tears! You always fall so fast and get obsessed with random guys. What happened with that hottie from Morgan Stanley you met at Catch?" Tracy asked. She was always onto the next best thing and quick to seductively slip her slender frame out of her designer clothes and into bed with different men. Lawyers, delivery guys, businessmen, wannabe entertainers—she wasn't picky, as one-night stands were customary for the thirsty vixen. Charlotte considered her sexual prowess more masculine than feminine. Tracy worked hard managing her popular nail salon empire, and she played equally hard in the dating field. She relished late-night partying and seducing young men before coldly disposing the wide-eyed out-of-towners, giving them a harsh dose of NYC reality: A pretty face is easy to replace.

"But Tracy, I love him and I'm sure you'll think this is stupid, but I thought we'd get married. Jorge even said he'd want me to take his last name *when* we get married. It seemed like a good sign!

I even planned how I'd incorporate his Mexican culture into our big California wedding." Charlotte broke down in sobs.

"Yes, that is stupid, and I don't have time to talk about a married guy when there are so many better options." Tracy carefully reached for her Birkin with her freshly manicured hand. "You guys can stay as long as you want. My new boy toy is waiting for me in the East Village. He's auditioning for Cirque du Soleil, and last night, he twisted me into positions I didn't even know existed. It's time to give my stomach muscles another workout." She breezily fled the scene of tears to rush downtown for another X-rated sexapade.

"That was so rude. I wish she'd understand my feelings." Charlotte knew deep down that Tracy cared for her and was simply exercising tough love as she often did during their ten-year friendship. "Maybe she has a point about falling too fast for Jorge, but a little compassion would be appreciated."

"Don't worry about Tracy, she has good intentions. Please forget about Jorge. Char, he's a really bad person. His poor wife. You don't want to be with a cheater. You're going to meet someone so much better, I promise!" Sofia reassured her.

"Thanks." Charlotte blew her nose. "I have to compose myself before a media dinner at Angelino's SoHo with a new *Eater* journalist. I'm not in the mood."

After a final hug, Charlotte was back in the commotion of the city—sirens, crowded streets, and nowhere to hide. She received a text. *Guapa, just landed in Atlanta. Are you ok? You seemed upset. Let me know. I've been meaning to tell you that it's better to email instead of texting. Besos. J*

Jorge's request to correspond via email infuriated Charlotte. He obviously wanted to prevent his wife from seeing her texts, as if she was a sneaky mistress. The thought made her sick! With red hair and green eyes, Charlotte stood out in a crowd, often utilizing the argumentative skills bestowed upon her by her trial lawyer father to advocate for those treated unjustly. Arrogant people who cut in line or swiped subway seats designated for the handicapped particularly incited her, and she publicly humiliated those on the receiving end of her wrath. She was no shrinking violet, and she certainly had no intention of enabling Jorge to betray his wife.

For the hundredth time that day, hurt gave way to anger. Charlotte threw her phone into her bag and stomped to the nearest Angelino's. Instead of wasting another precious second on Jorge, she'd have a drink and compose herself before dinner.

As soon as she entered Angelino's Park Avenue, chatty hostesses stopped midsentence and anxiously turned their attention toward her, sprinkling amicable greetings with compliments about her appearance. Reigning as the public relations director for one of the hottest global restaurant chains definitely had perks. Always welcomed with open arms in seven Manhattan locations and sixteen additional establishments throughout the world, she'd started the job after grad school when she was twenty-five years old. With three successful Angelino's at the time, the co-founders, Marco Giovannetti and Chef Lorenzo DeSantis, ran with an influential crowd. Their restaurants were packed with international jetsetters, celebrities, politicians, socialites, and trendy locals. The high-end clientele enabled Charlotte, a novice PR girl, to procure press exposure in tabloids and celebrity-focused media outlets. New Yorkers and visitors alike wanted to dine where their favorite reality stars, athletes, actors, and even the mayor regularly ate.

Ten years later, as Angelino's opened locations around the world, Charlotte was required to oversee every pasta ribbon cutting ceremony, scout new sites, review investor proposals, and liaison with international franchise teams for brand awareness and quality control. Although such business development duties didn't typically fall under the "public relations" umbrella, and her repeated requests to discuss a raise went unanswered, Charlotte had to admit that she liked her job.

The friendly hostess escorting her to the bar was a nice bonus. Most of the restaurant staff went out of their way to be pleasant to Charlotte, looking for insider information about the bosses and believing she could offer solutions to their grievances. After all, she spent a significant amount of time with the owners, sitting in on press interviews and joining them on international trips to launch new locations.

Charlotte's head throbbed from crying, but she tried to distract herself by deliberating over the new cocktail list. Angelino's Berry Happy Margarita. *Jorge loves margaritas....* Mamma's Martini. *I had a martini last night with Jorge....*

As tears welled up, Charlotte heard a familiar deep, husky voice. "Hey, Red, why you so upset?"

It was Ray James, the hottest bartender in NYC. She was surprised to see him because he usually worked at the SoHo location.

"What's up with my favorite ginger? You sad or something?"

Ray had a way of making improper English sound cool. Tall, muscular, and oozing sex appeal, his black hair, slightly hazel eyes, and bronzed skin made his ethnicity a mystery. Was he a mix of

African and Caucasian? Or maybe Latino and something else? Whenever anyone asked, he said he'd never met his dad. Nobody knew if James was even his real last name. But the ladies didn't care about such technicalities as they drooled over him. He was notorious for bedding both customers and staff.

Charlotte enjoyed a casual flirtation with Ray but never took him seriously because with his incredibly good looks came bad boy behavior. Allegations of assault (he claimed the other guy spit on his sister), odd tattoos, and the fact that he was a twenty-eight-year-old man whore kept her away. But she appreciated attention from an attractive guy after her traumatic night.

"I'm dealing with a loser, but I'll bounce back. Don't worry, *Ray*." Charlotte teased him by over-enunciating his name. It was a sultry way to catch men off guard and draw them in. Naturally a pro flirter, this time she only half-heartedly batted her eyelashes over bloodshot eyes.

Ray leaned in. "Yeah, bounce over to my place and forget that scrub," he whispered, letting his lips lightly brush her earlobe. A customer watched with curiosity while a tingling sensation ran down her neck. Ray's hotness was irresistible, even during times of distress.

Out of the corner of her eye, Charlotte spotted hostesses gawking, and she instantly snapped back into work mode. "Let's keep it professional. I'll take a glass of red. It's freezing outside, and I want to warm up before I head down to SoHo for dinner." Charlotte turned her attention to her phone to answer emails.

"Yes, ma'am. Your usual Pinot noir?" Ray projected confidence.

"Sure, thanks." Charlotte frantically composed a message, responding to a media request about a famous newscaster who recently brought a mysterious date to Angelino's.

* * *

As Charlotte's Uber pulled away from Angelino's Park Avenue toward downtown, her anxiety deepened when she saw Dr. Radcliff calling. During her routine gynecologist appointment, she had complained about hot flashes. Turning thirty-five a few days earlier meant she was too young for menopause. She wasn't pregnant and had no idea what was going on. The doctor had ordered blood tests to investigate.

"Hello? Dr. Radcliff?" Charlotte wondered if her apprehension was evident in her voice.

"Hi, Charlotte. Sorry to call on a Sunday, but it's the only time I can do follow-ups before my vacation. Would you like to hear your results now?" She sounded dreadfully serious.

"Yes, of course." Charlotte disguised the fear in her voice, appearing poised like a true publicist.

"Well, it's a rather dire situation if you plan on having kids. Is that important to you?" Dr. Radcliff's attempt to soften her voice was obvious.

Charlotte's heart tumbled into her gut. "Yes, of course. What's the problem?"

"You have a condition called premature ovarian failure." Dr. Radcliff fell back into an impersonal tone. "Fortunately, it's different than menopause, which is a good sign that you might still be able to get pregnant."

Charlotte said nothing as she rolled the window down a few inches for some air, restraining the urge to throw up. The doctor continued, but her words were a blur. Something about her ovaries not working, probably needing to do IVF with her partner, the clock quickly running out, and see a fertility specialist as soon as possible.

Taking a deep breath, Charlotte tried her hardest to sound composed. "Thank you for all the information. Is there someone you recommend?" She disguised her anguish so well that she didn't recognize her own voice. Her tone completely hid the suffocating despair.

"Absolutely! Dr. Donovan has an office near mine, and she's fabulous. Get your partner geared up and make a baby! You probably only have one to two years left, and it's unlikely you'll conceive naturally, so go now. You'll be glad!" Dr. Radcliff sure sounded chipper considering the horrible news she delivered.

Charlotte jotted down the number and politely hung up before burying her head in her hands. With her dreams of Jorge fathering her children engulfed in flames, she lacked the partner she needed to build a family.

* * *

At dinner with the *Eater* reporter, Charlotte geared up to tell the infamous "Emergency Landing Story," and when she began the anecdote of Angelino's conception, words flowed effortlessly, complete with intonations and exclamations. She shared the tale so often that it automatically streamed out of her mouth, as if it was pre-recorded and someone pressed "play," allowing her mind to occasionally drift freely during the spiel:

"The co-founders of Angelino's, Marco and Chef Lorenzo, met at a wine tasting about twenty years ago. Both were young, dashing Italian immigrants living the American dream. Lorenzo had recently graduated from culinary school and was looking for a job, while Marco imported wine from his uncle's vineyard in Tuscany and had a side gig as a club promoter to meet girls.

One day, they decided to go to a Depeche Mode concert in Vegas. Marco brought bottles of wine—this was before 9/11, when you could bring liquids on the plane. They passed out from drinking so much by the time they approached Sin City, until the flight attendant jostled them awake to put on their seatbelts. They were completely disoriented when the captain came on the intercom and informed passengers that something was wrong with the landing gear, and they'd circle the airport to burn fuel and figure out the best way to land.

Passengers were crying and praying—it was sheer pandemonium. They thought they were going to die! Can you imagine how scary it was?

Holding hands with each other, Lorenzo said a prayer his nonna taught him. But soon Marco stopped crying and yelled at Lorenzo for organizing the trip in the first place. The chef shouted back and said drinking so much of Marco's overrated wine gave him a headache, and he wished he'd never met him. Arguing ensued for an hour until the captain instructed them to brace themselves for an emergency landing. They quickly forgave each other, making a pact: If they survived, they would show their gratitude to humanity by opening a restaurant in New York to serve the best pizza and pasta in the city. Typical Italians! Always thinking of food!"

Charlotte customarily added laughter at this point, delighting in the listener's reaction. Today she faked it and let the "audio" continue to play:

"Sure enough, the plane slid and spun without landing gear, nearly slamming into a building. When they finally stopped in a nearby field, they careened down an inflatable slide to get off the aircraft. Once safely on the tarmac, they embraced each other. Marco said, 'We made it! Now we're going to open a restaurant with the best pizza and pasta in America!'

And that's exactly what they did! Lorenzo named it Angelino's because he believes that God sent a baby angel to save them from a crash. Look closely at the frescos throughout the restaurants for little hidden angels—in the flowers, the pasta, the sunset. You can spot them camouflaged throughout the art.

So, when they opened their first location on Fifth Avenue, it was packed with Marco's club friends—entertainers, models, party people. His crowd put them on the map. Angelino's also has very high-quality Italian cuisine, thanks to Chef Lorenzo, and a fun, casual atmosphere. It's a recipe for success! And we've expanded to twenty-three locations around the world. Angelino's is everywhere and growing!"

Charlotte paused and took a bite of her asparagus risotto, relieved that she finished the speech. "Would you like another glass of wine?" she asked.

The reporter laughed and said, "I was so captivated that I didn't realize I finished my drink." People's interest in the story of how Lorenzo and Marco's near-death experience inspired the creation of Angelino's always amused Charlotte.

When the *Eater* woman finally left, carrying an Angelino's bag filled with jars of gourmet pasta sauce and a bottle of wine, Charlotte wandered in the snow, her mind whirling out of control over Jorge being a married liar. When she caught herself fantasizing about sleeping with him, she rebuked herself. Her window to conceive was closing, and she needed to find a legitimate husband ASAP. She pulled out her phone and shed her NYC armor to confide in her best friend.

"Hello?" Grandma McPherson always sounded cautious when she answered.

Comforted by the familiar voice, Charlotte teased her, "Hi, Grandma, it's your favorite granddaughter."

The chuckle on the other end of the line warmed her heart. "You know I love all my grandkids, but you're special. I'll admit it if you don't tell the others."

Charlotte smiled. "Because I call you the most."

"You sure do. Where are you?" Grandma McPherson could never keep up with the globetrotter.

"I'm back in New York."

"What time is it there?"

"Almost 9 p.m., but I have some bad news. Jorge and I broke up." Charlotte braced herself for her grandma's reaction.

"What happened?"

Taking a deep breath, Charlotte explained that he was married.

Without missing a beat, Grandma McPherson replied, "Son of a gun. You'll have to forget about him and meet someone new. Don't waste time with married men."

"I know, that's what my friends said, too. But I really love him, and the doctor says I need to hurry up to have a baby. I thought he'd be the one."

"You're in love with the idea of Jorge, but he isn't who you thought he was. Pick yourself up and meet someone new so you can give me more great-grandkids. And tell me all about the next one. Nothing gets past me."

"Thank you, Grandma. You're always on my side." She wanted to hug her. "Are they treating you okay in your community?" Charlotte worried about her in an assisted living home, but her aunts insisted it was the best place for an eighty-nine-year-old to be somewhat independent and still have easy access to caretakers.

"They sure are. A nice man moved in across the hall, and there's a new nurse who is real nice. She brought me some cookies the other day. Sometimes I get a bit lonely, but I can't complain. I had sixty years with your grandpa, so I can't complain, Charlotte.

They're treating me real nice here." She tended to repeat herself but was otherwise sharp.

"I'm glad you're content, and I'll visit you next time I'm in California. I love you so much."

"I love you too, and I'll be waiting for you. I'll tell the ladies at poker that Jorge turned out to be a big rat, but we'll still root for you to get married. Be patient and it'll happen. Everything will be alright."

Although her grandma provided solace, tears cascaded down her face later that night as she brushed her teeth for bed. Shamefully, she reached for a Xanax and took half a pill to help stop crying. Charlotte remembered the last time she leaned on the anti-anxiety medication when she was grieving over her dead father. Jorge's betrayal and the news from Dr. Radcliff took her back to a dark place. But, as she drifted to sleep, she decided that after surviving the death of her father, she would absolutely survive a breakup and being fertility-challenged.

* * *

The following weeks consisted of ignoring Jorge's emails, preparing for the Angelino's Tokyo opening, and spontaneous charity work. Charlotte's neighbor recruited her to assist his husband's rescue charity to help homeless pups. She spearheaded a campaign to match friendly canines with injured veterans. The rewarding work lifted her spirits and kept her from falling into depression.

At their group manicure appointment, Charlotte and Sofia politely feigned amusement as Tracy shared sordid details about her liaison with the head of a brokerage firm, complete with naked selfies of the masked lovers. She bragged, "He wants me to screw him on a different employee's desk every Tuesday night. I told him I'd consider it if he invests in my next location. But he's so huge and rock-hard that I'll do him anytime, anywhere, regardless."

Charlotte quickly changed the subject and informed Sofia and Tracy that she had a big announcement. "I've decided to accomplish two goals by the end of next winter: lock down a husband and get a raise."

"Focus on effective methods for the best results." Tracy related to objectives and accomplishments. "What will you *do* to get the guy and the raise?"

"My job requires me to travel around the world, and I'll use work opportunities to meet new guys. I'm dedicating the next four seasons to dating as many men as possible and finding 'the one' before my thirty-sixth birthday. The raise will happen as soon as I corner Marco and Lorenzo in New York to talk about it." Charlotte sought solutions. "I can't discuss it during a trip because if they refuse, we'll be stuck in the same hotel and I'll want to kill them."

"You're right. They get nasty when people ask for more money, and it'd be a nightmare if you couldn't get away from them." As the daughter of an Italian immigrant father and an American mother, Sofia understood Lorenzo and Marco, and she worked with them five years longer than Charlotte. "But I like your idea to find a guy within a year. Go for it!"

"Are you excited about Tokyo? I've always wanted to go there!" Tracy loved adventure and perked up as she steered the conversation to the topic of travel.

"I guess so. The Japanese team planned a very detailed opening party. Marco invited his people, and Lorenzo isn't bringing his annoying new girlfriend, thank God." Charlotte heaved a sigh of relief.

Tracy couldn't hide her curiosity. "Who does Marco know there? He has so many hot friends, but are they Asian?" Raised by her tight-knit Chinese family after immigrating to the US as a child, she had an aversion to dating Asians, calling them too predictable.

"I'm not sure. His friends aren't my type, but maybe I'll be pleasantly surprised." Charlotte planned to fake it until she made it, even as Jorge still weighed heavy on her heart.

Chapter 2

ANGELINO'S SPRING STAFF MEETING

Lovesickness over Jorge plagued Charlotte. She was so distracted lamenting the breakup that she forgot about the Angelino's Spring Staff Meeting until the morning of the event. Every quarter, Angelino's hosted a company-wide meeting inside their flagship on Fifth Avenue at 9 a.m., giving everyone enough time to travel to their locations before lunch service started. The corporate staff and chefs, as well as managers, waiters, bartenders, and hostesses from the "front of the house" were forced to attend. Only lower-level kitchen employees (cooks, bussers, baristas, and dishwashers) were exempt from the brutal smackdown.

The corporate staff sat in a row at a long table in the front of the room. The chef and the restaurateur reigned between members of their executive team. Lorenzo had a unique, edgy style of wearing his white chef jacket over faded blue jeans while keeping his thick brown hair cut chin-length. In contrast, Marco wore elegant suits with suspenders, no tie, and his jet-black hair slicked back.

His dreams of being a couturier were shattered when he was forced into his family's wine empire at a young age—perhaps the deep-seated cause of his habitual angry outbursts. Lorenzo proudly displayed a slight belly because he said thin chefs were frauds, while Marco was slim and on the shorter side but boasted that his manhood compensated for his height handicap. Charming the ladies came naturally; they easily seduced conquests with their genetically endowed skills and ultimately broke hearts around the globe.

Joining the Italians at the head table were know-it-all Jessica Howard from Human Resources, miserable Melvin Brown from the Accounting department, and de facto CEO Jack Goodman. Although Jack provided the funds to open the first Angelino's, he opted for anonymity and tried to stay behind the scenes. The "silent investor" quietly pulled the corporate strings and calculated feasible expansion models. Marco and Lorenzo reaped the glory of Angelino's because it was their creative spunk and vast knowledge of Italian cuisine that propelled it to such a high level of success. However, it wouldn't have been accomplished without Jack's financing, and he often restrained them in business matters, proving to be the voice of reason. With only 48 percent ownership of Angelino's between the two of them (Marco held 38 percent, while Lorenzo possessed 10 percent), the hotheaded Italians had no choice but to yield to Jack who owned 52 percent of the company.

As public relations director, Charlotte McPherson was included on the main panel, opting to sit on the far end of the table in case things got heated. And they always did. Lorenzo was overly emotional, while Marco was unhinged, unpredictable, and relished authority—one never knew which direction the agenda would sway. Did the cook ruin the Bolognese sauce? Why did the hostess at Columbus Circle frown at a customer? Which waiter failed to clock in on time? Anybody's head could end up in the guillotine, usually for no good reason.

Charlotte found the shouting and drama extremely inappropriate and couldn't fathom why the human target of her bosses' rage was often treated with respect and even adoration just a few hours after being victimized. She was terrified they'd turn on her and subject her to their admonishment. After ten years of the same repetitive scenario, she summed it up to Italian passion. They love you one minute, hate you the next, and then love you again. Despite intense emotions, they quickly forgave whoever sparked their anger.

To make matters worse, before Marco took the floor for the grand finale, the corporate staff was expected to speak. Jack always yielded his time for efficiency. The rest of the panel, on the other hand, savored the spotlight. Jessica, a brainy African American, prided herself as "the enforcer" while she recited a litany of rules to deaf ears as the staff focused on their phones. Melvin, an angry middle-aged man, spoke with a cringe-worthy lisp. Charlotte would sympathize if he weren't so terribly cruel (she once comforted a waiter crying in the hallway after Melvin humiliated him for throwing away a bottle of olive oil with a spoonful remaining). After she spoke to the staff, Chef Lorenzo addressed food issues. Constantly accusing servers of not doing enough to encourage customers to try his specials, he repeatedly questioned why diners opted to order Angelino's bestselling Margherita pizza instead of his latest kale pesto gingered branzino or beef raspberry carpaccio concoction. (Charlotte often diplomatically tried to convince him that people want Angelino's famous pizza, not his gourmet foo foo!) Then it would be Marco's turn to belittle, berate, and bemoan while his chef-partner stood by his side for reinforcement.

Charlotte pulled off her jacket and reached into her bag for her notebook to prepare her brief remarks as employees from all seven Angelino's NYC locations filed into the converted meeting space, happily sharing hugs and cheek kisses with colleagues they hadn't seen since the last meeting. She typically thanked managers who helped her place celebrity stories in the press and acknowledged those who accommodated media dinners; she shared good news about notable guests and recently published articles featuring Angelino's. To conclude, she always gave everyone an update on upcoming restaurant openings, as well as those in the pipeline. She intentionally ended on an encouraging, positive note before the staff had to endure Lorenzo's whining and Marco's fury that would surely follow.

Today's meeting was no exception. True to form, Jack decided not to talk, Jessica gave her monologue, Melvin grumbled about excessively high electricity bills, Charlotte showered the group with gratitude, Lorenzo whimpered about his specials being neglected, and then Marco stood up to speak. Lorenzo crossed him arms to look tough while his partner geared up and let loose.

"You guys need to pull your shit together! When I see bad attitudes from waiters talking to customers, it pisses me off so much. I don't care if you had the worst day of your life, I really don't give a fuck. I don't care if your wife left you or your boyfriend cheated on you or you got in a car crash, it isn't the customer's fucking problem. They came here to eat, not deal with your bullshit. Fuck! I'm so pissed off!" Marco kicked his chair backward. "You guys think you can do whatever you want, and you don't care about what me and Lorenzo say! You have a job because of us! We don't need you!

We'll replace you tomorrow! Angelino's is Marco and Lorenzo, and we can find someone else to do your job!" Spit spewed from his mouth as he pounded the table.

Charlotte kept her head down and glanced sideways, catching a grimace spread across Jack's face.

"Marco, Marco, calm down, it's ok-uh." Lorenzo moved his hands up and down while he spoke with his thick Italian accent. He animatedly tried to defuse Marco. "We have so many things wrong here we need to talk about. First, we have a big problem-uh." Lorenzo took a deep breath after a dramatic pause. "Why, please tell me why, the calamari taste like condoms? It's a nightmare! My God-uh!"

A skinny hostess from Belarus, notorious for hooking up with rich customers, leaned into a stunning Serbian waitress and asked, "He say calamari taste like condom? How he know? He eat condom?"

Shushing spread throughout the room because Angelino's veterans knew that if Lorenzo heard people talking over him, he'd lose his temper and prolong the meeting. He could flip like a switch when he was riled up and yell as loudly as Marco.

"I no understand. Where you taste calamari condoms? Which location?" an Italian manager from Angelino's SoHo asked.

"All locations! It's bullshit! Why don't you tell the cook to make it the right way-uh?" As Lorenzo reached his breaking point, the manager who didn't keep his mouth shut found himself on the chopping block.

While the calamari condom debate raged on, Charlotte's mind drifted backed to Jorge. Once texting was off limits, he emailed eloquent letters daily. She wasn't sure if his utterly intoxicating words stemmed from his Yale education or his colorful Mexican heritage. He was so poetic, so romantic. She never answered the emails but couldn't deny her disappointment the first day she didn't receive a letter from him.

The commotion of the manager shouting in Italian, followed by silence as he crossed his arms and stared defiantly out the window, snapped Charlotte back into the present gathering. Lorenzo and Marco exchanged disgusted looks as Jack adjourned the meeting.

"Alright, everyone, we covered enough today. Remember to send Jessica your current phone number as she requested, and Charlotte will update you via email once Tokyo's open so you can let all your customers know about it. Thank you." Jack put out fires whenever Lorenzo and Marco started them. Often.

The staff marched out, relieved to dash off to their jobs. Charlotte exchanged a few cordial words with Jack, and then tackled her work. She edited marketing materials, participated in a phone interview about American restaurants franchising in India, met with a board member from Meals on Wheels, and finally stopped by a wine preview party at Angelino's 72nd Street.

After nearly falling asleep during the subway ride home, she yawned as she packed six perfectly rolled up dresses and some business casual clothes in her carry-on suitcase. She intended to look great while respecting local customs during her first trip to Asia. The next morning, after a blowout to tame her unruly hair, Charlotte troubleshot a double booking in the private party room at Angelino's Columbus Circle during her ride to the airport. Undeterred by slow traffic, she was eager for a trip to open doors for new possibilities.

Chapter 3

TOKYO

Charlotte checked into Japan Airlines at JFK for her flight to Narita and rushed over to the business class lounge, where she instantly heard distinctly loud Italian chatter. Oblivious to other guests, Lorenzo and Marco laughed boisterously into their speakerphone call with the accused manager from the calamari fiasco. Less than twenty-four hours earlier, they nearly punched him out. Typical. The dispute long-forgotten, the three Italians were friendly again. Jack sat nearby with his head buried in *The Wall Street Journal,* ignoring the animated conversation. Charlotte approached to give obligatory cheek kisses.

"*Bella Carlotta! Come stai?*" Lorenzo always greeted her pleasantly.

"What took so long? We're about to go to the gate." Marco was grumpy again.

"My Uber moved at a snail's pace. If only I'd been able to ride with you guys and your driver," she quipped before adding a dose of sweetness. "The important thing is that we're all together and we're going to have a fantastic opening in Tokyo!" Jack watched her with an amused expression.

"Does everyone have their bags?" Charlotte assumed a logistical leadership role on their foreign trips. "Lorenzo, is that your phone charger plugged into the wall over there?"

"My God-uh! Thanks for reminding me!"

Another disaster averted.

It was a relief to settle into her airplane seat, separate from the team. Jack passed by on his way to the bathroom and uncharacteristically teased her, "Are you sad to sit far away from us?"

"I think I'll manage. I can catch up on sleep." She tucked her blanket around her. The trip was just what she needed to forget about Jorge. A new adventure always helped erase the past.

Fourteen hours later, the group disembarked and found the Japanese delegation waiting to receive them. Lorenzo, Marco, and Jack were whisked away in an SUV to the Imperial Hotel, while Charlotte was sent in a sedan to her lodgings.

Charlotte's annoyance over unexpectedly being housed in a different hotel than her bosses turned into discomfort when she found herself in the lobby of a dormitory-style building full of Japanese men without another woman in sight. In her room, the bed was too small, and a brick wall stood a mere six inches from the outside window. A tiny bathroom, not much bigger than a phone booth, housed a basic plastic sink and a toilet. It took her a minute to discover a showerhead directly over the toilet and a drain in the floor.

Before she could unzip her suitcase, Marco texted her to hurry up and meet them in the lobby in five minutes. She fumed to him that it might take her a while since she was inconveniently staying so far away.

The hotel staff, all male, didn't speak a word of English. She repeatedly asked, "Where is Imperial Hotel?" but they simply smiled and nodded. Finally, Charlotte pulled out her phone, searched Imperial Hotel Tokyo, clicked on the Japanese translation and showed it to them. Eureka! They pulled out a map and drew directions just as she realized she should've used Google Maps on her phone.

Twenty minutes later, after a harrowing walk past train tracks, under a bridge and through narrow passageways, Charlotte scanned the lobby of the Imperial Hotel but couldn't find the Italians. Marco texted her and told her to come up to his room; the others were tired of waiting and already left for the restaurant. Jet lag nagged at Charlotte as she yawned in the elevator. When she saw his spacious suite, she told him about her miniature "motel" packed with men.

"Seriously, it feels like I'm in a brothel and it took me twenty minutes to walk here, it's a miracle I didn't get lost. They should have put me in the same hotel with you guys. It's so much more convenient."

"Well, you can stay in my room." Marco winked as he pinched her waist.

Charlotte deadpanned while she stared directly in his eyes. "That's so nice of you," she said with sarcasm. "But where would you sleep?" She held her head high before turning toward the door to leave. "After a fourteen-hour flight, it'd be nice to have adequate accommodations for a business trip. But I'll make the best of it."

On the way to Angelino's, Charlotte observed bustling streets through the car window. She'd never visited such a monolithic place. Tokyo's homogeneous population was different than the big cities mixed with several ethnicities she was accustomed to. Usually the only redhead in various situations, this time she seemed to be the only Caucasian woman amid a sea of Japanese.

The restaurant crew was hard at work, and after months of emails and video conference calls, Charlotte happily met the local public relations team in person. Their immaculate organizational skills and attention to detail impressed her. She also admired their trendy fashion style and was intimidated by their thin bodies.

Charlotte was naturally slender, but at the age of thirty-five, pasta and pizza tastings at Angelino's showed on her waistline. She used belts, fit-and-flare dresses, and even Spanx to disguise the extra weight gain around her belly. The petite Japanese women left her feeling self-conscious and she made a mental note to shed ten pounds before summer.

Lorenzo worked diligently with the kitchen crew while an eager interpreter mediated a dispute regarding portion sizes. The Japanese wanted pasta dishes plated about a third of the size of the NYC servings. "No! No! No! This is too small! It's all wrong-uh," he persisted.

"Chef Lorenzo, our chef say people in Japan no like waste food and they no eat so much." The interpreter tried to plead the case, before darting over to the GM who was explaining to Jack, in broken English, why the Angelino's logo had to be altered to fit on the menu. The interpreter spoke to the GM in Japanese, resulting in a great deal of nodding between the two of them. Finally, the GM explained to Jack that food portions must be much smaller than large American-style servings. Jack typically avoided the intricacies of menus and food preparation; however, a peacekeeper was needed to resolve the conflict. Within two minutes, he set Lorenzo straight and they moved on to the next issue: The pizza chef wasn't making the dough thin enough.

Battling with jet lag dizziness, hunger, and obligatory politeness to her formal Japanese colleagues, Charlotte skillfully assisted the animated Italian duo. Keeping with Angelino's foreign opening practices, there was no break between work and dinner. She tested a slice of pizza with Marco when Lorenzo informed them that the Angelino's Tokyo franchisee, Mr. Yamamoto, planned an elaborate welcome dinner, and they needed to leave immediately to meet him at The Palace Hotel.

Charlotte ran to the bathroom and washed her hands, applied face powder and freshened her lipstick. Unsatisfied with her appearance, she assured herself that it would be a dull business dinner and soon she'd be asleep in her little hotel room.

During the car ride, Marco mentioned he was inviting friends as he texted nonstop on his phone. "Are you sure it's appropriate to bring people?" Charlotte foresaw a problem. "Mr. Yamamoto was a serious guy when I met him in New York."

"*Si Carlotta! Si!* It will be fun-uh!" Lorenzo interjected while Marco ignored her.

Dinner began calmly when Mr. Yamamoto, along with two other Japanese businessmen and the interpreter, greeted Lorenzo, Marco, Jack, and Charlotte. Soon after an impressive selection of food was presented, Marco announced that his friends were in the lobby. Charlotte asked what she was eating, and the waiter proudly named each item, many of which she recognized, but "basashi" was unfamiliar. Meals consumed at Nobu didn't prepare her for this truly authentic experience. (The next morning, much to her dismay, Lorenzo explained that she had consumed horse meat.)

The door burst open, allowing Marco's sexy friends to flock to him, covering him with hugs and kisses. An awkward tension descended upon the room. The girls were stunning, no doubt, their stilettos lengthened their thin legs, and their hair was perfectly coiffed. However, their short dresses, heavy makeup, and loose mannerisms made one wonder if they earned their money on their backs. Lorenzo yanked one onto his lap, while another pulled out a cigarette and aggressively ordered the waiter to bring her tequila on the rocks. Mr. Yamamoto hid his annoyance as he gave a very slight bow to each woman Marco introduced.

Charlotte and Jack exchanged disapproving glances while Lorenzo turned his back to Mr. Yamamoto to woo his new conquest. Charlotte fished in her bag for her phone with the intention of discreetly texting Jack to tell him that the inappropriate invasion of party girls appeared to irritate Mr. Yamamoto. Just as she grasped it, the door swung open revealing a tall, handsome, blonde, Nordic thirty-something-year-old who ecstatically walked toward Marco with outstretched arms.

"Eric! You made it!" Marco jumped up and embraced him. "Come, meet everyone."

Charlotte let her phone slip back into her bag while standing up to shake his hand. She rose whenever she was introduced to someone because it gave her a chance to stretch her legs while exuding confidence and friendliness. She caught Eric's eye before Marco yanked him away to introduce him to Mr. Yamamoto and the girls. A waiter, or maybe it was a guardian angel, placed a chair for Eric between Charlotte and Marco.

Jet lag didn't prevent Charlotte from batting her eyelashes and getting to know Eric Sorenson. He quickly revealed that he moved from Chicago to Tokyo after his father was named United States Ambassador to Japan, enabling him to live near his parents and younger sister. He launched a consulting business (presumably aided by dad's connections) that was doing great. While completing his undergraduate studies at New York University, he ate at Angelino's at least three times a week and brought his family whenever they visited. Marco befriended his parents and they stayed in touch. Eric was eager to satisfy his prosciutto pizza cravings at the new Angelino's Tokyo.

Clearly, he was raised with a silver spoon in his mouth and Charlotte treaded cautiously with blue bloods. Her parents pinched their pennies to grant her a top-level education, but she accepted the fact that her middle-class California background excluded her from many elite clubs and gatherings on the East Coast. While she might be invited for a weekend in Nantucket with a well-connected family, she assumed they wouldn't want her to marry into their lineage. Hence, she tended to date self-made finance guys, techies, or open-minded attorneys who accepted her West Coast roots. Eric, on the other hand, was so cute and charming that nothing would hold her back.

"Marco is the best! I'm glad he invited you here," Charlotte gushed with sudden energy. "The new Angelino's is fabulous! It's a huge space in the heart of Roppongi. Are you coming to the opening party tomorrow night?"

"Now I am." Eric looked deep into Charlotte's sparkling eyes. "Why didn't Marco tell me about you? I would've showed up on time."

Charlotte smiled and blushed. "Oh, thank you."

"Do you want a ride back to your hotel? Are you staying at the Imperial with Marco?" Eric moved quickly.

The wine shed away Charlotte's inhibitions as she whispered in his ear. "Actually, the Japanese delegation put me somewhere else. It's so tiny that I don't know how I'll fit in that little bed."

"I've a driver outside, he'll take us to your hotel for a nightcap. Let's ditch this group."

Game on.

After dessert, they exited properly. Charlotte said polite good-byes to Mr. Yamamoto and the other Japanese men. Marco was so engrossed in a girl that she skipped him. Charlotte noticed Jack's scowl of disapproval when he realized she was leaving with Eric. Momentarily annoyed by his reaction, she refused to let it slow her down.

Lorenzo, on the other hand, gave his blessing, "*Bravo!* Go have fun together!" He kissed their cheeks. "See you tomorrow! *Ciao!*"

In the car, Eric was in great spirits as he blasted hip-hop.

"Are drivers necessary in Tokyo?" Charlotte wasn't sure if she should be impressed or concerned.

"I got a DWI in the states after I crashed my car into a tree." Eric was nonchalant. "I broke my leg but nobody else got hurt."

"That's scary. When did it happen?"

"A few years ago. I promised Dad I'd always use a driver in Japan, so it won't happen again while he's ambassador and we'll avoid an international incident. You know, bad press and all that shit." Eric lit a cigarette.

"You're lucky you're in Japan because hardly anyone smokes in the US anymore." Charlotte hated cigarettes.

Eric laughed. "Oh, are you the morality police? Maybe you can handcuff me later and teach me a lesson." He pulled her close and playfully bit her neck.

Before Charlotte could kiss him, the driver announced that they reached her hotel. Eric looked out the window. "Why did they put you here?"

"Thank you! That's what I thought. I'm supposed to stay in the same place as my bosses."

"This is a place for Japanese men to have very short term, low-cost places to sleep."

"You mean, like a brothel? Do they have women come for sex? I totally got that vibe—"

"No," Eric interrupted. "There probably isn't prostitution, but it's not a place for a girl. I can't leave you here. Do you want to stay in my little sister's place? She's in Ecuador for a nonprofit project. It's empty."

"Eric, that's so nice of you! Thank you!"

"I'm sure you'll make it up to me." He nuzzled her neck with his chin.

Eric's driver escorted Charlotte to gather her suitcase. It was even darker and scarier inside than earlier in the day, making the move to a gleaming high-rise a huge relief. The trip was getting better and better!

The apartment resembled a hotel suite with few traces of Eric's sister except for a couple of framed photos she noticed as he showed her around and explained the security details. "I'm going to be a gentleman for once in my life and leave you here to sleep. I've an early meeting tomorrow. Damn, I shouldn't have drunk so much...You have my number if you need anything. Okay?" He looked ready to bolt.

"Sure! Thank you so much. I really appreciate it." She hugged him, luring him to stay, but he broke free to text his driver.

"Rest and get rid of that jet lag so we can go out tomorrow night after the Angelino's party." He paused for a second, smiled as he looked into her eyes, grabbed her, and gave her a strong, deep, passionate kiss. Charlotte was taken aback, in a good way. She leaned in for another, but he pecked her on the cheek and sprinted out.

"You're such a tease!" she yelled after him.

Smiling as she prepared for bed, she realized she'd forgotten about Jorge all day. As she drifted asleep, she gave thanks for Tokyo and savored the thrill of meeting Eric.

* * *

Charlotte's brain turned cartwheels to keep up with the grand opening activities for Angelino's Tokyo. It started with a mad dash to the Imperial Hotel to meet Lorenzo and Marco. As usual, Jack was away on his own agenda and Charlotte felt relieved to escape his judgment. Marco was surprised she hit it off with Eric, and Lorenzo didn't remember meeting him.

After a quick breakfast, a driver arrived to take them to the restaurant. The Japanese team booked three interviews with major publications before the press luncheon. Charlotte sat in on media interviews to provide information and wrap it up on time. The Italians were magical with the press—warm, animated, funny, and cool. Women fell in love with them and men wanted to be them. The Emergency Landing story enticed journalists who devoured anecdotes about celebrity customers.

Charlotte assumed the interviews went well until a reporter nervously pulled her aside, explaining that he couldn't understand Lorenzo's accent and needed his tape recorder transcribed. To make the deadline, she realized with irritation that she'd have to complete it during the two-hour window she set aside to get ready for the opening party.

Meanwhile, the press luncheon was a huge success. Lorenzo and Marco charmed the attendees, all of whom were women. They took turns on the microphone, welcoming them to Angelino's, praising Japanese culture, and detailing each dish served. Guests savored every bite of the pasta, carpaccio, and pizza tasting menu. However, Lorenzo disapproved of the honey jars waiters provided to accompany the focaccia. Jack came to the rescue, resurfacing during the luncheon and convincing Lorenzo to adhere to local customs and not take additional condiments as a personal insult. After all, they did keep the menu authentically Angelino's.

The Italians espoused endless energy during the second round of press interviews while Charlotte slouched with fatigue. She regretted drinking alcohol the night before and wondered what time it was in NYC, how she'd survive after just five hours of sleep, and when she could peel off her high heels.

Back in her lodgings, with just two hours to spare before being picked up for the opening party, she raced through the transcribing, copied text of the Emergency Landing story from the Angelino's website, and pasted it into the document.

While resting her eyes with a short nap, the doorbell rang, and a huge bouquet of roses greeted Charlotte with a note: *Good luck with the opening, Char. See you tonight! X Eric*

Without a spare moment to daydream about her new prince charming, Charlotte showered, applied makeup, and slipped into a sexy black Dolce & Gabbana dress (she thematically wore Italian designers to Angelino's opening parties). Always a bundle of nerves at her events, she couldn't relax until she rounded everyone up for the speeches and the pasta ribbon cut was complete.

Ambassador Sorenson agreed to join the Italian consul general in Tokyo for the ceremony. Charlotte was impressed that Marco booked him but also wondered self-consciously if the diplomat knew she was staying in his daughter's apartment and kissing his son. She intended to make a great impression and toyed with the idea that the ambassador might one day be her father-in-law. Everything was happening so fast!

When Charlotte was introduced to the ambassador, she only had a few seconds to say a polite salutation, as the program was about to begin. The local team surprised Lorenzo and Marco with a stupendous performance from a Japanese opera singer while Charlotte scanned the crowd of stylish Japanese guests, looking for Eric. Jack appeared lonely as usual. Charlotte forgot about his judgmental scowl the night before and felt sorry for him. But where was Eric?

A Japanese ballerina took the floor and gave a two-minute performance around a cherry blossom tree. Charlotte gave up on Eric when the speeches began, focusing instead on the run of show. There was a specific order for the speakers: Mr. Yamamoto was to start, followed by comments from Lorenzo and Marco to thank individuals like the investors and chefs. Ambassador Sorenson would give closing remarks before the Japanese GM and hostesses rolled out the ten-foot-long pasta ribbon. At that moment, Charlotte would hand Ambassador Sorenson the giant scissors to cut it.

Charlotte's stress level soared as Marco ripped the microphone from Mr. Yamamoto and thrust it to Ambassador Sorenson. It wasn't the correct order. The ambassador's public speaking acumen enabled him to improvise as he thanked Mr. Yamamoto for a warm welcome and made positive remarks about America and Japan sharing a special relationship through cultural exchanges including those in the culinary world. The interpreter had her own microphone and rattled off several Japanese sounds for every English word spoken by the ambassador.

Then Marco took the floor, unable to contain his ego as he spoke nonstop for ten minutes while the crowd's attention waned. Guests looked at their phones, peeped at their watches, and Charlotte glanced around for Eric. Finally, the interpreter finished translating Marco's speech and it was Lorenzo's turn. "We love Japan and we hope you love Angelino's! Viva Tokyo!" He threw his fist in the air while the crowd cheered. With no need for the translator, Charlotte signaled the staff to roll out the pasta ribbon while she handed Ambassador Sorenson the giant scissors. It was the perfect photo-op.

After the ribbon was snipped, handshakes completed, and DJ turntable spinning, the ambassador snuck away without goodbyes. As Charlotte watched him leave, she felt a tap on her shoulder. It was Eric.

"There you are!" Charlotte was relieved. "Did you see the pasta ribbon cutting ceremony? I met your father for a second."

"Yeah, I came in as it happened. Dad had to leave for another function, but that's cool you met him." Eric yawned. "Long day."

"No worries, you're here now!" Charlotte beamed. "Would you like a tour of the restaurant?"

"Sure, I think you'll be the sexiest tour guide ever. Nice dress, by the way," Eric said, sizing her up.

Charlotte blushed while grabbing two glasses of Prosecco from a waiter carrying a tray full of drinks. The tour included the wine cellar, private room, bar, and main dining room. They noshed on pasta samples and drank more Prosecco. The noise level prevented meaningful conversation and Eric suggested checking out a bar nearby. The party was in full swing as Marco charmed a group of beauties. Lorenzo was absorbed in kitchen chaos and Jack had disappeared as usual. The coast was clear for Charlotte to slip out unnoticed.

Outside, Eric made an unexpected suggestion. "Charlotte, it'd be nice to talk somewhere quiet instead of a bar. Do you mind? I have to leave tomorrow for London, and I can't drink too much."

"Of course. But why are you going to London?" Charlotte was concerned. They just met twenty-four hours earlier and she feared he'd forget about her.

"I have a few meetings and I might stay in Europe for a week or two since I'll already be out there."

The realization that Eric was geographically undesirable sunk in, but Charlotte maintained hope. "You should come to New York since you'll be right over the pond."

"Actually, I thought about it because I could do some meetings and see NYU friends. I might even go to Chicago for a few days, but I'm still deciding. Let's have dessert at Joël Robuchon's place, La Boutique. It's nearby and they have a quiet corner." Eric grabbed Charlotte by the hand and whisked her off.

Settled into a booth at the boulangerie, the conversation flowed seamlessly. They talked about their families, friends, politics, and even religion. Eric was raised Lutheran and Charlotte was brought up Catholic, practically the same thing in their opinion.

Eric inquired about her last relationship and Charlotte remembered adulterer Jorge. Skillfully, she maneuvered the conversation back to Eric because she believed that men loved to talk about themselves while women ought to leave them guessing. He confided that he went through a difficult breakup with a Brazilian model a few months prior but abruptly changed the topic. Charlotte suspected he still had feelings for the woman and was happy to steer the discussion back to current events.

The evening was ending as the café cleared out. "I can't believe you're leaving tomorrow," Charlotte sighed.

"I know, it sucks. I want to get to know you better." Eric paused. "When can you leave Japan?"

"I leave Friday afternoon at the same time as my bosses."

"And when do you have to be back in New York?" he asked.

Charlotte wasn't sure where the conversation was headed but she liked it. "Monday night or even Tuesday morning. I always get a day off after foreign openings."

"I was thinking about going to the Cannes Film Festival for a few days to see my director friend. Maybe you can fly out Friday, we hang, and then go to New York on Monday."

"I love that idea!" Charlotte exclaimed. "I went last year but didn't think I'd make it this year because of this opening."

"It's a twelve-hour flight from Tokyo to Paris and then you'll change planes and fly down to Nice. I can hop over from London

Friday morning, but you won't get there until late Friday night if you catch a flight out of here in the afternoon."

Charlotte was determined to make it work. "Any time after 3 p.m. is perfect. I'll see Marco and Lorenzo off and then fly to meet you…. But I'm not sure about the ticket situation."

"Don't worry. I'll get you to Nice and home to NYC. My travel agent will arrange it. Just email me your passport details."

Eric had all the answers and Charlotte barely contained her excitement. "Cannes will be so much fun! I'm friends with Wyatt Ashcroft. He has the best party up in the hills."

"Yeah, I know." Eric sounded impressed. "My friend took me last year."

"I was there, too!" Sometimes she was dumbfounded by how the world could be so small.

"Yet it took the Tokyo magic for us to finally meet." Eric put his hand on her inner thigh, giving Charlotte a tingling sensation.

"Actually, it was the Angelino's magic," Charlotte cooed.

"Ha! If you insist! Marco is lucky to have you, such a sexy brand ambassador," he inched his hand up higher. Charlotte felt slightly too turned on and shifted a few inches away, reluctant to engage in public displays of affection.

"Can you get us in Ashcroft's party?" Eric asked as he pulled out a cigarette. "I have the rest of the weekend covered."

"Absolutely. I received an email invitation a few days ago but didn't have a chance to decline. Now I'll RSVP for both of us." Charlotte was thrilled everything was turning out perfectly.

After playful flirting during the ride back, Eric escorted Charlotte into the apartment building lobby. Inside the elevator, he pushed her against the wall and kissed her strongly as his hands roamed beneath her dress, his fingers sneaking into her bra, caressing her breasts. They made out in the lift, hallway, suite entryway, on the couch, and finally in the bedroom. Eric threw her on the bed and pulled her dress over her head. Charlotte felt him aroused as he straddled her and unbuttoned his shirt. With a flash of fear, she worried the situation was out of her control.

"Eric, wait. Can we slow down?" Charlotte needed to catch her breath.

He looked dejected. "What's wrong? I thought you were into me?"

"Nothing's wrong, I'm totally into you. But we should pace ourselves," she reasoned.

"Okay, yeah. Sorry. It's cool. I should head out." Eric stood up and re-buttoned his shirt.

"Are you upset?" Charlotte asked, concerned.

"Nah, it's okay. I just feel such a connection with you. It's hard to stop." Eric looked at his phone.

"I feel a connection, too. And I'm sure we'll get closer in France. I think with the jet lag, the press luncheon and the opening—"

"It's fine, don't worry. I can't stay here and not touch you." He walked toward the door. "Send me your passport info in the morning."

Charlotte jumped up, ran to him, and hugged him. "We'll have lots of time in Cannes. Okay?"

"Sure. Get some sleep." He didn't hide his annoyance.

Uneasiness settled into the pit of Charlotte's stomach as she washed her face for bed. It was a shame to end the evening on a sour note and she hoped he'd still bring her to France. *Bing!* Her phone email alert interrupted her thoughts. Realizing it was morning in NYC and she hadn't checked her emails in over five hours, she braced herself for a barrage of messages. Her blood boiled at the sight of the first email's subject line:

Re: WHERE THE FUCK DID YOU PUT MY STAPLER!!!!

Melvin. He was so vulgar and rude. The body of the message was blank. Exhausted, emotional, and sleep deprived, her fingers trembled with rage as she typed:

> *Melvin,*
>
> *I didn't touch your stapler! As you know, I'm in Tokyo, working myself to death for Angelino's. Don't ever use profanity to accuse me of something I didn't do. Shame on you!*

Bing! Melvin responded immediately:

DON'T GIVE ME SHIT. THEY SAY YOU TOOK IT. FUCK YOU.

Charlotte composed a nasty response, edited it three times, added exclamation points, and then stopped herself from sending it. She subdued her redheaded temper and reminded herself of the famous expression: Revenge is a dish best served cold.

The next morning at breakfast, the Angelino's team got an earful from Charlotte. "Melvin has no right to speak to me like that. Completely unprofessional."

"*Bella*, I'm sorry. He's so mean. Just ignore-uh." Lorenzo shook his head disapprovingly.

"Did you take his stapler?" Marco asked in all seriousness.

"I'm here in Tokyo with you guys! How could I take it?"

Jack stepped in. "I'll talk to Jessica about it, she can remind Melvin about appropriate workplace behavior. He needs a refresher from Human Resources."

"Jesus. Getting a lecture from Jessica is torture," Marco spoke from experience because she had reprimanded him several times over the years. "Are you happy now?"

"I'm not out to punish Melvin, all I ask is that he respect me." Charlotte grew weary of the topic and was satisfied she got him in trouble with Jack. "The driver is out front. We should head over to Angelino's for the menu meeting with the GM."

During the ride, Charlotte received a text from Eric. *Hey Sexy, taking off soon to London. My travel agent has your info and she'll email your tix. See you in Cannes.*

Charlotte had a good feeling about Eric. She knew France could be the stepping-stone to something serious with him—she was already three steps ahead, fantasizing about giving birth to mini Erics.

The rest of the day flowed smoothly despite the usual drama between Lorenzo and the foreign culinary team. There were numerous taste tests, a blogger luncheon, two media interviews, and a late dinner with Mr. Yamamoto. It was the first night that Angelino's was open for business, and he didn't want the NYC corporate staff to waste space reserved for paying customers, so he took them to Gonpachi, a buzzing dining institution popular with tourists.

Many sake shots later, Charlotte ate delicious shabu-shabu and watched as Mr. Yamamoto and two of his colleagues laughed loudly while shouting in Japanese. Jack appeared unhappy and clearly wanted to leave while Lorenzo and Marco typed nonstop on their phones. As Charlotte checked her phone to see if Eric had landed in London, Mr. Yamamoto and his colleagues stood up abruptly, bowed, and said *sayonara*.

The group from NYC jumped up and exchanged awkward goodbyes with their Japanese associates. Jack extended his arm for official handshakes, Western style, while Charlotte gave a slight bow before remembering that respect in Japan is measured by the depth of the bow. She haphazardly followed up with a bow so deep that her hair fell into soy sauce on the table. Lorenzo and Marco grabbed the Japanese gentlemen by their shoulders and kissed each cheek. Thankfully, everyone besides Charlotte and Jack were too drunk to notice the messy farewell.

"Thank God! They're gone! Let's meet the girls at the club-uh!" Lorenzo slurred.

"Let's go. They're waiting." Marco pounded one last shot of sake and walked toward the exit.

"I'm heading back to the hotel," Jack said.

Relieved, Charlotte started to ask for a ride, but Lorenzo set them straight. "No, we only have one driver. You come with us. If you don't like it, you leave-uh." Lorenzo and Marco were drunk and determined to meet the girls. Jack and Charlotte were drained but lacked transportation to flee.

They were promptly ushered into the club with plush half-circle booths, bottle service, sparklers, semi-naked cocktail waitresses, an elevated DJ stand, and American rap booming through the speakers. Four scantily clad women waited for them in a reserved booth, two Japanese and two Eastern European. Lorenzo and Marco were in their element, gyrating, drinking, and chatting up the girls. Jack sat stone-faced and Charlotte fake sipped her vodka soda while using every ounce of energy to dance next to their table.

A few minutes later, Lorenzo left for the bathroom while Marco made out with a girl and Jack typed on his phone. The coast was clear for Charlotte to slump down into the booth.

When Lorenzo returned, he pulled her up frantically. "Let's get out of here!"

"What happened? Are you okay?" Charlotte had never seen him so upset. Jack stood up.

"The bathroom. Unbelievable what they do-uh!" Lorenzo was shaken.

"Did you walk in on a couple having sex?" Unfortunately, Charlotte had witnessed club bathroom fornication before.

"But no!" Lorenzo exclaimed. "Not boy and girl, but two boys and girl-uh!" He stormed off toward the door. Jack followed and Charlotte looked toward Marco, but he was preoccupied with his tongue down the throat of his companion. Charlotte bolted out and jumped in the car after Jack. Lorenzo was still shaking.

"But what about Marco?" Charlotte dutifully tried not to ditch him.

"It's fine. We'll send driver back-uh." Lorenzo seemed determined to escape.

Content to leave, Charlotte relaxed into the tranquility of the car ride while Lorenzo stared into space in a state of distress. Apparently, even the ladies' man had limits.

Charlotte rashly washed her face, too tired to bother with stubborn mascara stains, and forewent her regular night cream application. She was on a mission to at least brush her teeth but was so fatigued that squeezing toothpaste felt like a herculean task.

Bing! Charlotte shuddered when her phone chime reminded her that it was Wednesday morning in New York and an email avalanche would soon follow. She read the first message:

> *Re: Melvin's Stapler*
>
> *Hi Charlotte,*
>
> *We found Melvin's stapler in his desk.
> Apologies for the mix-up. We thought you used
> it when you prepared your press packets.*
>
> *Have a safe trip back to NYC.*
>
> *Best wishes,*
> *Jessica*

After breakfast the next morning, the Japanese delegation planned a day of sightseeing before the Influencer Tasting at Angelino's. Jack tended to other business and Lorenzo skipped the tour to participate in the kitchen training with the Japanese culinary team. He feared their cooks couldn't replicate Angelino's menu and was convinced the marinara sauce tasted like "tree bark-uh."

Marco and Charlotte set off with a translator and driver. It wasn't the first time the two adventured together while the rest of the NYC team was occupied. They usually got along well, but there was often a bit of sexual tension. Like a chameleon, Marco hid his anger issues and utilized his Italian charm for conquests and had dated several women from Angelino's, including a hostess he married and divorced a few years later. Charlotte was aware he found her attractive but assumed Jack stopped the restaurateur's advances when she first started at Angelino's.

As for Charlotte, sometimes she was infatuated by Marco. He looked refined in his custom-tailored suits, wore incredible-smelling cologne, and drove like a racecar driver. Although she enjoyed his creativity and occasional kindness, she loathed the way he yelled at the staff and threw temper tantrums. She also resented him for underpaying her and making inappropriate remarks. Ultimately, she wanted to keep things professional.

First stop was Imperial Palace. Charlotte and Marco strolled through the gardens and engaged upon an unusually deep conversation. He confided that he was starting to burn out because he was working too much and he was ready to settle down again and have another child, hopefully a girl, to add to his three sons from previous relationships. She listened and provided polite responses but didn't volunteer any personal information.

Next, they headed to Harajuku Cat Street where he tried on some bright shirts over his suspenders and Charlotte advised him on the best choices. After lunch, at one of the city's Depachika food halls, they went to Koishikawa Botanical Garden to catch the remnants of cherry blossom season and then jumped in the car to visit Shibuya Crossing, perhaps the busiest intersection in the world; people rushed in all directions at the flick of a light. Marco made her record videos of him walking back and forth several times while he laughed and threw his fists up in the air. She giggled at his happiness and enthusiasm.

The guide offered to conclude the tour with Sensoji Temple, Tokyo's oldest temple, founded in 645 AD. Marco was uninterested, but Charlotte insisted. She'd heard about fortune cards distributed at temples and sought signs about her future with Eric.

Throngs of people waited to enter the structure. Security officers roped off the entrance and kept crowds waiting on the other side of the square. Every fifteen minutes, they removed the rope, allowing a few hundred people to enter. Charlotte stood anxiously while Marco flashed her a frown.

"Don't worry, it'll be worth it when we get our fortunes." Charlotte hoped to appease his superstitious side.

"It is called *omikuji*. You find out future," the translator beamed.

As the security officers drew the ropes back, the crowd flooded into the square, sweeping Charlotte with them. The translator disappeared and Marco surged a few feet ahead. Charlotte was suffocated as bodies crushed together, then a hand from behind her squeezed between her legs. A finger penetrated through her dress but was blocked by her underwear. Her body tensed up she lurched forward, broke free, and whipped her head around to identify the perpetrator. Fists clenched, anger rushing through her veins, she was ready to attack the pervert. But all the men within arm's distance stared straight ahead, avoiding eye contact. She wasn't sure which one deserved a black eye. As the pushing continued, she worried she'd faint.

She screamed, "Marco! Help!" Someone grabbed her arm and she feared it was the groper. Much to her relief, she heard a familiar voice.

"Hold onto me." Obnoxious Marco turned into Superman.

"Someone groped me, it was so scary," Charlotte said, shaking.

His face turned red with fury. "Who did that? Show me! Which one?" Marco shouted.

But when she looked at the men staring past her as if she didn't exist, she realized it was impossible to identify the scumbag. "It's okay. We'll never find him. I'll stay close to you. I doubt he'll be back," she said, deflated.

"Are you sure you're okay?"

Marco's genuine concern touched her. Masking her distress, she replied, "I'm fine, thanks. Let's get our omikuji. Hopefully, we'll hear good news."

Traditional steps were required to obtain an omikuji. Charlotte inserted a coin into a container to make a small offering. Then she picked up a metal box, shaking it several times before turning it over and allowing a single stick to fall out. The stick had a kanji number that the translator helped her match to a number on one of the many drawers set before them. Charlotte opened one and withdrew a thin piece of paper with Japanese script. She watched intently as the translator read it.

"Very good fortune!" The translator read it aloud:

> *Your wishes will be realized.*
> *A sick person recovers.*
> *Taking good care is important.*
> *The lost article will be found.*
> *The person you are waiting for will come.*
> *Building a new house and employment are good.*
> *When you make a trip, be careful.*
> *And marriage is VERY good.*

The translator clapped. "Congratulations!"

"Thank you so much! I love the last part about marriage! I can't wait to start a family—"

"Let me try." Marco forcefully shook the box, causing sticks to jam together, blocking the opening. Jiggling it in different directions eventually allowed one to free itself and catapult across the wooden table. Charlotte reached for it, but Marco snatched it up first. The translator helped him locate the correct drawer, instructing him to gently pick up the omikuji on top. Instead, he carelessly grabbed at the top sheet, jerking several out. He shoved the extra pieces back into the drawer. "Here, read it," he demanded as he gave his omikuji to the translator.

"Oh no. Very, very bad, Mr. Marco. I so sorry." The translator looked genuinely concerned.

Marco's anger rose. He shot Charlotte a stern look and then barked at the translator, "What does it say? Tell me!"

She did as instructed:

> *Every year, your servants get fewer and you will*
> *be alone.*
> *Even if you stay in bed, you never get well.*
> *It's too dangerous for you to bring boat to shore.*
> *Just like a dragon loses its treasure ball, you lose hope.*
> *Your wishes will not be realized.*
> *A sick person will never recover.*
> *The lost article will not be found.*
> *The person you are waiting for will not come.*
> *Building a new house is not good.*
> *Making a trip, marriage, employment are bad.*

The translator stood frightened. Charlotte broke the silence. "Well, maybe—"

"This is all your fault! You made me come here!" Marco shouted.

"But I didn't know you'd get a bad fortune." Charlotte defended herself.

"Mr. Marco, no worry. Just superstition," the translator reassured him.

"You told Charlotte it's real! I hate this shit! Now I have bad luck!"

Charlotte was at a rare loss for words and sought ways to remedy the situation when the translator interjected. "We have tradition to get rid of bad fortune. You tie over there, and bad fortune gone. You leave behind." She led Marco to an area with several fortunes tied to long silver rods. Charlotte stayed behind and watched with curiosity as Marco carefully tied his fortune and said a prayer while making the sign of the cross. Evidently, he thought his Catholic God could beat the Buddhist curse.

The car ride to the influencer event at Angelino's reeked with tension. Marco's dour mood filled Charlotte with guilt for forcing him to visit the temple. They had a different driver from previous days, and when they finally arrived at the restaurant, he turned around and said to her, "You hair nice. I like red."

"Thank you! You're so sweet!" Charlotte gushed. It was the first time during the entire week that a Japanese man paid her a compliment. Something was askew in the busy city and she suddenly realized what it was: acknowledgement from local men.

"It's so nice to get a compliment from a Japanese guy," Charlotte contently told Marco.

"Maybe it's because of your good fortune." Marco stormed ahead of her and into the restaurant with a door slam. Apparently, he'd need time to recover from Sensoji Temple.

* * *

The event was a success; the influencers loved the food and endlessly snapped pictures while holding up peace signs. The farewell dinner that followed was uneventful. Lorenzo seemed wiped out from a long day in the kitchen and there were no surprise visitors. Jack slipped in late and Mr. Yamamoto adjourned the meal early. Everyone retreated to their rooms to rest.

The next morning, the refreshed group chatted during breakfast, ready to complete their last day. Charlotte informed them that she'd ride with them to the airport before flying to France and would return to the office Tuesday morning. Jack appeared perturbed but Charlotte didn't dwell on it. The team headed to Angelino's for a local magazine photo shoot and one final taste test. It would be the last time the NYC delegation would meet with the Japanese group.

Sadness struck Charlotte whenever work trips concluded because she'd probably never see the foreign team together again due to the high turnover rate in the restaurant industry. Managers were fired, PR companies replaced, waiters quit. It was impossible to predict who would stay.

The shoot went well, and the Italians pleased the photographer with creative poses. Mr. Yamamoto brought his business partners and they seemed delighted with the food. When Lorenzo asked them to make the portions bigger "like we do in New York-uh," Jack cut him off, putting the matter to bed before the translator could relay the message.

When it was time to leave, there were the usual awkward goodbye exchanges. Lorenzo and Marco startled Mr. Yamamoto and his colleagues with cheek kisses, Jack forced handshakes, and Charlotte bowed deeper than before. They exited the building and rode up an escalator to reach their car. Suddenly, they heard shouts of "Viva Angelino's! Viva Angelino's!" They walked to the railing and looked down at the restaurant. Out front, the entire staff, from managers to dishwashers, stood outside smiling, shouting, and waving goodbye.

Inside the car, emotional from their kind gesture, a tear ran down Charlotte's cheek. She caught Jack watching her with concern.

Marco asked, "What's wrong with you?"

"I feel sad to leave them. They're all so nice." Charlotte quickly composed herself. Lorenzo and Marco shrugged and turned their attention back to their phones while Jack paused for a moment, looking away as soon as their eyes met. Deep in thought, Charlotte stared out the window for the entire ride to Narita International Airport.

Chapter 4

CANNES

harlotte flew westward to France, while the rest of the Angelino's group headed eastbound back to NYC. Amused as she was to literally travel around the world, she was beyond excited about seeing Eric. He booked a room at Hotel du Cap, which impressed her because it was difficult to get a reservation at the luxurious landmark during the world-famous Cannes Film Festival.

After a peaceful journey from Tokyo and a quick layover in Paris, she boarded the ninety-minute flight to Nice. Charlotte squeezed into a middle seat between a mother nursing a baby and her five-year-old son cooped up next to the window who declined Charlotte's offer to switch seats. Despite the language barrier, she enjoyed playing mom and assisting the boy with his Legos and snacks. The endearing innocence of the child reinforced her maternal desires.

A text from Eric greeted her when she landed. *Welcome Sexy! Driver has sign with your name. See ya soon!*

Charlotte adored Nice. Although she couldn't see much during the dark drive, the familiar crisp freshness in the air brought back pleasant memories of her previous visit. Within half an hour, she arrived at the hotel. It was nearly midnight and Charlotte stood underdressed in jeans and a pink cashmere sweater among a sea of gowns and tuxedos flooding the lobby. The driver escorted her to the front desk and spoke in French to the reservation specialist who instantly presented her with a key and sent her off with a bellhop.

They entered a moderately sized room, elegantly decorated with a mint green floral bedspread and matching curtains, lush cream-colored carpet, a mahogany Edwardian antique desk, plush sitting chairs, and antique nightstands on each side of the bed. Eric left swim shorts and a few t-shirts strewn around the room. Charlotte stowed her suitcase in the closet and quickly showered. She had already texted Eric when she arrived to ask where to meet.

Thirty minutes later, she was ready but no sign of Eric. She texted again. *Hey, not sure if you got my message, I'm ready to meet you*

No response.

Fifteen minutes later, she tried again. *Hi... Where are you?*

No response.

She sat on the bed, disconcerted. Was his phone dead? Were the texts delivered? Finally, she called him. It was nearly 2 a.m. and she needed to reach him.

Eric picked up on the fourth ring. "Hey Char!" he shouted over loud music.

"Hi Eric! Did you get my texts?" Charlotte yelled back so he could hear her.

"Easy, babe, you're screaming in my ear. Yeah, I got your texts, but the thing is I'm at this dope party and there's no way I can get you in because they're so strict," he said unapologetically.

Charlotte hid her annoyance. "Well…Okay…. How long will you be there?"

"It's just starting, but I'll see you in the hotel later. Gotta go. Bye, sexy!" Eric hung up.

Collapsing onto the bed in frustration, Jorge flashed in Charlotte's mind—he'd never dismiss her like Eric. But Jorge was married, and she must forget about him.

She was famished, having slept through the dinner served on the flight from Japan to Paris, which made her especially moody about Eric blowing her off. She planned on taking him to Wyatt's party, yet he didn't have the decency to reciprocate with an invitation tonight.

Wyatt. Charlotte missed her mysterious friend. She curled up in bed and yawned sleepily as she reflected on memories of him.

Chapter 5

LOS ANGELES

During her undergraduate studies as a communications major at the University of California, Los Angeles, Charlotte struggled in a class called History of Cinema. Assuming it would be an easy elective, she panicked over the unexpected workload requiring her to analyze avant-garde movies. For help with the course, she befriended a film major taking the class as a requirement. They remained close after graduation, and she occasionally brought Charlotte to movie screenings.

Charlotte had recently started her Angelino's job when she was invited to the *Complicated Life of a Water Bottle* premiere. The movie was at the forefront of the recycling movement and credited by many for sparking an environmental revolution. Critics heaped praise upon the work that juxtaposed a water bottle's journey to a landfill with the cycle of an abusive relationship between a truck driver and an insurance company receptionist. The film was hailed as a masterpiece and garnered Oscar buzz from the moment production started. Elusive Wyatt Ashcroft was the writer, director, and producer.

Ashcroft was an enigma in Hollywood, keeping a low profile while producing mega blockbusters before transitioning from action films to environmental activism. A-listers desperate to work with him accepted pay cuts to star in his offbeat masterpieces. His background was murky, and legend had it that he ran away from abusive parents when he was a teenager before starting his career in Hollywood and producing his first hit at the age of twenty. In his late thirties, at the time of the new film release, he had never been married and was rumored to follow the Mormon faith, abstaining from alcohol, coffee, and even soda. A genuine tree hugger, he advocated vegetarianism to help sustain the planet. He was lanky, due to his height and diet, with shaggy brown hair that fell into his bright blue eyes. Ironically, he was extremely camera shy and rarely photographed.

The premiere fell on a holiday weekend, allowing Charlotte to fly into LA late Friday night and out on a Monday red-eye to return to work by Tuesday. She stayed with her friend in West Hollywood and planned to visit her family in Orange County.

An entire block on Hollywood Boulevard was closed to traffic, allowing room for paparazzi, fans, and guests who descended upon historic Grauman's Chinese Theater for the screening. Charlotte's friend worked for the studio releasing the picture and had reserved prime seats for them both. The film finished to a standing ovation around 11:30 p.m. Due to the time difference with the East Coast, it felt like 2:30 a.m. to Charlotte, who decided to end the night while her friend stayed to chat with colleagues.

Charlotte maneuvered through street closures to the corner, looking for a taxi, when a steady rain began to fall. Yes, rain in Los Angeles—such a rare occurrence! Without a car in sight, she ran with determination as her pale periwinkle dress soaked into royal blue. Lacking an umbrella and defenseless against Mother Nature, the small purse she held over her head barely kept a tiny patch of hair dry.

Three blocks later, Charlotte scurried down the street, taking brief moments of shelter next to buildings and under awnings while seeking transportation. The area was deserted, only a few cars whizzed by, spraying water each time. A black town car slowly crept up next to her as a tinted rear window lowered to reveal a guy with tousled hair and sunglasses. "Are you okay?"

"I can't find a taxi anywhere. I'm getting drenched." Charlotte remained composed, even though she was on the brink of a meltdown. "Do you know where I can get one?"

"That depends, how'd you like the movie?" the stranger joked.

Charlotte realized he must have been at the premiere also, easing her apprehension. "It was great! And it was dry! I'm sorry, I'm so wet, I can't think straight."

"Can I give you a ride somewhere?" He cracked a lopsided smile.

"Sure. I'm going to West Hollywood, it's close," Charlotte said as she opened the door, forcing him to slide across the backseat. Normally, she'd never jump into a stranger's car, but she felt safe since he attended the premiere. "Sorry to barge in, but I had to get out of that rain. I'm Charlotte," she extended her arm for a handshake as he removed his sunglasses to look closer at her, revealing his piercing blue eyes.

"Wyatt Ashcroft." He shook her hand gently, as if it was priceless china.

"Wait, you're the Wyatt Ashcroft who made the movie I just saw?" She slicked her wet hair back from her face to get a better look at him, but instantly got lost in his intoxicating eyes.

He nodded sheepishly. "Yep."

Charlotte paused for a moment to catch her breath and let the realization that she was sitting next to Wyatt Ashcroft sink in. "It's an honor to meet you," she said in the most confident voice she could muster.

"Are you an actress?"

"Not at all," Charlotte giggled nervously. "I'm a publicist for a restaurant group in New York, but my friend works for the studio and she invited me tonight." She added with a hint of irony, "She stayed behind to network."

"Which restaurant?"

"It's called Angelino's. We're on the East Coast and we'll open here someday." Charlotte was new to the company, but Angelino's often came up in conversation whenever she met someone.

"Angelino's is great! I like the one in SoHo." Wyatt subtly checked out her body before returning his eyes to hers. "Do you want to go to Mel's and get a milkshake?"

The entire situation seemed surreal. Charlotte was soaking wet, completely discombobulated, and in a car with Wyatt Ashcroft. The *legendary Wyatt Ashcroft* and he'd invited her to hang out! Milkshakes at midnight seemed so unorthodoxly innocent.

"I'd love that!" Exhilaration replaced Charlotte's fatigue.

Wyatt directed the driver to Mel's, an iconic twenty-four-hour 1950s-style diner on Sunset Boulevard. Rain fell steadily when they bolted from the vehicle, but Charlotte no longer cared. Wyatt was in great spirits while she jittered with excitement—typical first date anticipation. They settled into a booth, and Wyatt proved he was indeed a milkshake connoisseur.

"If they blend it too much, it's watery and doesn't have the right texture. They can't overmix." His steadfast conviction amused Charlotte.

"Yes, consistency is important, it's a big issue at Angelino's. If Chef Lorenzo catches one of the cooks altering his recipes, it's like World War Three, except the ammunition is gnocchi and truffles. Pots and pans go flying when things get really bad."

Wyatt laughed. "A witty sense of humor in addition to ethereal beauty. Very captivating. Tell me your story."

Spellbound, Charlotte waited a second. "Well, I grew up south of here in Newport Beach. I never really fit into the 'California Girl' stereotype because of my red hair and pale skin—"

"Red hair is known to be a fire that ignites the imagination," Wyatt interrupted.

Charlotte smiled shyly before continuing. "I have two blonde, tan younger sisters who are very athletic and will spend their entire lives in SoCal. I went to UCLA for undergrad and then graduate school at Columbia for my master's in communications. I fell in love with New York, but I didn't know what I wanted to do after graduation. My family urged me to come home, but that sounded like defeat to me, so I jumped on this opportunity at Angelino's right after my twenty-fifth birthday. I've only been there about a month, but I'm learning so much. It's fast-paced, and I'll get to travel internationally for new locations. And…. I'm happy to be here with you!" Worried she sounded starstruck with her last comment, she quickly added, "Now it's your turn. What's your story?"

Wyatt looked deep in thought. "I'm good at reading people and I can tell you like adventure, but I sense you've left things out. Interests? Challenges?" He raised an eyebrow. Charlotte sat tongue-tied. He shrugged and continued, "Maybe I'm more complex because I'm twelve years older than you—"

"Oh, age is just a number!"

"If you say so. As for me, I had a very difficult childhood. I grew up on a ranch in Utah, and I try to forget the horrible way my father behaved toward my mom and my siblings. There were seven of us—"

Charlotte interrupted, "Seven? That's a lot!"

"Yeah, a big Mormon family. By the way, is that shake thick enough?"

"Absolutely! It's perfect! Would you like to try?" Charlotte asked and immediately wondered if she was too forward.

"Sure, let me taste it. I'm not usually into strawberry, but duty calls. And you can try my chocolate shake to experience pure perfection." Wyatt handed her his shake while he wrapped his lips around Charlotte's straw. She couldn't believe they were already sipping out of each other's drinks, and she cherished the sudden intimacy.

"So, as I was saying, I try to forget most of my childhood. But the one joy I savored was going to the theater to watch classic movies. My aunt took us about once a month, and it was pure happiness for me. She was a little nutty and she'd take us to adult movies. So, I saw things like *The Godfather, Deliverance, American Graffiti, The Exorcist*—"

"Wait, your aunt took you to see *The Exorcist?* How old were you?"

"I think I was around ten years old. That's what I mean, she took us to inappropriate movies, but inevitably, it helped me as a filmmaker. Most kids were watching cartoons at an early age while I was exposed to masterpieces. Beyond that, I was in a bubble because my mom homeschooled us. I didn't interact with other kids besides my siblings, and I was the oldest. The rest were girls except for the two youngest boys who were too little for me to bond with. I didn't have much of a childhood in the physical sense, but my imagination still had the innovation of a young mind, and by sixteen, I ran away to Hollywood to make movies. Eventually, I combined my childish idealism with adult intellect and that's what enabled me to succeed in this town." Wyatt paused to take another sip of his milkshake.

Charlotte was in complete awe. She'd met intriguing people over the years, but nobody compared to Wyatt Ashcroft. He was absolutely fascinating.

"Am I boring you? I don't usually talk this much." Wyatt suddenly appeared self-conscious.

"Boring me? Not at all. You're amazing!"

Wyatt smiled. "That's a good endorsement." Charlotte noticed a slight blush spread across his cheeks.

"I mean, you're very interesting. You've really accomplished so much. You came here with a dream and you made it happen in the City of Angels." Charlotte worried she sounded moonstruck instead of like a potential girlfriend. She already decided that he was Mr. Right. The knight in shining armor who picked her up on Hollywood Boulevard, gave her shelter from the rain, invited her out for milkshakes, and mesmerized her with his story.

"That's correct. I made it happen, but it wasn't easy. I'm kind of a quiet guy. The party scene isn't my thing. I mean, sometimes I host events because it's required in the industry. But the alcohol, drugs, actresses trying to date me to get famous…none of it's for me." Wyatt stared out the window, as if studying the rain.

Instinctively, Charlotte reached out and took his hand in hers. "But you create movies that are changing the world. This film tonight has the potential to help the environment and put an end to plastic waste. I only went because it was a hot event, but now that I saw your message on the big screen…I think about the environment differently. And the story of that poor woman living with the abusive truck driver really touched my heart."

"It did?" Wyatt stared deep into Charlotte's eyes, filling her with an electrifying sensation mixed with inexplicable longing, compassion, and familiarity, as if they had been soul mates in another time and another place.

"Do you two want anything else?" The waitress startled them out of their trance and held the bill out in front of Wyatt.

"No thanks," he retracted his hand from Charlotte's and fumbled with his wallet.

She couldn't believe the waitress had the audacity to interrupt such a beautiful moment.

The magic didn't return. Charlotte tried to rekindle it, but Wyatt ended the night. At least he suggested exchanging numbers, but then he quietly gazed out the car window during the ride.

When they reached Charlotte's stop, the driver jumped out and stood beside the car with an umbrella. She turned to Wyatt and said, "Thank you for the most memorable milkshake I've ever had." Then it happened. Charlotte gave him a tender, sweet, gentle kiss on the lips while he sat motionless. With a sly smile, she hopped out of his car, hurrying toward the apartment complex while the driver followed, protecting her with an umbrella.

When she reached the building, she turned around and saw Wyatt staring at her with a blank expression. She gave one final wave and dashed inside.

Charlotte lay sleepless that night as thoughts of Wyatt danced in her head. It was the strongest connection she'd ever felt with a guy. She was convinced her feelings were mutual and he'd see her again before she headed back to New York. Or maybe they'd plan a date soon on the East Coast. But to her dismay, he only responded politely to her thank you text the next day. *It was nice to meet you Charlotte. Stay in touch. Wyatt*

For the next ten years, they met occasionally for decaffeinated tea or milkshakes, sometimes even lunch or dinner. Charlotte tried to reignite the spark she believed was consensual the first night they met, but Wyatt put her in the friend zone. He threw epic parties and often extended an invitation through his assistant. She was grateful to be included, but there was something inside her that always wished for more with him.

Now she was thirty-five, still working at Angelino's, and her eggs were dying while she waited for a guy she barely knew to show up at her hotel room. Wyatt had created several more hit movies since their milkshake night, but he was approaching fifty and had never married. Occasionally, there were rumors about a girlfriend, but he was never photographed with a date, and one could assume that his relationships didn't last long. It was Wyatt, not Eric, who Charlotte dreamed about as she drifted to sleep.

Chapter 6

CANNES

"Hey, sexy! Do you normally sleep in your dress?" Eric's drunk bellowing woke Charlotte.

Disoriented, she momentarily forgot where she was. "What time is it?"

"It's like 7 a.m. and that party was insane! Totally dope! Sorry I couldn't get you in. I hope you're not mad." Reeking of cigarettes, he crawled into bed next to her and wiggled his hand inside her dress and up her leg.

She inched away—tired, hungry, and miffed. "It would've been nice to see you last night instead of sitting alone in the room, all dressed up with nowhere to go."

"Why didn't you go out? If you've got connections to Ashcroft's party, I figured you'd be fine on your own." Charlotte remained silent. "Look, I didn't fly you out here to be in a bad mood. I said I was sorry."

"No, it's fine. I'm just tired and hungry." She tried to brighten her voice.

"Well, here's the menu, order room service." Eric tossed a folder on the bed next to her. "I'm jumping in the shower. Get me a burger if they have one, if not, any kind of omelet is fine. Make sure you ask for fries or hash browns and sausage," he continued talking after he entered the bathroom and closed the door. "I need something to soak up the alcohol from all those vodka shots last night."

Charlotte flipped through the menu and realized that Eric might not be the prince charming she thought she'd met in Tokyo. Before she could dial room service, his phone beeped from the nightstand and she saw a message flash on the screen. *Nice meeting you! I can't wait to see you in New York! Kisses*

Her body tensed up, but she managed to place the food order. Eric emerged from the bathroom jovial. His overly energetic behavior made Charlotte wonder if he was high on drugs.

"So, who did you hang out with last night?" she inquired.

"This buddy of mine from NYU—you'll meet him tonight— and a girl he brought. She was okay, but sort of throwing herself at me. I told them I had a hot redhead waiting at the hotel." He grabbed Charlotte and kissed her passionately, redeeming himself.

His towel dropped to the ground, revealing his chiseled muscles and an extremely excited body part standing at attention. He cusped the back of her head with one hand, keeping his lips locked on hers and rolling his tongue inside her mouth, while his other hand unzipped her dress and slid into the back of her panties, gently stroking between her legs. Unable to contain themselves, they fell into bed locked in each other's arms. Just as Charlotte was about to insist on using protection, room service knocked on the door with their order. They untangled out of their embrace and Charlotte composed herself while Eric let them in. Once the food was set up, they sat on a balcony overlooking the courtyard and consumed a delicious breakfast complete with stimulating conversation. All was forgiven, and they settled into "happy couple" mode.

After the meal, Eric napped while she went to the gym to work out until she finally crawled into bed next to him as he slept. Jet lag combined with exhaustion from the draining week in Japan hit her at once. Getting ready for Wyatt's party would require so much effort and she just wanted to stay in and snuggle…

"Charlotte! Wake up!" Eric shook her.

Startled out of a deep sleep, Charlotte mumbled, "What happened? What's wrong?"

"It's nine o'clock! We're going to be late for the party!" He was in a panic.

Shocked they had slept for nearly ten hours and unsure where she'd find energy, Charlotte asked, "Are you sure you want to go?"

"Ashcroft's party? Of course! That's why we came here!" Nothing was going to stop him.

Charlotte rolled out of bed and dragged herself into the shower. She assured Eric that the party wouldn't be good until 11 p.m. and they had plenty of time, but unfortunately, not enough time to eat dinner. Then she remembered that Wyatt always had a delicious spread of food at his shindigs. They'd be able to eat there.

The theme was "Dream Green Vegetation" in honor of Wyatt's latest film to stop deforestation in the Amazon. Charlotte wore an emerald-colored cocktail dress she had fortunately packed for Japan and plucked some leaves from a tree near the balcony to create a wreathlike crown to place on top of her red mane. Eric donned an apple green tie and handkerchief with a beige suite and green cufflinks. Charlotte laughed when he showed her his matching green socks.

Excitement filled the air during the car ride to Wyatt's rented villa up in the hills. "Will you introduce me to Ashcroft? I've never met him." Eric lit a cigarette as he spoke. "I want to tell him about an idea I have."

Typical. Everyone wanted to get close to Wyatt. But he was so evasive; it was nearly impossible to schedule a meeting with him. Just like the Great Gatsby, there wasn't a trace of him at many of his own parties. Everyone had a blast eating, drinking, and dancing, but the next day, nobody remembered seeing him. Charlotte hoped he'd be out of sight while she was with Eric. She always had a crush on Wyatt, although she accepted the fact that he didn't want anything more than friendship. She'd attended many of his parties over the years, usually with a female friend. A few times she'd brought dates and luckily Wyatt never surfaced on those occasions. She assumed it was just a fortunate coincidence. Charlotte said a silent prayer that she wouldn't have to introduce spoiled Eric to humble Wyatt.

* * *

The driver pulled up to a grand entrance, arguably the best villa in Cannes. Two statuesque women wearing skimpy green bikinis embellished with fresh leaves ushered Charlotte and Eric into the entryway. They were handed green cocktails, which they sipped while they scanned the room for familiar faces.

Unbeknownst to them, Wyatt observed guests arriving from a second-floor window. Charlotte looked delightful in her green dress and ivy-adorned fiery hair. He noticed her date say something in her ear and she threw her head back in laughter. He watched intently as Eric spun Charlotte to face him and gave her a passionate kiss. Wyatt shuffled away and hibernated in his bedroom for the rest of the night, missing his entire party.

* * *

"Eric, we can't make out in front of everyone." Charlotte appreciated his kisses but not in public. "Let's find your friend from NYU."

They headed into the garden as the DJ started spinning. Eric whirled her around the dance floor for nearly half an hour before they decided to take a break and eat. As expected, the buffet featured everything one could desire: lobster, ribs, filet mignon, sautéed chicken breast, grilled octopus, and salads among plentiful side dishes. They each prepared a plate of food and joined a table where a friendly Greek couple struck up an interesting conversation before leaving to dance. Eric put his arm around Charlotte as she rested her head on his shoulder. When she turned to hug him, she stopped herself upon seeing his distorted expression.

"What's wrong?" Charlotte asked.

"She's here." Eric stared into the crowd in disbelief.

"Who?" She squinted.

Eric's eyes stayed glued on someone. "Marcela, my ex."

Charlotte followed his gaze to a tall, thin, gorgeous brunette wearing a skimpy green sequin dress and matching green stilettos. The life of the party, she was dancing, clapping, and shouting to the music. She was carefree and fun—a startling contrast to worry wart Charlotte. Marcela flipped her hair over her shoulder, spotted Eric, and stopped dead in her tracks. The former couple locked eyes until she slowly made her way over to them, fixated on Eric, as if she was in a trance.

He stood up as Marcela approached, and when she finally reached the table, she threw her arms around him and the two embraced. "I missed you," she said with a deep Brazilian accent.

"I missed you too, my darling," he held her with emotion.

"Hi, I'm Charlotte." She tried to introduce herself, but Marcela ignored her. Instead, she whispered to Eric, causing him to look at his forgotten date.

He leaned into her ear, "Hey, Char, I hope you understand. I need some time with Marcela." Charlotte glared at him perplexed. He continued, "We were together for so long and we have to talk about things." Eric turned away with Marcela's hand in his.

"Sure, but how long will you be gone?" Charlotte asked, but they had already taken a few steps and quickly disappeared into the crowd.

She sat down, completely stunned. One minute, she thought Eric could be her future husband, and the next minute he ditched her for a Brazilian bikini model. She reminded herself that she had known him for less than a week, but it still stung.

That was it. Eric had abandoned her. Charlotte searched for Wyatt, but he was nowhere to be found. She even texted him, but he didn't answer. An hour later, the Greek couple bumped into her and mentioned that they saw Eric leave with "that incredible Brazilian dancer." Charlotte went back to the hotel on her own, sad and defeated.

Eric sent her a text. *Hey Char, I hope you understand, Marcela is the love of my life. Enjoy the room, I'll send someone to get my stuff. Have a safe trip back to NYC!*

The flight home worsened the situation. There was always something disconcerting about being up in the sky, vulnerable and little in such a big universe. She sulked about Eric but fixated on Wyatt's behavior and wondered why she hadn't seen him at his party. Although they were just friends, he was the most genuine man she'd ever known, and she wished he'd spend more time with her.

When she walked into her empty, lifeless studio on 56th Street, she felt invisible. There was no one to give her a hug and welcome her home. No boyfriend, kids, not even a pet. After calling Grandma McPherson and updating her on another failed romance, she responded to a customer email complaint about loud music at Angelino's SoHo and collapsed into bed, falling into a deep, dark, heavy slumber.

Part 2

SUMMER

Chapter 7

NEW YORK CITY

Like most New Yorkers, Charlotte embraced June because of the great weather and the start of vacation season. However, her workload increased drastically, as the restaurants were booked with graduation parties and wedding showers. Angelino's was a favorite destination among New Yorkers with something to celebrate (the mayor even threw his son's bar mitzvah there). Charlotte's calendar was jam-packed as she made appearances at bookings associated with vendors. For example, when the law firm representing Angelino's held their intern orientation lunch in a private room, she stopped by for a few minutes to make sure everyone was happy. Such visits weren't part of her job description, but she conscientiously provided an extra touch of customer service.

Adding to her chaotic schedule, Charlotte was required to attend the launch of Angelino's Mumbai. The situation was unusual; she'd already spent two weeks in Goa opening the first Angelino's in India, and she never attended subsequent franchise openings in foreign markets. Although she appreciated the first visit to India (philosophical locals, picturesque beaches, and exotic spiritual culture), one work trip there was enough.

Much to Charlotte's chagrin, the franchisee was so delighted by her diligence that he insisted she take part in their first big metropolitan location. Meanwhile, she craved stability in New York while nursing wounds from Jorge and Eric. A few weeks of rejuvenation would restore her mental clarity to be a better judge of character and at least do a background check before becoming emotionally attached.

"Jack, I'm still exhausted from Japan. And besides the fact I'm on the committee for my dog charity and I'll have to miss our annual gala, the Indian PR team already proved themselves, and they can handle their second opening." She tried not to whine. "Do I really have to go?"

"I'm sorry, Charlotte, I don't blame you. I'm relieved to skip this one, but the franchisee says they're investing so much money in two locations and the least we can do is send our head of PR."

She bit her lip and made one last attempt to get out of the trip. "But there's no way Melvin will pay my travel expenses."

"You're right. The Indian team is paying for everything. Don't worry, it's only three days. It'll go by fast."

By the time she arrived at her coveted nail session with Tracy and Sofia a few days later, Charlotte was in a completely foul mood and immediately vented, "I'm so mad I have to go back to India! I was just in Japan and France and now I have to fly again. It's seriously taking a toll on my mental and physical health. How can they expect me—"

"Enough, Charlotte! You're so spoiled. You met a great guy in Tokyo who whisked you to Cannes and took you to Wyatt

Ashcroft's party and now you get to go back to India, yet you complain about it." Tracy shook her head in disapproval while blowing on her nails.

Taken aback, Charlotte looked at Sofia who stayed out of the dispute by burying her head in a magazine. She turned back to Tracy. "Yeah, I met a 'great guy' who ditched me at a party that I took him to. I got him into Wyatt's party, not the other way around." She was incensed. "And I have to fly for hours with Lorenzo and Marco, smile and kiss ass to our investor. It isn't fun. In fact, it's major pain. Why don't you understand that I'm exhausted from traveling so much?"

Tracy backed off a bit. "Well, I guess I don't understand because I spend twenty-four seven working on ViewPoint Nails. I'd love to travel just a fraction of the amount you do."

For the first time, Charlotte suspected that she might be jealous. This revelation surprised her because Tracy was smart, stylish, and extremely successful. *The New York Times* recently put her on a list of Top Female Entrepreneurs Under Forty, and she had several offers to open ViewPoint Nails in other cities, including Chicago and Philadelphia.

Charlotte softened her tone. "You're right. I should be grateful for my travel opportunities. I think I'm just irritable from being let down by Eric and, of course, that asshole Jorge."

At the mention of Jorge's name, Tracy's face grew red. "Charlotte, Jorge never wronged you. Did you ever ask him if he was married? If you really wanted to know, you would've asked. But you jumped into a relationship, like you always do, and avoided the topic. Now you act like the victim."

"Are you serious? He's the biggest lying scumbag on the planet! What the hell are you talking about?"

Sofia jumped in. "You both need to calm down. Let's go get a drink. You're arguing about stuff that doesn't matter."

"You're right, none of this matters. Just remember that, Charlotte," Tracy said as she rose up to leave. "I need to do some work in my office. You guys can stay as long as you want."

Charlotte sat stunned while Sofia asked, "Aren't you coming with us to Angelino's?"

"No, I already have plans with that baseball player I met last week. You guys have fun," Tracy said over her shoulder as she stormed down the hall.

"Why is she being such a bitch?" Charlotte arrived at the nail salon unhappy, but now, she was livid.

"Try not to get upset, Char, she has to refinance and find new investors. I think she's too stressed out." Sofia was the peacemaker again. "Let's go eat, but we should go to SoHo to avoid running into Marco uptown. He'll be there with his sons."

Charlotte felt a shift in her friendship with Tracy. The traitor lacked empathy about Jorge's deception, and when she initially told her about Eric ditching her in Cannes, Tracy didn't offer words of comfort. Instead, she asked if there were any hot guys at Wyatt's party.

Tracy and Charlotte had traveled the world together before ViewPoint Nails opened and they were inseparable running around NYC. But recently, they seemed to have little in common, and Charlotte found her to be shallow and outright mean at times. Maybe the only thing that bound them in the past was nightlife.

At the age of thirty-five, Charlotte's interest in clubs and random hookups had vanished. She desired a husband and kids while Tracy was stuck in her twenties.

Chapter 8

MUMBAI

Charlotte wore her game face when she bumped into Lorenzo and Marco at the American Airlines check-in counter for their red-eye journey to India. Although she wasn't in the right frame of mind for another foreign trip, especially one lacking the buffer of Jack, she marched forward like a true PR professional.

"*Bella! Carlotta!*" Lorenzo gave his usual sweet greeting while he kissed both cheeks.

"You're on time," Marco grumbled.

Charlotte tried to sound chipper. "Yep, there's no traffic this late. Are you guys ready for India?" The Italians were already too busy on their phones to bother responding.

They approached the counter and Charlotte received the unsettling news that she was booked in coach. For work travel, she insisted on business class (an appreciated perk for physically demanding openings, especially since she could only afford economy when she financed her personal trips). She had uncharacteristically neglected to confirm her seat assignment when the Indian travel agent sent her the ticket, further evidence that she hadn't quite been herself the last few months. With no time to protest, Lorenzo and Marco whisked her into the business class lounge (as their guest) on the pretense that she should eat as much food there as possible before take-off because she'd starve on the plane. They reminded her that the tickets were reviewed and approved by Melvin and she should've told him if there was an issue. After all, they lectured, she was responsible for double-checking the entire team's tickets, including her own. She fired off an email to the travel agency and cc'd the franchisee with the request to upgrade her ticket for the long flights home.

Fantasizing about ways to get revenge on Melvin, she piled pasta on her plate when she felt a slight tap on her shoulder. She spun around with rage, food sliding off her dish, as she expected to find Marco bothering her as usual. Instead, she came face-to-face with Wyatt.

"Oh my gosh! What are you doing here?"

Wyatt stepped back in fear. "You look upset."

"Oh no. I thought you were my boss. He's annoying sometimes." Charlotte followed Wyatt's gaze to the plate she held lopsided, with nothing left on it. "Oh. Oops." She awkwardly crouched down and used her fork to scoop up rigatoni from the ground.

"Hey, what are you doing on the floor? I lost my phone!" Marco barked.

Charlotte turned crimson as she bolted upright and desperately tried to separate her nemesis from her crush. "Let's go back to your seat and look," she said as she shooed Marco toward the couches and turned to Wyatt. "I'll be right back!"

"Do you know that guy?" Marco asked.

"What guy? Let's find your phone. Did you check your bag?" Without asking, Charlotte ransacked his tote to no avail and then shouted at him, exasperated, "Marco! It's right there in your pocket." She ripped the phone out of his pants and tossed it on the table. "I just need a second." She dashed back to the buffet counter, leaving Marco scratching his head.

Wyatt was watching her as she raced back toward him.

"Sorry about that!" She smiled while catching her breath.

"Are you okay?" he asked.

"Of course. Just helping my boss. So, what are you doing here?"

"Did you find his phone? He seemed pretty stressed."

"Yep. Phone found. No worries. Where are you going?" Charlotte tried again to change the topic.

"India. My first time. I was in New York and an agent recommended a retreat to recover from a complicated project I finally completed. It's supposed to turn me into a yogi," Wyatt joked.

His grin made Charlotte's heart skip a beat. "That's so nice," she squeaked out.

"What about you?"

"Just work. We're opening another Angelino's in India. This time in Mumbai. We must be on the same flights." She noticed that her voice sounded nervous.

"I'll be in Mumbai for a few days before the retreat to meet with some Bollywood people. It's a huge industry."

Wyatt gazed deeply into her eyes, or maybe she was just imagining it. "Are you staying at the Four Seasons?" she asked.

Wyatt shook his head no. "I'm staying at The Taj Mahal Hotel."

"I heard it's really nice. Do you want to come to our Angelino's opening? I mean, I know you don't like to do parties, even though you throw some great ones. But, maybe, you'd want to come to this, even though it isn't as glamorous as yours are. But of course, you're invited. It's the day after tomorrow." The senseless rambling was cringe-worthy.

"Sounds good. Text me the invite." Wyatt cocked his head and smiled again.

"Hurry up! It's time to board," Marco growled.

Shaken from her trance, Charlotte quickly introduced Wyatt to the restaurateur and the chef. He was congenial to the Italians, who had no interest in meeting him. They murmured quick greetings before whisking her off.

During the wait at the gate, she noticed Wyatt board with the first-class group. If he spotted her in the crowd, he didn't send any signals. She was able to board with Lorenzo, Marco, and the rest of business class, but she was directed immediately to the right when they entered the plane, while the two men headed to the left toward their plush seats.

In her chaotic cabin, complete with howling babies and arguing adults, Charlotte cursed Melvin while she squeezed into her tiny spot covered with plastic. Her knees indented the seat in front of her, but at least she was next to the window. Charlotte skipped her usual skincare routine and poured herself a glass of water to hydrate during the first seven-hour leg of the trip to London. After a two-hour layover, they'd fly another nine hours to Mumbai.

Somewhere over the Atlantic Ocean, Charlotte was lost in a dream. She stood on a beach watching Eric dance with his Brazilian until a wave washed over her. When it retracted, she was entangled in a peacefully loving embrace as soothing lips caressed her neck and made their way down her chest and along her breasts.

Her body flushed with a warm tingling sensation as her dress evaporated, exposing her flesh to the man gingerly leaving a trail of kisses around her naval. She discovered Wyatt on top of her as another wave swept past them. With a crash, a stream of urine ran down her leg.

Jolted awake, she discovered her lap was soaking wet. Completely disoriented, she was in disbelief that she had peed herself, but within seconds, she realized her plastic cup of water fell into her lap when the seat in front of her reclined backward into her tiny space.

"Crap!" Charlotte thrust the empty cup off herself. The cabin lights dimmed as passengers slept, including her snoring, heavyset neighbor she needed to rouse to access the bathroom. Relieved she hadn't urinated but discomforted by her wet lap, she tapped the man a few times and was eventually met with an angry scowl. Eyes heavy with fatigue, she dragged her suitcase down from the overhead bin and fished around until she extracted a pair of underwear and bright pink stretch pants. They were meant for the gym, but it was better than having a damp crotch. Changing in the tiny bathroom, she narrowly avoided stepping in a puddle someone had left on the floor.

Charlotte dried up the seat with thin napkins from the flight attendant and tried to go back to sleep. But she was wide-awake, thinking about Wyatt the rest of the flight to London. Her feelings for him and his behavior confused her. He seemed happy to see her at the airport, but she refused to get her hopes up again because he made it clear in the past that he wasn't interested in her romantically.

During the London stopover, Marco took a moment from reminiscing about the soft flatbed in business class to question Charlotte. "Why are you wearing exercise pants? Change before you get to India. This is a business trip."

The delivery was bad, but she knew he was right. She'd look foolish if they went straight to the restaurant when they landed. Fortunately, she had options in her carry-on luggage, allowing her to wear a professional, albeit uncomfortably tight, pair of black slacks for the final nine-hour leg of the trip. Wyatt was out of sight and Charlotte wondered if he'd stayed in London for a night or continued on their next flight.

Not surprisingly, she was only allotted a few hours' rest before heading to Angelino's Mumbai with Lorenzo and Marco. She hadn't slept upon arrival. Instead, she stared out the window of the Four Seasons, thinking about the shantytown below, unable to comprehend the poverty housed next to her luxury hotel.

"Why are you so quiet?" Marco demanded during the car ride to Angelino's.

"Sorry, I'm just tired. Do you need anything?" Charlotte tried to do a good job despite her fatigue. Marco shrugged and stared out the window.

The PR team and GM greeted the NYC crew with open arms at Angelino's, and the beauty of the restaurant awed Charlotte. The Italian artist had quit midway through painting the frescos due to creative differences, and the new Indian muralist had a unique style, creating a patriotic flair by incorporating national symbols, like the Lotus flower, Indian peacocks, and Bengal tigers alongside typical Angelino's images of wine vases, pasta, and olive trees. Within the vibrant walls were large tables made of oak with bright yellow leather chairs. Colorful bouquets and candles adorned each table, while the central bar area was erected before a massive wall stocked with wine bottles from floor to ceiling.

The Indian chef from Goa emerged to greet them. Lorenzo whisked him off to the kitchen to philosophize about pasta sauces. Marco retreated to a corner to call his kids and Charlotte sat down at the bar to check emails. Later in the afternoon, she joined the team on the floor as a Hindu official tied red strings around their wrists and recited affirmations in a spiritual ceremony complete with incense and chanting to bless the new location.

When evening fell, Charlotte was too exhausted to attend a formal dinner. For the first time since she'd started at Angelino's, she politely asked Lorenzo and Marco if she could stay in her room and rest. Lorenzo acquiesced but typical Marco insisted she attend the meal in the home of the franchisee.

"It's just a few hours. You're coming," Marco ordered.

Dutifully, Charlotte showered, slipped on a black, knee-length dress, and fastened a gold belt around her waist to cover her slight tummy bulge. She paired matching gold stilettos with a clutch and pulled her hair back into a tight ponytail because there was no time for a blowout. She accessorized with gold jewelry and wore minimal eye makeup, accenting her mouth with red lipstick.

Dinner turned out to be particularly troubling, as she had a fear of food poisoning. Her uncle nearly died when he ate unpasteurized ice cream sold outside the Taj Mahal, thus her mother warned her to stay away from all Indian dairy products, advice Charlotte heeded while working at Angelino's Goa. The formal dinner in a private residence limited her ability to monitor the fare.

The home was located on the top three floors of a high-rise building. An estate manager handed everyone a glass of Champagne before leading the group on a tour. The views were spectacular and the interior was an eclectic mix of modern furniture. The plants particularly impressed Charlotte, as the vegetation made the habitat feel lush and breezy. There were countless bedrooms, a movie screening room, and even a basketball court that doubled as a tennis court.

The franchisee arrived with his elegant wife and Charlotte instantly greeted them with respect. She had met them a few times in Goa and NYC and found them to be polite and kind. Lorenzo charmingly kissed the wife's hand and Charlotte watched her blush as he told her she was the most beautiful woman in India.

Feeling a grumble in her stomach, Charlotte's eyes lit up when they entered a large, formal dining room. She was by no means an Indian food connoisseur, but she loved the traditional dishes she ordered whenever she ate the cuisine in the US: chicken tikka masala, vegetable samosas, and naan. She was relieved to find them all on the table with an incredible buffet of additional dishes. The franchisee graciously invited everyone to sit down, pulling a chair out for Charlotte and, of course, his wife. She listened to him with interest while he proudly described the delicious items laid out before them: papadum (thin, crisp, disc-shaped cooked dough), raita (a condiment made from yogurt, cucumber, and mint), saag paneer (spinach with Indian cheese), sambar (lentil-based vegetable stew), Navratan korma (creamy vegetable curry with cream and nuts), aloo matar (potatoes and peas in a spiced creamy tomato sauce), malai kofta (veggie balls with sauce), kheema (ground beef with peas), and beef vindaloo (extremely spicy curried beef).

They ate with pleasure as Charlotte relished Indian Zen. Her mind wandered to daydreams about Wyatt's forthcoming appearance at the opening. She forgot about the uncomfortable flights and her reluctance to make the trip as she chewed her food.

For dessert, they ate kheer (milk-based pudding), gulab jamun (deep fried dough balls dipped in sugary syrup and flavored with saffron and rose water), gajar ka halwa (carrot pudding), and kulfi (frozen dairy dessert similar to ice cream). Remembering her uncle's near-death experience, Charlotte skipped the kulfi.

Lorenzo and Marco dozed off during the car ride back to the hotel while Charlotte stared out the window, wondering what it'd be like to grow up in a caste system. Deep in thought as they drove past a filthy market, she suddenly snapped to attention with the troubling realization that she did indeed eat dairy at dinner. How could she be so careless?

Panic set in as she tried to recall what she'd consumed. Her stomach tightened, while official names slipped her mind. She remembered the pudding for dessert, the white sauce with the mint and cucumber, and the Indian cheese in spinach. Charlotte was terrified by the time they arrived at the Four Seasons. They proceeded through the police checkpoint complete with bomb sniffing dogs and metal detectors (security remained tight since the Mumbai terrorist attacks in 2008). She barely said goodnight to Lorenzo and Marco before racing up to her room, tearing off her dress, and running to the bathroom where she sat on the toilet and clenched a trash can, waiting for the inevitable. But nothing happened. Eventually she cautiously tiptoed to her bed and crawled beneath the covers. She tossed and turned all night, worried she'd have to race back to the bathroom. Surprisingly, her stomach was fine the next morning. She even managed a workout at the hotel gym before meeting the Italians for breakfast.

The day flew by as Charlotte sat in on numerous interviews with her bosses. As she predicted, the local PR company had everything under control. Feeling useless, she watched Indians bobble their heads as they successfully completed their work. At least she had time to call Grandma McPherson to check on her before dealing with the latest crisis in NYC involving a customer who'd gotten locked in the bathroom with his three-year-old daughter at Angelino's SoHo and screamed for help until a waiter on the other side forcefully pushed the door open, allegedly striking the child's face.

They retreated to the Four Seasons to change for the opening party. Charlotte wore a silky violet Prada dress with dangling gold earrings and the same gold stilettos as the night before because she forgot to pack one of her black high heels. Her red hair cascaded down her back, fresh from a blowout she'd managed to sneak in at a salon near Angelino's. She was determined to look good for Wyatt who promised to stop by toward the end of the event.

She darted off, upon arrival at Angelino's, to connect with the leader of the local PR team to ensure the pasta ribbon cutting ceremony flowed smoothly. They had it completely under control, more proof that Charlotte wasn't needed. But her anger dissipated with the thought of seeing Wyatt.

Lorenzo, Marco, and the franchisee made remarks before the consul general from Italy gave a speech in Italian that few people in the room understood. Once the ribbon was cut, the party was in full swing and Charlotte mingled with a crowd of flashy women dripping in jewels, couture dresses, and designer handbags. Just when she thought the evening would be drama-free and she could relax, Marco barreled toward her and grabbed her arm. "Get Lorenzo! The newspaper wants a picture of us with an actress."

Grinding her teeth with annoyance, she ran throughout the party trying to find Lorenzo. She stormed the kitchen, teetering in her stilettos, sinking into the floor mat rings while holding her hair in a low ponytail to prevent stray strands from falling into food. She edged past the pastry chef and saw Lorenzo berating an Indian cook over the pesto sauce. She inched her way through the steamy chaos and shouted, "Lorenzo! Marco needs you for a photo op!"

Startled, he turned to face Charlotte just as she took a step closer. Her heel wobbled on the edge of the mat and jolted her forward. To prevent falling, she thrust her hand toward the counter, but instead it landed on the edge of the sauce bowl, flipping it and dousing the front of her dress with the subpar green concoction. She gasped as Lorenzo grabbed her waist, saving her from landing in the salad station.

"*Carlotta!*" he exclaimed with concern. "Be careful! You could be hurt-uh!"

She was uninjured but drenched, and Wyatt would be there within an hour. She rushed to the restroom while Lorenzo and Marco smiled with the Bollywood beauty, haphazardly leaned over the sink to wash the front of her dress with soapy water and then crouched under the hand dryer for a good twenty minutes, ignoring quizzical stares from women waiting in line for toilets.

Flustered by the pesto debacle but not broken, Charlotte rested her back against the wall to catch her breath while she surveyed the crowd. She felt a familiar excited, throbbing beneath her chest, provoked by the thought of seeing Wyatt. She hoped he wouldn't notice the faded stain on her dress. Trying to relax, she noshed on pizza, fantasizing about how she'd greet him.

Lorenzo stormed out of the kitchen. "My God-uh! It's a mess-uh!" His fury slipped him into an even heavier accent. Before she could respond, he continued, "They don't use our imported buffalo mozzarella!"

Charlotte was indifferent to the ingredients at Angelino's, and although she appreciated Lorenzo's devotion to quality control, she avoided kitchen disputes. She shrugged and gazed back at the crowd, taking another bite of pizza. Her lack of concern infuriated him even more.

"Do you know what they did-uh? They run out of buffalo mozzarella and go to the market and buy their own local cheese! Who knows about this cheese you're eating? It might make you sick-uh!"

Suddenly understanding the severity of the situation, Charlotte spit a mouthful of pizza into a napkin. Panic gripped her. The cheese she'd consumed wasn't from the same source as her gourmet dinner the night before. No, it was from one of those dirty markets that made her wince. Lorenzo stormed off, leaving her alone to digest the bad news.

As she tried to calm down and convince herself she was fine, Wyatt startled her. "Great turnout."

"Hi, Wyatt. Thank you for coming." Her voice cracked slightly.

His arms darted out from nowhere as he embraced her. "Congratulations!"

She briefly hugged him back before nervously transitioning into PR mode, "Would you like a tour, or some food? Although, we're not serving pizza at the moment due to a mozzarella shortage in the kitchen."

Wyatt laughed. "That's great. You're funny."

Unsure if he was complimenting her or not, Charlotte simply shrugged. "Guilty as charged."

He turned serious. "I hope you're not offended, but I just ate a nine-course vegan meal with a Bollywood producer, and I can't consume another bite."

Relieved that there was no risk from Angelino's cheese substitutions making him sick, she assured him that she understood and would happily invite him for a meal another time.

"Do you have to stay here all night? I have a driver who can take us to all the sites in the city. I've been researching the area for a few weeks and thought I'd be doing it alone. But if you'd like to join—"

"I'd love to go!" Charlotte looked over her shoulder and saw Lorenzo and Marco chatting at a table with the woman they were keen to pose with earlier. "I can leave any time."

"Let's explore Bombay." Wyatt held out his elbow so she could link her arm into his perfect nook as they ducked out together. Chatting freely, Charlotte asked why most Indians called the city "Bombay" instead of the government-mandated name "Mumbai." They embarked on a conversation analyzing colonialism and nationalism.

Her stomach felt fine and, having survived various forms of dairy the previous night, she concluded she was overly paranoid about getting food poisoning. After all, Indian dairy products should have improved since the time her uncle consumed the near-lethal dessert.

Wyatt was an excellent tour guide and she appreciated his attention to detail. He took her to an astonishing hilltop overlooking the Arabian Sea where the beautiful Basilica of Our Lady of the

Mount was built in the 1600s and then rebuilt in the 1700s. Next, they drove past the Gateway of India, a monument beside the sea resurrected to commemorate Queen Mary and King George V's visit to the city in the early 1900s. Reminiscent of those she saw in Europe, the massive arch was more than eighty feet high and made of concrete. Then they stopped for a cup of tea at Wyatt's luxurious hotel where he showed her the opulent lobby and mentioned noteworthy former guests.

"A headhunter called me the other day and asked if I'd consider joining the PR department of an international hotel chain," Charlotte remarked as she studied the intricate indoor balconies towering above them.

"And?" Wyatt tried to read her level of interest.

"Well, I gave it some thought. I've been so focused on getting a raise, but maybe it's time to try a different career path."

Wyatt nodded in agreement. "You're very talented and I was a bit…surprised to meet your bosses."

"You weren't impressed?" Charlotte teased. "They would've charmed your pants off if you were a woman. But they don't make an effort for new male acquaintances."

"But why should gender matter? Men and women are equal."

"Ha! Not at Angelino's." Charlotte rolled her eyes. "We're still in the dark ages."

"That's not right and you should consider this hotel job if it's a place that will treat you with the respect that you deserve."

Charlotte smiled. "Thanks, Wyatt. Your concern is appreciated."

"I mean it. The #MeToo Movement ushered in a new era. Take advantage of *it* and stop being taken advantage *of*."

"You're right. And I like working at Angelino's, but if I don't get a raise, I might quit." Charlotte crossed her arms. "I'll come up with Plan B if I need to."

"You'll get it. They'd be absolute idiots to let you go. You're like a treasure, irreplaceable."

Charlotte's heart fluttered. "Thanks! Let's check out more of the city before it's too late." Always a master at changing the subject, she walked toward the exit with him following a few steps behind.

They drove past an enormous gothic structure in the center of Mumbai called the Victoria Terminus. Bright with lights and so wondrous that UNESCO had declared it a World Heritage Site. One of the busiest railway stations in the city, it was built in 1888 and as Charlotte gazed at it, she was transported to another time period. Struck by how much influence the British had in India, she wondered aloud to Wyatt what it'd be like if they'd never set foot there.

Before she turned into a British imperialist, he took her to see the truly remarkable Haji Ali Dargah. Built without any European influence, the massive whitewashed mosque was flanked by marble pillars. Wyatt's eyes sparkled as he explained the legend that whomever prays there will get their wish fulfilled. But, just like a fairytale, they couldn't enter it because the shrine was in the sea and the pathway to reach it was submerged by the evening tide. They stood on the shore, admiring the structure while she pondered what people wished for and imagined their happiness when dreams were fulfilled. She caught Wyatt observing her reaction with intrigue, focusing more on her than the tourist attraction.

The Siddhivinayak Hindu Temple was a site to behold and the ancient architecture fascinated Charlotte. It appeared to be at least seven stories tall and looked as if large, peach-colored horizontal cylinders, accented with spires, were elegantly sculpted and attached together to create a cohesively alluring monument. It was a combination of strength and beauty. Wyatt explained that nearly 25,000 worshipers visited the 200-year-old temple every day seeking blessings. A childless lady with the hope of granting barren women children originally funded the temple. Suddenly reminded of her fragile egg situation, Charlotte resisted the urge to run inside and beg the Hindu deities for fertility. She wouldn't dare cause a scene in front of Wyatt, and it had already closed for the night.

Finally, they drove to the beach for a stroll on Marine Drive, immersing themselves in the night energy of the city. Tall buildings were alight, and he explained that the long, curved road was called "The Queen's Necklace" because the bright streetlamps created the illusion of a pearl necklace. Impressed by Mumbai, Charlotte wished she could stay longer, especially with Wyatt.

"The retreat is supposed to revive me and help me recuperate from work stuff that has me mired down." He stared at the sky pensively as he spoke.

A wave of concern washed over Charlotte. "Are you okay? What's been going on?"

"I'll be fine. I just need a break from industry politics. I'm trying to make films that impact society for a greater good, but I have lawyers hounding me about things like the size of actors' dressing rooms. The studio is supposed to handle it, but so many trivial matters end up on my desk. I can't work with unhappy talent, but their demands are often frivolous in the grand scheme of things." Wyatt sighed.

"I can imagine. Celebrities are lucky to earn a fortune while many talented people never make it to the big screen. I bet some take success for granted." Charlotte rolled her eyes.

Wyatt stopped walking and turned to look at her. "You're exactly right. They want to be in my films because they say they care about the environment. Then I find out that the studio flies them on private jets to our shoots."

"That's so hypocritical. What about you?" Charlotte raised an eyebrow. "Flying private?"

"Obviously not." Wyatt appeared insulted until he realized that she was teasing. "Never have, never will. Commercial flights are packed with different personalities trapped in a vessel thousands of miles up in the sky. Great fodder for future scripts!"

His excitement amused Charlotte. "I have plenty of material for you if you want to delve into the restaurant industry."

"I'd create the perfect ending complete with a promotion and bonus as Employee of the Year. Those Italians should kiss your feet for doing an amazing job," Wyatt quipped.

Charlotte laughed. "Thanks for the vote of confidence. I don't anticipate feet kissing but I'll take a happy ending anytime." Her mind drifted back to Dr. Radcliff's call, reminding her of her intense desire to get married and have children. She gazed into Wyatt's eyes and found warmth combined with understanding.

"You're a nice person. You deserve everything your heart desires." Wyatt turned back to the sky, allowing Charlotte to reflect.

It was nearly 2 a.m. and she momentarily felt anxious about getting enough sleep, working the next day, then flying at night. But her worries dissipated when she gazed at Wyatt as they wandered back to the car.

"Did you like the tour?" he asked as he followed her into their vehicle.

"I loved it." Charlotte looked at him slyly and contemplated reaching across the seat to touch him. "Do you want another tea, at my hotel?" It was a spontaneous offer and an attempt to prolong the evening.

Wyatt stared out the window, causing her to tense up before he responded, "Sure."

Her mind raced, convinced they were about to embark upon a turning point in their relationship. The arm linking, relaxed conversing, his compliments, and she even caught him looking at her curves (more than once) as she sashayed around the monuments. Together they'd inhaled the exotic intrigue of India. The stage was set for more exploration and she toyed with the idea of inviting him directly up to her room, transitioning into a physical relationship.

As they drove in silence through dark streets, her mind veered into over-analytical mode while her nerves pulsated. Worry consumed her thoughts and she felt a gnawing sensation grow in her stomach. She glanced at Wyatt who appeared perturbed and a gray cloud of anxiety descended upon her. Maybe the hotel rendezvous was a bad idea and he was thinking of a way to get out of it.

Five minutes into the ride, she spoke for the first time. "How far are we?"

"We're just a few blocks away," the driver responded. Those blocks felt like an eternity as war broke out deep inside her bowels. She didn't understand why she felt so nauseous about spending more time with Wyatt. Until, with a heavy sense of dread, she realized: *It's the cheese.*

Charlotte held it down as long as she could despite her unease. "Um, do you mind if we take a rain check on the tea?"

Wyatt looked at her with confusion. "Sure. But I thought you wanted—"

"I have to go!" Security officers had barely waved them through when Charlotte jerked the door open and jumped out, forcing the driver to screech to a stop.

A doorman at the entrance asked if she was okay. Unable to speak, she yanked off her heels, clutching them as she beelined through the lobby, praying for the strength to make it to her room. Stuck waiting for an elevator, she broke out into a sweat, frantically pushing the button until her knees weakened as she collapsed and threw up all over the floor. Heaving, she tried to hold the last bit back, but it refused to stay down as the elevator doors opened to reveal Lorenzo, Marco, and their dates. They simultaneously gasped when they found Charlotte reeling next to a pool of vomit.

"My God! *Carlotta!*" Lorenzo exclaimed in shock.

With every ounce of strength she could muster, she bolted into the elevator as they jumped away from her, narrowly avoiding the mess on the floor. She held down the button for her floor, ascending away from her speechless bosses, raced into her room, then straight to the bathroom for a diarrhea attack. It was official: Charlotte had food poisoning.

She dragged a pillow and bedspread into the bathroom to sleep on the floor when she wasn't sitting on the toilet or throwing up in it. The next day, she texted Wyatt, thanked him for the tour, and apologized for her hasty departure. Too embarrassed to tell him the truth, she gave him a lame excuse about having a press emergency for work. He didn't respond. She emailed Marco and Lorenzo (and cc'd Jack) to tell them that the cheese mistake left her bedridden. A hotel doctor examined her, ordered bed rest, and told her to wait an extra day to fly back to the US. Her bosses avoided a personal visit and instead communicated via texts before they departed.

Charlotte was deserted in Mumbai. The symptoms subsided by nightfall, but she stayed in bed, drank water, and ate crackers. Weak and depressed, she replayed her evening with Wyatt over and over in her head. It was dreamy until the damn cheese ruined everything.

Navigating the airport on her own the next day was harrowing. Her health improved by the time she boarded the flight, although her stomach muscles ached. Her seat wasn't upgraded, only the departure day was altered, and she cursed Melvin during the entire journey home.

Chapter 9

NEW YORK CITY

U pon returning to NYC, Charlotte took advantage of the personal day allotted to her after each foreign trip. With low spirits, she desperately wished for a new environment, remembering her dream of living in Paris to study French that she never pursued due to her demanding work schedule. She was lounging in bed, researching language schools, when she noticed a Craigslist ad from a French photographer seeking an apartment swap with a New Yorker for a month. It was the perfect scenario! She emailed him without hesitation and plotted how she could temporarily escape her job.

Charlotte was pulled away from web surfing to address an inquiry from *People Magazine* about a reality star's husband dining with his alleged mistress at Angelino's Fifth Avenue. She had a casual friendship with the wife and deliberated contacting her to warn her about the story when she received an email from Sofia with the subject line: *Did you know about this?*

The message linked to a *Page Six* article about Ambassador Sorenson's son's pending nuptials to a Brazilian model. Eric was engaged to Marcela!

She read the details about their engagement party at The Boom Boom Room, which was graced by notable attendees from the diplomatic and modeling worlds. Shocked that it happened so fast, Charlotte theorized that Eric must have proposed during the Cannes weekend or soon after. Although her "courtship" with him was too brief for her to be devastated, she felt left behind, remaining single and haunted by fertility issues.

Trying to distract herself, Charlotte perused other sections of *Page Six* when an entry in *Sightings* made her blood freeze: *Wyatt Ashcroft spotted at exclusive Atmantan Wellness Spa in India with mystery brunette.*

Struck by nausea, Charlotte read the item five times to search for deeper meaning about his interaction with the horrid woman who repulsed her even though she didn't know who she was. *Page Six* stories were usually accurate, but just because he was "spotted" with someone, it didn't mean he was madly in love. They could simply be friends. She knew celebrity press often sensationalized innocent facts to sell publications and garner more clicks, and she reasoned that she'd been in public with him several times and could've been a "mystery redhead spotted with Wyatt Ashcroft." Charlotte tried to disregard the item, but she curled up with her pillow and worried he was offended by her rude on-the-brink-of-vomiting departure after their magical Indian night tour. A true PR girl found a way to spin a sticky situation into a golden opportunity, but she'd run out of honey.

Charlotte needed a shoulder to cry on, but Grandma McPherson was playing cards with her friends and compassionate Sofia was swamped organizing the Russian culinary team who recently arrived in NYC to train. Tracy was the last person Charlotte would turn to for empathy as they'd barely spoken the last few months and she didn't foresee things improving anytime soon. Their Sunday gatherings were a thing of the past and she needed to find a new place to get her nails done.

Loneliness reared its ugly head and the hours dragged on until she realized that it was time to do something drastic. She longed for a change of scenery and the apartment swap with the Parisian provided a perfect window of opportunity. She texted Jack. *Can we talk after the staff meeting tomorrow?*

Chapter 10

ANGELINO'S SUMMER STAFF MEETING

W ith her body still reeling from India and her spirits down, Charlotte dreaded another painful staff meeting. She faked a smile and made pleasant conversation upon arrival. She listened to Jessica rattle on about the new uniform policy and bit her tongue when Melvin decried a manager's wastefulness for switching trash collection companies without consulting him. Charlotte wasn't speaking to him since the stapler incident and she vowed to give him the silent treatment until he apologized. Deep down, she knew he'd never say he was sorry, but at least now she had an excuse not to talk to such a hateful man.

Speaking out of turn, Lorenzo rose to express his outrage about waiters forgetting to offer fresh Parmesan to compliment certain pasta dishes. After his cheese purveyor questioned why purchasing had declined, the chef studied hours of surveillance video footage to solve the mystery and threatened to release a list of culprits if the injustice wasn't immediately halted. Servers shifted in their seats uncomfortably and Charlotte silently predicted that the cheese vendor would soon receive a massive order.

During her turn, she spoke energetically about the opening of Angelino's Mumbai, briefly stopping midsentence at one point as she had a flashback of running away from Wyatt, crippled by food poisoning. Quickly regaining her composure, she acted her part until the end. "The last item I'd like to share pertains to Angelino's Greenwich! We're just two weeks away from the opening, and we need to cross-promote because many of your business lunch customers live in Greenwich. We want them to take their families to Angelino's for dinner and we hope their wives will lunch there. Please inform everyone about this new location. We'll have table cards and promo materials for the check folders by the end of the week. Our first Angelino's in Connecticut! Let's spread the word!" Charlotte sat down with enthusiasm waxed on her face.

Then, it was time for the tirade. Charlotte braced herself for the inevitable.

Marco began eerily soft-spoken, showing off his henna tattoos from India and tranquilly describing the new "*bellissima*" location. Then, Lorenzo interrupted to tell everyone about the Indian chef using the wrong cheese.

"We must always buy the best! Don't use crap-uh! *Carlotta* ate the bad cheese and threw up all over the hotel in front of everyone! She slept on the floor next to the toilet and couldn't fly home! It was a catastrophe!" Lorenzo threw both hands in the air.

Charlotte wanted to hide under the table as the entire staff turned to look at her. Flashing a closed-lip smile, she shrugged her shoulders and nodded her head. She caught a few expressions of concern from colleagues, but out of the corner of her eye, she saw Melvin covering his mouth, trying not to burst into laughter.

"And we need to talk about something else." Lorenzo frowned as he looked at the floor. Everyone braced themselves, ready for the explosion. "Marco…"

It'd be worse once Marco took over. The short beast stood up next to Lorenzo and tucked his thumbs under his suspenders, his face crimson with rage. Everyone held their breaths.

"Where's Ray?" Marco said in a steady voice as he looked around the room.

Ray raised his hand, confident and brave. Charlotte noticed his sexy, bad boy persona again. It was hard to miss.

"You motherfucker!" Marco went full steam ahead. "We know what you're doing! Lorenzo saw you on the cameras when he was looking for Parmesan cheese! You're giving away free cappuccino and espresso! Do you think we're fucking stupid? You thought you wouldn't get caught? Fuck you!" Marco threw both of his middle fingers up in the air.

"Marco, Marco. Let him speak-uh," Lorenzo motioned his hands downward to try to calm him while the staff subtly gave Ray sympathetic glances.

The bartender was unfazed. "Yeah. Sometimes when a customer eats at the bar, I'll give them coffee after their meal. It's no big deal."

"No big deal?" Marco was even more fired up. "Who the fuck do you think pays for that coffee? How can Melvin pay the bills if you're giving shit away for free?!"

Melvin was in hysterics, giggling and shaking his head in agreement. Charlotte thought he might pee his pants with excitement.

"If you want to talk, we can do that after the meeting. There's no need to involve the entire company." Ray got up and walked out.

A stunned silence fell upon the room. Charlotte noticed his toned body as he was leaving. A rebel without a cause. She was completely turned on, along—she was certain—with many fellow female and male employees.

While Marco recovered, Lorenzo lowered his voice. "Guys, make customers pay for the coffee, for everything. Don't give it away free-uh."

"Yeah. If we catch you, we fire you." Marco sounded deflated by Ray's departure.

From that day on, Ray was a hero at Angelino's because when the bosses treated him like a dog, he bit back. He proved he had self-respect and wouldn't tolerate abuse. Marco ordered Jessica to fire Ray immediately, but she said it was illegal to dismiss him without following the "Three Warning Rule." According to her, in the state of New York, employees required three disobedience warnings in writing before they could be fired. Although it sounded odd to Charlotte, she never questioned Jessica, the human resources expert.

A few days later, Sofia informed Charlotte that Ray and Jessica slept together a week before he was berated at the staff meeting. The affair made much more sense than a "Three Warning Rule." For the first time in her career, Jessica had done something unethical and lied to her superiors about the law. Ray was that irresistible.

* * *

As promised, Jack met with Charlotte after the meeting. She disclosed how rough things had been. There were problems in her personal life, and she was overworked. She begged him for a sabbatical to take a month off and go to Paris and study French.

"Charlotte, that's impossible. Maybe two weeks, but that's all," Jack said.

As uncomfortable as it was, Charlotte used her last piece of ammunition. Taking a deep breath, she admitted that instead of taking adequate time off after her father's death, she'd lost herself in work and she couldn't keep going without a break.

He massaged his forehead a bit. "When is the Greenwich opening?"

Charlotte sweetened her voice as she smelled victory on the horizon. "It's two weeks from tomorrow."

"Anything big on the calendar after that?"

"No, just a few events in the Hamptons, nothing major. Lorenzo and Marco will be with their families in Italy during July. They won't even notice I'm gone, and most of our regular customers will be traveling." Charlotte watched Jack nod his head in agreement.

After a minute, he said, "Fine, go to Paris. I'll tell Jessica you're taking two weeks of vacation and you have a personal matter to handle for a week away from NYC, but you'll do some work remotely. Stay very low-key; don't post tourist pictures on social media."

"That'd be amazing! But it's only three weeks…" She was determined to take a month-long leave.

"The final week will be like a business trip in France. I'll intro you to some people to meet with. We're in talks with a big shopping center developer in Paris, so it'll be good to have you there. You'll check out some locations and meet a few people. But you'll only get paid for three out of four weeks that you're away. We can't pay you for the 'personal' week. Deal?" Jack put out his hand.

"Thanks so much, Jack," Charlotte went in for a hug and felt Jack's body stiffen as she threw her arms around him. It was all set!

Chapter 11

GREENWICH

One of the most affluent cities in America, Greenwich, Connecticut, was known for large estates, picturesque scenery, and its hub of financial institutions. Only forty-five minutes by train to Manhattan, it was one of the most desirable suburbs of NYC. Before Angelino's signed a lease there, Charlotte had only been a handful of times to watch polo matches and attend parties. She loved the trees and quaint feeling of the town, but it wasn't a place for single girls. It was for families: moms and dads, sons and daughters. Maybe she'd be a Greenwich wife someday, but for now, she was a city girl.

Charlotte spent opening week shuttling back and forth between NYC and Greenwich. Angelino's didn't hire an outside PR firm, as they expected her to handle the work because of the proximity to Manhattan. It was easy breezy since local media was already familiar with Angelino's, and in PR, the first half of the battle was gaining name recognition in a new market. Charlotte didn't face that challenge in Greenwich because anyone who spent time in NYC or read tabloids knew about Angelino's and its celebrity clientele. For those who didn't know about it, they'd soon find out because the restaurant was destined to be popular with locals.

During opening night, Lorenzo, Marco, and the investing partner gave speeches with the first selectman and town administrator before cutting the pasta ribbon. Charlotte surveyed the crowd and saw a sea of blonde women in Tory Burch and Lilly Pulitzer dresses on the arms of dapper men in three-piece suits. Many couples reminded her of nice Orange County folks from back home. She felt slightly envious, as she longed to be on the arm of a handsome husband.

Tracy waltzed in after the speeches, late of course. Charlotte was in no mood to see her. Flashy as usual, Tracy donned a tight, sexy, gold dress and high stilettos. Heavy makeup partially masked party girl fatigue, and she immediately downed a martini to take the edge off. She couldn't drink a simple glass of Prosecco like everyone else. Instead, she forced the bartender to make something special. Typical high maintenance Tracy. Her demands irked Charlotte.

"Hi, Tracy, how are you?" She greeted her at the bar with an airy cheek kiss.

"There you are. I've been so busy, but I knew you'd be disappointed if I didn't come," she said, as if she did Charlotte a huge favor.

"Thanks for making it. You look exhausted. Is everything okay?" Charlotte didn't care but thought it was the right thing to ask.

"Yeah," Tracy said as she gulped down the rest of her second martini. "I met the hottest guy, twenty-three, from Ohio. Ripped body. He moved out here to model, best sex *ever*. I think I only got two hours of sleep."

Charlotte was tired of hearing about Tracy's conquests. It had been amusing a few years ago, but now it seemed ridiculous. "Wow. Are you going to see him again?" It was a half-hearted question.

"I don't know. I'm talking to three other guys, and I need to focus on this financing round I'm doing for ViewPoint." Tracy looked wearily at Charlotte. "Where's Sofia? Are there any hot guys here?"

Charlotte spent the rest of the evening making pleasant conversation with the guests. She tried to say hello to everyone at Angelino's opening parties, and she usually had about an 80 percent success rate. Tonight's crowd was manageable, and she met nearly a hundred people.

At one point, Charlotte looked across the room and caught Tracy chatting with a handsome man in a suit. She watched as they laughed and clinked drinks. Charlotte felt a bit nostalgic about the good times they shared over the last ten years. They'd traveled, had adventures, cried and laughed together. But their friendship was different now and perhaps irreparable. She had no intention of telling Tracy about the month she planned to spend in France, for fear of making her jealous.

Sofia interrupted Charlotte's thoughts, grabbing her by the arm, "Come on, Char! Let's get the photographer to take a picture of us with Tracy in front of the Angelino's sign!"

The camera clicked away. It had happened so many times in the past, the redhead, the Italian, and the Chinese, all striking sexy poses. Diversity combined with high fashion thrilled photographers, and many pictures landed on local society websites. They endured the blinding flashes for the sake of getting that one perfect shot. Charlotte had a premonition that it would be the last time the three women were photographed together at an event.

Chapter 12

PARIS

Charlotte loved everything French and traveled to the south of France twice but had yet to explore Paris because she was waiting to go with someone special. When that person never surfaced, she realized she'd have to see it on her own. Studying French was the perfect excuse to spend a decent amount of time in the City of Lights, and the apartment swap was an affordably convenient arrangement.

Challenges began as she slid into a taxi at Charles De Gaulle airport and tried to explain the address in French until reluctantly showing the confused driver a printed email from the apartment owner:

> *Hello*
>
> *So my address:*
> *6 rue des Prouvaires 1st district*
> *Tell the driver it's near les Halles and that he has to take the street rue du Roule from rue de Rivoli.*

The gate is a big blue iron gate between
2 restaurants on your left.
Then you press the bell with the name Chevallier
and I will answer and come down to help you.
The code of the gates are: 1st gate: 6304 2nd gate: 8174
I think you have everything you need.
I am shooting today but will not finish late so will
be on WhatsApp by the end of afternoon. Kiss

After several wrong turns and confusion, Charlotte finally called the apartment owner and put him on the phone with the driver. Five minutes later, she was in front of the big blue gate; the tall French photographer with a head full of dreads smiled through the iron bars. He grabbed Charlotte's luggage out of the trunk while she paid for the taxi, and then led her up five winding stories to the very top unit.

Completely out of breath by the time she stumbled through the front door, she was relieved to discover an adorable apartment. Just like the pictures, the living area contained two sofas facing each other, separated by a coffee table, and a television mounted on an adjacent wall. A large desk occupied a nook, while the kitchen was small like those in NYC, but at least it was a proper walk-in. Dangling strings of beads separated the queen-sized bed, flanked by two night tables, from the rest of the living area.

Charlotte was drawn to the 360-degree views of the city. Because the apartment was located at the top of the building, possibly a servant's quarters decades ago, each wall had small windows providing glimpses of the skyline. She was grateful to move into an authentic Parisian abode.

Her enthusiasm escalated when the Frenchman gave her a tour of her new neighborhood. They were mere steps away from the famous shopping street rue Saint-Honoré, a ten-minute walk to Musée du Louvre and beautiful parks, like Jardin des Tuileries, and another twenty-minute walk to Jardin du Luxembourg. The central location compensated for the five-flight trek up to the apartment. Charlotte had struck a goldmine with the housing swap!

She couldn't remember the last time she'd felt so optimistic. Refreshed and excited about the adventures she planned to enjoy in the elegant city, she resisted the urge to skip and laugh aloud. Instead, she maintained her composure and expressed her gratitude to the handsome Frenchman who gave her the chance to live, eat, and breathe all that Paris had to offer. She suggested treating him to dinner and he gladly accepted.

As they settled into their seats at his favorite sidewalk café in Le Marais, a hip area that reminded her of a more exotic version of New York's SoHo, they chatted happily. Charlotte nearly pinched herself while she sipped red wine and ate steak frites with the handsome Frenchie. She was in Paris! He told her about his childhood, daily life in France, and his career as a photographer, while she described growing up in California and her love for New York City. She encouraged him to network and make connections, giving him phone numbers for models and agents she befriended during her clubbing days. She had thoughtfully left Angelino's gift cards for him in her apartment. He'd have a great time in New York while she absorbed Paris. It was serendipitous!

Charlotte climbed up the steep circular staircase to reach her new home, slightly tipsy from the alcohol. They had a great night, and she felt a crush brewing but quickly squashed it. After all, he was leaving at 5 a.m. to catch a flight to NYC. Despite his charm, it was extremely awkward to sleep in the small apartment with a stranger just a few feet away on a sofa. Charlotte tossed and turned until she heard him slip out sometime before dawn to catch his flight. Finally, she could relax.

When she woke up, she had missed two texts due to the time difference. Jack wrote. *Did you make it? Will connect you with a few people to meet.*

Another text followed. *Hi Charlotte, just arrived in NYC for a meeting tomorrow. I'm free tonight if you'd like to join me for dinner. Wyatt*

His message made her heart sink. Disappointed about missing him in NYC, she second-guessed her decision to take a sabbatical by herself. Also, she worried her non-reply may have hurt his feelings or made her look flaky since he wouldn't see her response until he woke up in the morning.

She drafted a few texts before sending the final version. *So sorry I missed you! I'm in Paris for a month, studying French. Let me know if you visit, otherwise I hope to see you in August when I'm back in NYC.*

It was time to explore. She walked endlessly for hours, taking in the sights, stopping occasionally to sit on park benches and live in the moment. Vive la France!

Charlotte began French language school the next day and fell into a routine for the rest of the week. She woke in the mornings to a barrage of texts and emails from NYC delivered while she was sleeping. After rapidly answering them, she dressed, practiced her French at the corner boulangerie where she ordered a café au lait and croissant, and then walked three blocks to her school on the top floor of a seven-story building. The elevator was so slow that she usually climbed the stairs to class. Her classmates were eclectic: a teenage girl from Seattle, an elderly man from Chicago, and two middle-aged women from Madrid. The teacher was a petite Parisian suited in black slacks, a white button up shirt, leather loafers, and a colorful Hermès scarf draped over her shoulders. Class lasted three hours, with a thirty-minute break, and one hour of homework was assigned each day.

After school, Charlotte was free to explore. She visited museums, strolled through parks, and ate at cafés. Often alone during the initial four days of her trip, she utilized the opportunity for self-reflection. She thought about mistakes she made in the past with ex-boyfriends, the pain of losing her father, pressure she felt from herself and her family to get married, and she wondered if she'd ever have a chance with Wyatt.

Charlotte also evaluated her friendships. She could count on Sofia, but Tracy proved to be a major disappointment. Had she always been so shallow? Or had Charlotte simply outgrown her antics?

And then, there was Angelino's. She gave the company ten of her prime years, and it was time to stand up for herself. They paid her $75,000 for work that warranted $150,000. She questioned why she stayed there and felt compelled to make a career shift but didn't know where to go.

By Friday night, she was ready to socialize. Charlotte enjoyed the half-hour walk to Buddha Bar from her apartment to meet an old classmate for a drink. The restaurant was packed, and they had a fun chat until her friend had to run to meet her boyfriend for dinner. Charlotte stayed behind for one more drink and briefly flirted with a cute guy at the bar. But when his date showed up, she realized she had misread his motives, or maybe he was just another cheater. Unaffected, she walked home along rue Saint-Honoré, feeling blessed. She had her health, freedom, and she was in a wonderful city.

Before bedtime, she sent a few messages on Facebook to the international crew in her network and connected with a German college friend visiting Paris. She met him the next day at a dinner party on the Left Bank held in his friend's large, sparsely decorated flat. A guest suggested heading to Hôtel Costes. This hot spot was on Charlotte's bucket list, and it was on rue Saint-Honoré, fairly close to home.

Charlotte understood why it was so trendy as soon as she entered the hotel. A relaxing aura created by sensual music, dimmed lights, and flickering candles set the sexy vibe as she soaked in the buzz of chatter throughout the space. She recognized English, French, and Arabic spoken amongst the crowd. Impressive antiques surrounded by hues of velvety red created a seductive space for the upscale crowd—European chic, sophisticated, and stylish.

They squeezed into a corner table and her friend ordered a few bottles of wine for the group. Charlotte was on her second glass when a man approached and exchanged cheek kisses with everyone. He reached Charlotte and let his eyes run up and down her body before saying, "*Enchanté.*"

Charlotte stood up to kiss his cheeks, feeling extra confident, thanks to the wine. In her high heels, she was a few inches taller than the balding Frenchie, but he was in great shape. She guessed he was about fifty-five years old. But an energetic fifty-five. A charismatic fifty-five.

He looked deep into her eyes and grinned. "*Je suis* Pascal."

"I'm Charlotte. Nice to meet you," she said as she smiled back. He had charm. She was intrigued, and the feeling was mutual.

"American?" he asked.

"Yes. I should practice my French, but I'd hate to misspeak to someone who looks so debonair." Charlotte's eyes lingered on him.

"Don't worry, I speak English. I used to live in Florida." Pascal helped her back into her seat.

"What were you doing there?" Charlotte wanted to know about this intriguing Frenchman. Most importantly, was he single?

"Well, after we won the World Cup, I broke my arm in a motorcycle accident and went there for reconstructive surgery and physical rehab."

"Wait, you won the World Cup? Like, for France?" Charlotte wished she knew more about soccer. Coming from a family of red-blooded Americans, she was well versed in baseball, basketball, *American* football, and even tennis. But not soccer—and she wanted to say something witty about it.

"Yes, for France. 1998. How old were you then?" Pascal laughed.

Charlotte avoided the question and continued, "You must be a national hero. But you don't sound French when you speak English. Your accent's perfect."

"I moved to England when I was sixteen and spent most of my career playing there. Maybe you heard of Manchester United and Arsenal?"

The teams sounded vaguely familiar. Usually skilled at making pleasant conversation, this time, she was stumped. Maybe it was too much wine or perhaps it was Pascal's intoxicating hazel eyes.

It didn't matter because he didn't seem bothered. "They're big teams in England and when I wasn't playing for the French national team, I was always around English speakers. Where are you from in the US?"

Charlotte launched into her story and Pascal interjected frequently, demonstrating empathy and interest in her life path. He was easy to talk to and they conversed nonstop until their group fizzled out and it was just the two of them left at the table. He had three kids in their twenties who lived in England with their Dutch mother, whom he divorced the previous year. After twenty-seven years of marriage, they had drifted apart.

Charlotte gladly accepted his offer to drive her home in his immaculate Range Rover. He asked if he could hold her hand while they cruised along the shining streets of Paris, giving her the sense of adventure she wished for when she embarked on the trip. As they arrived at her flat, Pascal said he was busy the rest of the weekend but invited her to lunch on Monday. Charlotte agreed without hesitation and he offered to send his company's driver. With only three weeks left in France, this blossoming summer romance was exactly what she needed.

Monday couldn't come soon enough. Charlotte went about her usual routine but cut class a few minutes early to run home and get ready. The driver was punctual, but Pascal wasn't in the car. From what she could decipher with her meager French skills, they were going to pick him up from a meeting. After a short ride, the car stopped and Pascal jumped in, looking serious in his three-piece suit. He greeted her with cheek kisses.

They rode over to trendy L'Avenue restaurant near Champs-Élysées. Pascal said hello to the hostess and a few people dining as they made their way through the outdoor garden area and inside to a private corner table. Charlotte liked the ambiance and looked around the room with contentment. It was classy and sophisticated; she couldn't afford to lunch there on her own and she was grateful that Pascal invited her.

Charlotte ordered the spicy tuna tartare with avocado for a starter and jumbo shrimp risotto as her main course, while Pascal opted for artichokes, asparagus and Parmesan-Reggiano as an appetizer, followed by sole. Men with healthy eating habits fascinated her. She reconsidered the heavy risotto but didn't dwell on it.

True to his French heritage, Pascal insisted they share a bottle of wine with lunch. He studied the list, and because they both ordered seafood, he opted for white. The waiter nodded with approval when Pascal chose the 2009 Pape Clément Blanc. Upon the first sip, Charlotte remarked that it was the best wine she'd ever tasted. She had a decent understanding of wine, thanks to her job at Angelino's, but by the end of her first glass, she made a mental note to Google it when she returned home because it was so exceptional. (She later learned that it was a unique combination of Muscadelle, Sauvignon Blanc, Sémillon, and Sauvignon Gris.)

Conversation flowed smoothly as they discovered more about each other. Although the constant buzzing of Pascal's phone annoyed Charlotte, he apologized profusely and explained that it was "business." She had no idea that retired athletes were so busy. He took calls and spoke rapidly in French or Spanish for a few minutes before turning his attention back to Charlotte. After a full fifteen minutes without interruption, the waiter presented the dessert menu. She moistened her lips as she contemplated the options, but before she could deliberate with Pascal, his phone rang again. "Sorry, this is my ex, I have to take it." He bolted from the table and out of the restaurant.

Charlotte pondered what it would be like to date a divorced man. She'd thought Jorge was divorced, but he wasn't a good barometer, as he turned out to be married. Pascal was a true divorcé. A bit perplexed, she watched him out the window. He smoked a cigarette and seemed stressed out, until he started laughing. After spending an evening and an afternoon together, she mused that she didn't know him very well. She went back to examining the dessert menu until he startled her with his reappearance. "See anything you like? I'm sorry to do this, but I have to run back to my office for a meeting, I lost track of time!" Pascal motioned to the waiter.

"Yes, time flew by." Charlotte was disappointed he had to go.

"I'd like to take you to dinner tomorrow night if you're free." Pascal typed on his phone while he talked.

Charlotte perked up. "Sure, that'd be great!"

Pascal gave the waiter his credit card and spoke rapidly in French and turned back to Charlotte. "He's going to charge my card, but I told him to bring you any dessert you want. I need the driver to take me to my meeting and your flat is the opposite direction. Stay here, have dessert, coffee, whatever you want, and finish the rest of this wine. It's too good to waste!" He stood up and kissed her cheeks before she could maneuver out of her seat.

"Oh, okay—"

"Here's twenty euros for a taxi to take you wherever you need to go. I'll text you tomorrow about dinner. Practice your French with the waiter. That's why you came to Paris!" Pascal chuckled as he dashed off.

Charlotte didn't know what to make of the situation. She felt slightly objectified as she stared at the money conspicuously left on the table in full view of others. She quickly tucked the twenty-euro bill into her wallet and after some thought, decided not to be upset because he behaved like a gentleman—treating her to a wonderful lunch and paying for her ride home.

She pulled out her phone to Google him, surprised she hadn't done it sooner. In NYC, everyone wanted to know what everyone else "does." Upon meeting someone, no time was wasted before the infamous question was asked: "What do you do?" Charlotte usually inquired instantly with new acquaintances. But she was turning into a Parisian because she'd known Pascal for three days and they'd spoken for hours, yet she never asked what he did for work after retiring from football.

Thanks to Wikipedia, she discovered that Pascal Renaud was born into a working-class family in La Rochelle. His father was a bus driver and his mother cared for special needs children. As Pascal mentioned, he'd gained fame and stature as a professional soccer player but had to retire shortly after his World Cup appearance due to an ankle injury. He'd lived in the US for a few years and later became involved in the management side of an English team before leaving soccer altogether and focusing on business interests in real estate and telecommunications. Evidently, in the early 2000s, he'd parlayed his soccer fame and connections in South America to team up with an expanding telecom company as a brand ambassador, bartered for shares in the company, and made a hefty profit.

Charlotte placed her phone on the table and took a minute to think. Pascal was much more successful than Jorge, Eric, or any other man from her past, and he was self-made. Finding a man who'd made it on his own excited her. It took a combination of extreme intellect and burning ambition to create something from nothing. Men capable of such achievements reminded Charlotte of her father, who'd earned money fixing cars as a self-taught mechanic to pay for law school. Without help from his poor Irish immigrant parents, he exemplified the American Dream by diligently climbing ladders in the legal profession until he was able to launch his own law firm. Pascal shared a similar path with her father, albeit in different industries and different countries. Perhaps it was a stretch to compare the physically gifted athlete to her father, but they both impressed her with their work ethic and hard-earned success.

And the Frenchie smelled so good. Whatever cologne he wore lingered long after he was gone. She took another sip of wine and let her imagination run away with fantasies of undressing him and feeling his body against hers.

Staring out the car window, exhilarated by wine and lust, whizzing through historic streets, Charlotte's thoughts roamed during the ride home, dreaming of a life with Pascal. Eager to find out if he wanted more kids, visions of rearing French babies pranced in her head.

* * *

She was brought back down to earth that evening when she was forced to see one of Jack's contacts. He was a Canadian businessman involved with a food hall concept in Paris and there was a chance for Angelino's to be part of the project. They met at his hotel, Le Meurice, conveniently near her flat. Ultimately, soaking in the grandeur of the luxurious palace-style structure made the meeting worth the effort.

The Canadian only had an hour to spare, and she diligently tried to sell him on the idea of Angelino's in Paris by discussing the marketable aspects of the restaurant: family-friendly atmosphere, fabulous food, celebrity clientele, international renown, low overhead costs, and high profitability.

Satisfied with the meeting and encouraged about her future with Pascal, she leisurely strolled rue Saint-Honoré back to her dwellings. NYC seemed like the distant past. With an epiphany that she'd be fine if she left Angelino's to venture down a different career path, the possibility of taking a journey with Pascal was especially appealing.

The next day, Charlotte attended class as usual, but her homework was incomplete. Although she didn't want to waste the money spent on two weeks of classes, socializing with a potential husband took priority. The elderly man from Chicago, bless his heart, was the only student who finished his homework every night. Charlotte officially crossed to the other side with the rest of the slackers. Once she saw the text from Pascal confirming dinner, she couldn't concentrate on the lessons, as her mind was lost in dreamland.

After school, Charlotte raced home to shower and blow out her hair before carefully applying makeup and slipping on the knee-length navy ALAÏA dress she packed for a special occasion. With jittery nerves, she tiptoed barefoot down the five flights of stairs, purse dangling in one hand and stilettos wedged in the other. Ten minutes early, she hid behind the blue gate. Finally, she put on her shoes and emerged. The Range Rover was waiting, and Pascal jumped out to open the door. "Perfect timing!"

"I'm so happy to see you," Charlotte purred.

"Me too! We're going to my favorite restaurant in Paris, I know the owner. It's in Plaza Athénée." Pascal was in good spirits and Charlotte loved being a "we" with him.

"Sounds nice. Who's the owner?" she asked.

"Alain Ducasse. Maybe you heard of him," Pascal raised an eyebrow.

"Of course, I've heard of him! He's a legend! How do you know him?" Charlotte couldn't believe it. Coming from the restaurant world, she was more interested in famous chefs than entertainers. Chef Ducasse reigned over an elite gourmet empire and she was eager to dine at one of his restaurants.

"I know everyone, haven't you realized that yet?" Pascal took her hand and kissed it.

Dinner was a dream. Ducasse was missing, but the chef on duty served his tasting menu, sparing Charlotte the task of deliberating over what to order. She devoured everything—all eight courses, presented in small portions. Pascal carefully selected two wines to complement the food and enhance the evening.

Charlotte excused herself to the ladies' room before dessert. Upon first glance into the mirror, she realized she was tipsy and on the verge of drunk. When she was sure nobody was watching, she drank water out of the sink faucet. Determined to sober up to maintain poise, she intended to impress Pascal and ride this wave of positivity to the alter. She reapplied lipstick as her ovaries cheered. This was the one! Newly composed, she strutted back to the table. Pascal rose to pull out her chair.

"Do you have school tomorrow?" he asked as he took her hand and proudly held it on the tabletop.

"Yes, three more days left. I only paid for two weeks because I didn't know if I'd prefer roaming around Paris. I can always sign up for additional classes if I want." She doubted she'd continue, but it was good to have options.

"I'm flying to London early tomorrow for a meeting, but if you want to join me after class and spend a few days there with me, it'd be my pleasure...." Pascal raised her hand to his mouth and kissed it.

"Yes! I mean, I'd have to miss the last two days of school though..." Charlotte briefly hesitated only because she hated to waste her hard-earned money.

Pascal laughed. "I promise to speak to you in French. I'm an excellent teacher." He moved his hand to her knee and ran it beneath her dress toward her inner thigh. Charlotte wanted to pounce on him but controlled herself in the restaurant.

"That sounds nice." She tried to maintain a calm voice even though she needed to catch her breath.

A waiter arrived to take the dessert order. Pascal released Charlotte's leg and rattled off in French, choosing a few items. They discussed logistics during the rest of the meal. Pascal asked her to make her own travel arrangements and promised to reimburse her. Charlotte obliged and they agreed to meet sometime after his dinner the next night at the hotel in London.

She only received cheek kisses when he dropped her off, as he was in a hurry to get home to do some reading before bed. With no time for disappointment, she gleefully rushed to book a ticket to London, pack a bag for their two-night getaway, and call Grandma McPherson with the good news.

Chapter 13

LONDON

Instead of flying to England, Charlotte took the Eurostar and found it mind-boggling to travel by train for less than three hours between two foreign countries separated by a sea. Back home, it could take the same amount of time to get from one end of Manhattan to the other during rush hour traffic.

It was her first trip to London since her vacation with Jorge six months earlier. Although the wounds were still healing, she resolved to push those memories aside and focus on her new beau. Pascal wasn't as tall as Jorge and didn't have as much hair, but he was honest and legitimately divorced. Charlotte focused on the future and cooked up hypothetical plans featuring the Frenchman. She fantasized about what their kids would look like, where they'd raise them, and if they'd speak English with French accents until she dozed off, happily dreaming of domestic life with her new man.

The train pulled into Paddington Station, waking Charlotte as it slowed to a stop. She made her way to Chiltern Firehouse, an exclusive hot spot in Marylebone. As the attractive women at the front desk greeted her and led her up to Pascal's lodgings, she marveled at the stylish crowd in the garden relaxing with pre-dinner cocktails. Along the way, Charlotte inquired about the history behind the hotel and discovered that it was a real fire station in the 1880s. Since transitioning into one of the trendiest hangouts in London, it frequently hosted parties with A-listers, but the staff wasn't allowed to elaborate. Charlotte laughed and told them she'd seen it all at Angelino's; she could only imagine what went on in such a popular hotel.

The room was darling, complete with a fireplace, antiques, marble bathroom, and one big bed. Charlotte stared at it for a moment with the realization that she'd soon consummate her relationship with Pascal. She was apprehensive because she hadn't slept with anyone since Jorge and the first time with a new lover was always awkward; she hoped they'd have chemistry. Her phone buzzed with a text from him. *Darling, starting dinner. Relax and eat at the hotel. Be back around 11pm. Bisous*

After showering and changing into a simple white sundress and heels, Charlotte touched up her makeup and headed downstairs for dinner. She was granted access to a special lounge reserved for hotel guests and VIPs and self-consciously found a seat among a crowd of twenty-something skinny girls. Sucking in her stomach, she remembered when she looked like them, but time and pasta had altered her appearance.

With her weight in mind, she ordered a low-calorie vodka soda. A young, vibrant redhead who quite possibly just waltzed off the cover of *Vogue* jumped with glee as she greeted her hipster friends with dramatic hugs. A rush of insecurity motivated the elder redhead to change her order to a sparkling water with a splash of Belvedere vodka, convinced that it had even less calories than her previous choice.

Not realizing she was dehydrated, Charlotte downed the drink and ordered another. She quickly finished it and glanced at the menu but was interrupted by a cocktail waitress. "The gentleman in the corner would like to offer you a drink."

Charlotte surveyed a table of well-dressed Middle Eastern men. In a surge of confidence propelled by vodka, she responded, "Please tell him I said thank you, but I prefer to have company when I drink."

She giggled and turned her attention to a menu until she smelled potent cologne and looked up to see a confident grin on a short, hairy man with a very big watch. "What's your name?" He spoke with a thick accent.

"I'm Charlotte. And you?"

"Khaled. Where are you from?"

"New York, but originally California. And you?"

"I'm from here. I join you?" He pulled a chair out.

"Sure. But where are you from originally?"

"Kuwait. What are you drinking?" Khaled sat down, causing Charlotte to panic. She suddenly feared the hotel staff would gossip and tell Pascal she'd hung out with another man.

"Actually, I'm waiting for my boyfriend, so you don't need to buy me a drink. But thank you," Charlotte said awkwardly.

"Okay...We're leaving for dinner soon anyways. Can I get your number?" With no way out, Charlotte discreetly slipped him her business card and hoped the bartender missed the covert exchange.

After she'd finished her third sparkling water with vodka, the bartender convinced Charlotte to try an apricot ginger martini.

Declaring it the best drink she ever tasted, she drank two more while munching on nuts and people watching. She was nervous about sleeping with Pascal and alcohol took the edge off. So much so, that she had to steady herself when she walked to the bathroom. Officially drunk, she ducked into the elevator and escaped to her room to avoid embarrassing herself in public. She kicked her shoes off, squeezed out of her dress, and crawled under the covers before realizing that she forgot to pay the bill. Head spinning, she couldn't get dressed and go back down into the bar. Besides, it was almost 11 p.m. and Pascal would return soon.

Charlotte called the front desk and explained the situation. She asked them to charge the room for her drinks and add a 20 percent tip for the bartender who made the best apricot ginger martini she'd ever tasted. In fact, it was the only apricot ginger martini she'd ever tasted. Or was it an apple ginger martini? Unable to remember, she adamantly insisted they relay her compliment to him.

She noticed a text from Pascal apologizing that he wouldn't be back until midnight. The alcohol hit her, leading her mind down Sorrow Street. Her heart panged at the memories of her last London trip with Jorge and the betrayal she later uncovered. Tears fell as she thought of her dead father.

She considered texting Tracy because they had commiserated about the loss of their dads in the past. Then she remembered Tracy's hurtful defense of Jorge and decided she was the last person she should talk to. Instead, she called Grandma McPherson to reminisce about a man they both deeply loved. It was past midnight in London when they said their goodbyes just before Charlotte passed out.

A loud wheeze jolted her awake. It was daylight. She was in her bra and panties, and a contently snoring man slept next to her. For a split second, she thought it was Jorge until she realized it was Pascal.

Charlotte carefully slid out of bed, trying not to wake him, and slipped into the bathroom. She was startled by her reflection in the mirror—bloodshot eyes, mascara-stained cheeks, smeared lipstick, and matted hair. Head pounding, she drank water out of the faucet to kill the stale taste in her dry mouth. Next, she wiped the dried makeup from her face while quietly gargling with mouthwash. She returned to the room, grabbed her phone, and snuck back into the bathroom. It was only 7 a.m., but she'd missed several emails and text messages from the night before.

The first text was from Tracy, who she hadn't heard from since the Greenwich event. *I've been so busy, can you book a reservation for my mom's b-day dinner at Angelino's Park Ave? 7pm next Thurs. 10 people. You're welcome to join. Thx.*

Followed by another text. *Nice meeting you Red. Let's go out while you're in London. Khaled*

Realizing he was the guy she met at the bar, she instantly deleted the message.

The third text stopped her heartbeat. *Hi Charlotte, I made it to Paris. Might be too late to meet tonight, but I can do lunch or dinner tomorrow. Wyatt*

She sighed. *You won't believe it, I'm in London for a few days. I'm so sorry to miss you! I'll be back tomorrow night, will you be there?*

After she sent the text, she reread it to convince herself that it sounded good. His response startled her. *Nope. Going to Berlin for a premiere.*

Deflated, she replied. *Sorry to miss you, good luck with the premiere!*

"Darling, are you in there?" Pascal yelled from the bed.

Charlotte perked up and exited the bathroom, slipping her phone into her purse. "I'm right here."

"Get in bed," he demanded.

She crawled under the covers and feeling shy, she asked, "What happened last night?"

"The guys kept me out until 2 a.m. I'm so sorry, darling. You were sleeping like an angel by the time I got back, I didn't want to wake you." He rolled over and wrapped his arms around Charlotte, revealing his naked body. "Will you forgive me?"

Relieved, Charlotte used the situation to her advantage. "I'll forgive you this time, but don't let it happen again."

"I love a strong woman. Come here," he said as he pulled her face to his and kissed her softly, then passionately.

Instant chemistry surged throughout her body. Within seconds, he unfastened her bra, slid off her panties, and entered her. Charlotte didn't have a chance to think. She felt a brief rush of fear because they weren't using protection, but her mind went blank as she enjoyed the physical connection of him inside of her. For a fleeting moment, Jorge flashed in her thoughts. He was always adamant about using protection, as any married man would be. Obviously, Pascal didn't have the same concern.

Jorge quickly forgotten, she gave herself completely to Pascal. All day and into the night, they only took two breaks: one for breakfast room service and another for an afternoon nap. Charlotte wondered if all Frenchmen had such strong libidos, or maybe it was the special transatlantic spark between them. By nightfall, they decided to get ready for dinner at Sexy Fish nearby in

Mayfair. She showered, humming to herself when Pascal jumped in, startling her.

"I can't keep my hands off you," he said, nibbling her earlobe while he fondled her breasts. He pressed himself into her, showing that he was ready, lifted her leg and steadied it next to his waist, holding her against the wall, gyrating inside her as she released moans. Sex in the shower was a first for Charlotte. It was slippery and wet but incredibly sexy as she wrapped herself around him for balance. Like a nymphomaniac unleashed, she couldn't get enough.

They behaved during the taxi ride to the restaurant and flirted throughout dinner. Charlotte usually scoped out the scene and studied menus of new restaurants, but her mind was focused on her man, hungry for more sex with him. Sometime between the appetizers and the main course, he shared an idea. "Why don't we go to Cap Estel tomorrow instead of back to Paris?"

"Where's that? I've been to St. Tropez and Cannes, but I've never heard—"

Pascal interrupted, "It's a special place close to Monaco. I want to show you. Will you come with me?"

"Of course, but I only packed a few dresses and day clothes, I don't even have a bathing suit—"

"Don't worry." Pascal grinned. "We'll get everything you need there. After dinner, I'll ask the concierge at Firehouse to book a room and arrange tickets. Let's have another glass of wine."

Charlotte relished new experiences that didn't involve work. Pascal had never even heard of Angelino's before he'd met her, yet every place he took her was exceptionally cool. Back at Chiltern Firehouse, he sent her up to the room while he organized the next leg of their trip. Two hours later, she had dozed off when he returned.

"Sorry it took so long. I had a few drinks while they booked everything for us," Pascal explained. "We're leaving tomorrow at 8 a.m. for Heathrow. It's early, but we want to spend as much time as possible in Cap Estel." He undressed and removed his watch before climbing into bed. Charlotte dreaded the thought of waking up in a few hours, but she'd be a trooper and combat sleep deprivation. They had sex, but just one time because they were both exhausted.

Chapter 14

CAP ESTEL

For a taste of heaven, Charlotte would recommend a visit to the Côte d'Azur. Villas dotted the green hills rolling down onto sunny beaches while sleek yachts lined the horizon of pristine Mediterranean waters. Locals espoused a relaxing *je ne sais quoi* attitude, attracting tourists and jetsetters from around the world. Restaurants served fresh seafood and offered al fresco dining enhanced by exquisite wine. All was blissfully surreal as a typical day consisted of ocean activities, delicious meals, parties, and hopefully romance with a special someone.

Pascal blasted the radio as he raced their rented convertible out of Nice airport and along winding roads. Charlotte let her hair fly loose in the wind while she gazed at the sea. Thirty minutes later, they pulled into a narrow gated driveway. Pascal spoke into the intercom, the gate retracted, and they inched down a steep decline until they reached a grand entrance. Charlotte's eyes widened as she walked through the main doors. The large marble lobby housed a check-in desk along with ornate furnishings, while the far side of the spacious room's retractable glass wall sat open, exposing fresh air and stunning ocean views beyond its colossal balcony. Charlotte ventured out to survey the scenery. A saltwater infinity pool on the edge of a cliff fell into the sea, as Monaco stood proud in the distance.

Charlotte returned inside where Pascal was signing paperwork. "Is this a villa?"

"It's a family estate that they turned into a hotel." Pascal handed a bellboy money to send their luggage to the room and then he took Charlotte's hand, leading her outside. "I'll show you."

He escorted her around the massive estate, complete with lush gardens, fountains, two restaurants, plush sitting areas, a serene spa with an indoor pool, and a bar overlooking the ocean. Two other couples on chaise lounges sipped wine and laughed.

"Pascal, I love it here!" Charlotte hugged him and kissed his cheek.

"I'm saving the best for last. Follow me to our room." Pascal led her down a narrow path. She watched with curiosity as he used an old-fashioned church key to unlock the door and reveal a completely white interior room, accented with hues of navy blue. It was built into a cliff, allowing enormous sliding glass doors to open onto a balcony hovering over the sea below. The view was spectacular. Charlotte plopped down on the bed and stared out at the water, completely mesmerized.

"Come outside." Pascal took her hand and led her to the balcony.

The refreshing breeze, the view, and the handsome man with his arm around her made Charlotte felt like the luckiest woman alive. But she didn't have much time to soak it all in once he started nuzzling her neck, followed by passionate kisses. Soon, they were in bed, ready to consummate the room.

The next few days were heavenly. Charlotte and Pascal developed a routine without even leaving the hotel: morning sex, breakfast on the balcony, exercise in the gym, poolside reading, grilled fish and rosé for lunch, more sex, a nap, early evening swim at the private beach, sex, shower, dinner at the formal hotel restaurant, nightcap while stargazing, and bedtime sex. Wake up. Repeat.

It was the most sex Charlotte had in her entire life. She'd never met a man who turned her on so much. She didn't know if it was Pascal's French charm, the magnificent Hôtel Cap Estel, or maybe the fabulous rosé. Whatever "it" was, the entire weekend felt magical.

It was also the first time in ten years that she put her phone away and decompressed. When she wasn't lip-locked with Pascal, she chatted with fellow hotel guests, read French magazines, and zoned out. The workaholic had completely disconnected from her New York life.

By Sunday night, they decided to extend their stay until Thursday, when Pascal was scheduled to meet his kids on the Amalfi Coast. Charlotte wanted to travel with him, and it was her dream to visit Southern Italy, but he said it was too soon for her to meet his family. She was disappointed, but at least they had three more days and nights to enjoy together.

Once the glorious weekend came to an end, the mood shifted dramatically. Instead of waking up in Pascal's arms, Charlotte awoke to him yelling in French and Spanish. Outside on the balcony, he screamed into his phone about some sort of deal falling apart. She soon realized it was Monday and she hadn't checked her phone since Friday. Charlotte plugged it into the charger and positioned herself in the desk side chair to review missed messages.

There were a few from her mom and sisters asking about her new boyfriend and trip. Then, there were texts and emails from a manager at Angelino's SoHo. Reviewing the chain, Charlotte discovered that a waiter failed to inform a customer allergic to nuts that Angelino's chocolate cakes contain Nutella. Horrified, she read about the girl's allergic reaction, the ambulance, the angry father, and the ruined birthday dinner. She'd have to deal with the mess later, when it was daytime in New York.

The next text made Charlotte's heart sink. It was sent Saturday morning. *Hi Charlotte, Berlin was good, flew back to France to see you. Let me know when. Wyatt*

Another one delivered. *Heading to the Louvre to see some art. Are you free? Wyatt*

The last message was sent on Saturday night. *Tried calling. Heading to dinner and leaving tomorrow for LA. Let me know if you're around. Wyatt*

Charlotte felt uneasy as she texted back. It was the middle of the night in LA, but she couldn't wait. *I'm so very sorry! I just saw your texts, I diverted from Paris and went to the beach for a few days. I'm so sorry I missed you!*

He wrote back immediately. *You're too busy for me. Wyatt*

Charlotte was taken aback, unsure of how to interpret his text. Was he angry? Did he like her as more than a friend? If he'd give her some notice about meeting, there wouldn't be so many mix-ups!

Charlotte responded. *Never too busy for you! I didn't realize you were coming back to Paris, so I made other plans. I'm back in NYC in a few weeks and LA for a wedding in Sept. Can we schedule a time to see each other?*

She stared at the phone, waiting for a response. It never came. Charlotte reread the exchange a few times until she was jolted by a door slam.

"Cocksuckers!" Pascal was livid. "People always want to screw you!"

"What happened?"

Pascal laced up his running shoes with fury. "I'm dealing with a bunch of fucking wankers who want to blow this entire deal."

"I'm so sorry. What project—"

"I'm going to the gym. I need to be alone and run this off." Pascal's tone calmed down a bit. As he walked out, he said, "Sorry, darling. I'll meet you at the pool in an hour."

Charlotte had never seen this angry side of Pascal. He seemed more like the Wall Street sharks drinking at The Regency than the sexy European soccer player who wooed her to Cap Estel. Their morning routine of sex before the gym was over, and Charlotte turned her attention back to her phone. There was a message from a manager at Angelino's 72nd Street about an heiress bringing her twins for a pasta lunch date and the pizza chef giving them an impromptu pizza-making lesson. It was a cute story she'd pitch to the press.

Scrolling through messages, her eyes widened at an email from Jack with the subject line: *Paris Agenda*

She opened it and realized that Jack was coming to France to work for five days during her last week! Beyond perturbed, she searched her brain for the miscommunication between them. The silver lining was the fact that Pascal would still be in Italy with his kids during most of Jack's time in Paris; but still, she resented having to work alone with him during her vacation.

Charlotte hoped the sight of Pascal at the pool would sweeten her sour mood. Instead, she felt uneasy as she approached his lounge chair while he argued on the phone. The deal had apparently tanked even further. He slammed his phone down and crossed his arms with a huff, staring into the distance with fury.

"It's nearly 11 a.m., not too early for a sip of rosé," Charlotte said, trying to uplift Pascal.

"I'm sorry. I have some work issues." He stood up and collected his glasses and newspaper. "I'm going to the business center. Enjoy the pool and order whatever you want."

Charlotte tried to hide her disappointment. "Okay, but when will you be done?"

Pascal gritted his teeth. "My entire deal is a mess right now! Just relax and hang out." Seeing the hurt on Charlotte's face, Pascal softened his voice. "Look, I didn't think this would happen, but I'll sort it out by tonight, and we'll go to Monte Carlo for dinner. Does that sound good?"

"Sure."

"Great, I'll book something." Pascal was already walking away. "Besides, I'm sick of the restaurant here, three nights in a row was enough."

Charlotte loved the restaurant and wanted to repeat their euphoric routine of the past three days, but clearly, that wasn't an option.

* * *

With her London clothes exhausted and desperate for proper Monaco attire, Charlotte improvised with a bathing suit cover-up embellished with beads and gold threading that she bought in the hotel spa. She belted the vibrant turquoise wrap, transforming it into a mini-dress, and paired it with heels and a clutch. She'd easily blend in with women donning Cavalli and Givenchy dresses in Europe's most elite tax haven.

Pascal's mood improved as he sang along to music while they zipped through the curvy roads to Monte Carlo, the center of Monaco. When they pulled up to the valet twenty minutes later, he jumped out of the car and took Charlotte's hand as he led her up the steps of Hôtel de Paris Monte-Carlo and directly to Le Grill on the top floor.

"There's a surprise," Pascal said as they were seated near a window table.

Charlotte took in the panoramic views of the Mediterranean Ocean and the town below. "What is it?"

Pascal flashed that grin she found so irresistible. "Look up."

Charlotte tilted her head back and gasped. There was no ceiling! It had been retracted, bringing the sky into the opulent dining room.

"Look at the sunset through the window. By the time we eat our soufflé, we'll be dining under the stars." Pascal massaged her neck, filling her with warmth and contentment.

The meal was perfection. They both took a break from fish and ordered succulent filet mignons and drank fine wine. Le Grill was known for its soufflés; Charlotte chose the Grand Marnier soufflé, while Pascal opted for a berry variation. By the time dessert arrived, stars shone above, filling Charlotte with joy. After the perfect romantic dinner, she was eager to return to their little love nest on the cliff to finish the evening in bed. But Pascal had a different plan. He wanted to say hello to some friends at Jimmy'z, the best club in Monte Carlo, if not the world.

Italian sports cars, along with a few Mercedes and Bentleys for good measure, caused gridlock in front. The crowd clamoring to get in was glamorous and the vibe inside was electric. The sexy interior was filled with dark leather half-circle booths encompassing the large dance floor and several bars scattered throughout the area. Pascal took Charlotte's hand and navigated through the crowd. Part of the club was enclosed with a roof, while the rest was outdoors under the night sky. Cigarette smoke throughout the venue irritated her eyes and throat.

"There they are." Pascal pointed across the room. Charlotte looked in the direction of his finger and froze with fear. Straight ahead was a table of provocative girls, chugging shots and dancing wildly with…Lorenzo and Marco.

Sweat beads surfaced on Charlotte's forehead and armpits. She pulled Pascal back. He turned to her in confusion and said, "Come on! Why are you stopping?"

"I…I can't go over there," she stammered.

"Why not?" Pascal sounded frustrated.

She turned to him. "You're friends with Lorenzo and Marco?"

"Who?" He wanted to keep moving.

"Oh, thank God! I thought we were going to their table," Charlotte said with relief.

"Are you drunk? Hurry up, I don't want to lose them," Pascal said as he yanked her past Lorenzo and Marco's table. She ducked to blend into the crowd as she passed by. Soon she was out of their vantage point, and Pascal introduced her to his friends from Nigeria. She tried to make polite conversation but needed to flee before her bosses spotted her. The Italians thought she was working in NYC, and she didn't want to be discovered, especially after Jack had covered for her. She told Pascal she felt ill and needed to leave as soon as possible. Frustrated rather than concerned with her welfare, he reluctantly left his friends to follow her out the door.

During the tense ride home, he showed his displeasure. "You were rude to my friends."

Overwhelmed with guilt, she tried to explain. "I'm so sorry. I didn't mean to offend them. My bosses were there, and I had to hide because they think I'm in New York."

Pascal grew more irritated. "Why do they think you're there?"

"Well, it's complicated, but for me to get a month off to go to France, the CEO pulled some strings but asked me to keep it quiet from the other owners." She realized she sounded like an unprofessional liar.

"You're not allowed a vacation? They're obviously taking one."

"I can have vacation, but I took a month off. And they own half the company, so they obviously have more freedom than I do." Charlotte grew defensive.

"Strange job. Ten years and you have to sneak around like a teenager? Don't you have higher aspirations for your life?" Pascal asked.

"I'm trying to figure it out. Yes, ten years is enough at one company, but I'm not sure what else I'd do." She flashed back to what Dr. Radcliff told her about her fading ovaries and sadly added, "I thought I'd be married and raising kids at this point of my life."

Pascal softened. "But why didn't you marry and have kids? You'd be such a good mom."

Charlotte held back a tear and projected her best PR voice with the automated answer. "I just haven't met the right person yet."

Somewhat dramatically, Pascal pulled over to the side of the road, a bit too close to the edge of the cliff in her opinion. He turned off the engine and they sat in silence with just the murmur of the ocean waves crashing down below. He took a deep breath. "Charlotte, we've been having such a good time, but until now, I never knew what you wanted in life. I guess I should've known that you have the same needs as every other woman."

Charlotte timidly interjected, "By 'needs' do you mean marriage and children?"

"Exactly. And I definitely want to get remarried someday, that's for sure. The headaches I've had since my divorce…Women manage the home, organize meals, and sex is important too—it's a physical need. I want to remarry, and you have the right qualities." Pascal's endorsement of her spousal capabilities filled her with pride and her mood perked up. She hung onto his every word until his next statement. "But I don't want more kids."

She could practically hear her ovaries weeping. Fantasies of bearing Pascal's children had frequently waltzed through her thoughts during the trip. She even decided that if she "accidently" got pregnant and it was a girl, they could name her Estel in honor of the beautiful place they conceived her.

"I'm fifty-seven, I'm too old for more kids. I already have children who are thinking about having their own kids soon."

"You're not too old to have kids. Men your age and older do it all the time," Charlotte countered. "Besides, moms do most of the work anyways. It's not like I ever envisioned you changing diapers."

"So, you did think about having kids with me?" Pascal's voice squeaked.

"Of course I did! We've been sleeping together for nearly a week, without protection I might add, and I dropped everything to be here with you." Charlotte was indignant.

"Nearly a week? Come on, Charlotte. Don't you think it's a little too soon to have a serious marriage and baby discussion?"

After learning her lesson with Jorge, she decided to voice her needs at an early stage of the relationship to avoid another disaster. "No, it isn't too soon. We've spent a significant amount of time together, and I should be upfront and let you know that I want a husband and kids. I'm not looking for a summer fling."

"Well, alright. The lady knows what she wants. I appreciate that, but I need time to think about it. I mean, we didn't even know each other two weeks ago." Pascal was exasperated and Charlotte had to admit that he had a logical argument. She decided to soften a bit and try the "bees with honey" approach.

"You're right. I think I'm caught up in this strong connection we have, and I always feel like there's no time like the present. But you make a good point. Things are moving very fast. I don't want you to feel pressured. We should enjoy our time together and see where this goes."

He remained deep in thought for a moment and then he took her hand and kissed it. "Okay, let's do that. Thanks for your honesty."

They drove in silence to the hotel. As they walked through the deserted grand entryway, it felt as if they were the only two souls in the entire place. They retreated to their room and had sex.

In the morning, Pascal apologized that he'd have to work all day again, giving her time alone for self-reflection. He was right; it was happening so fast. Pascal was charming, witty, and a great lover, but was he the right man for her to marry? She knew she'd win the battle over having kids, but did she want to leave her family and friends in the US to base herself in France? She wasn't sure.

They enjoyed their last few days together in Cap Estel. When they parted ways at Nice airport, in front of the gate for her flight to Paris, fear and sadness washed over her.

"I miss you already." She hugged him, on the verge of tears.

"Darling, don't worry. It's just a week and then I'll be back in Paris before you leave for New York." Pascal kissed her passionately and flashed his irresistible grin before walking away. Charlotte wondered if she'd ever see him again.

Chapter 15

PARIS

After the whirlwind trip with Pascal, an odd quietness descended upon Charlotte back "home" in Paris. She enjoyed a relaxing weekend, her second to last, by spending time with friends visiting France. They hit cafés, galleries, parks, and traveled out to Père Lachaise Cemetery, where Jim Morrison, Chopin, and Oscar Wilde, among others, were laid to rest.

Then, the Monday clouds rolled in with Jack's arrival. He scheduled several meetings for them, and she found it odd that he wanted her to attend all of them, even those that didn't pertain to Angelino's. Spending so much time alone with him felt inappropriate.

"Paris looks like it's been treating you well, Charlotte," Jack said with a smile when she approached his table at their first lunch meeting. "You even got a little color. Have you been hanging out in the park?"

Feeling awkward, she resorted to upbeat small talk. "Merci! It must be a glow from the City of Lights." Charlotte sat down and took a sip of water. "Jack, I want to thank you again for giving me this break. I really needed it."

"You're welcome. You work hard for Angelino's and everyone deserves a vacation. I'm glad we could make it happen," he said as he gave her a wink. Alarmed by his unusually happy demeanor, Charlotte smiled back politely. She suspected he was flirting with her and didn't understand why they were lunching together in the first place. "Should I order a bottle of wine?"

"Um…" Charlotte hesitated. "Iced tea is good for me. It's a little early for alcohol."

"Suit yourself." Jack was unfazed. "I'm having a glass of red."

"You're blending in with the French already." Charlotte gave another forced smile. "So, I'm curious about these meetings. It seems like several don't involve Angelino's."

"You're right. Some are for other projects I'm working on, but it will be useful to have you with me." Jack scanned the wine list and ordered a glass from the waiter.

Charlotte was truly annoyed. "How can I be useful if it doesn't concern Angelino's?"

"Because a deal might not involve Angelino's now, but it might later." Jack dismissed her interrogation.

"It's great that you enabled me to be in France, but I don't want to spend all my time in meetings as a silent observer." Empowered by Pascal's comments about self-respect, she wasn't going to let Jack exploit her.

He grew serious. "Charlotte, there's more to life than Angelino's. You'll apprentice with me this week and I'll show you new possibilities." He sampled the wine the waiter poured for him and nodded in approval.

She perked up at the idea that Jack was trying to help her. "Oh, now I understand. I think of you as the CEO of Angelino's and I don't know much about your other projects." Using charm to soften things, she added, "You're always so mysterious." She batted her eyelashes as a slight blush spread across Jack's face. A little flattery went far with men.

Jack took another sip of wine and said, "I'm not trying to be enigmatic. I just choose to keep my business interests separate from Angelino's. I never took the official CEO title because I need freedom to do other things."

"But you're the only rational leader in this company. Lorenzo and Marco are reckless, and Melvin's pure evil," she said with disdain. "And don't you think the staff meetings are a complete circus? Marco curses everyone out." Charlotte had to get it off her chest.

"Yes, it's his way to flex his muscles. Remember, I have the majority interest of Angelino's, so I let him put on his show and step in during dire situations to reel him in." He punched his fist into his open hand.

"Feel free to use that fist in the next meeting to shut him up."

Jack laughed, a little too hard from Charlotte's perspective. "You're funny sometimes, Char! Very dramatic!"

"Thanks?"

"No, it's cute. But I see your potential. Maybe you'll outgrow Angelino's, and should you seek other opportunities, I'd like to keep you working in one of my businesses."

Charlotte adjusted her attitude. She'd have new insight into what Jack did and their work together in Paris could open new doors. "Thank you. Now I understand." She smiled, and this time it was sincere.

Over the next few days, Charlotte discovered that not only did Jack have keen business acumen; he also had a surprisingly cool personality. During their breaks, he even relaxed and made some amusing jokes about France, always "off the record." As much as she missed Pascal, it was refreshing to be in the company of a fellow American who understood her sense of humor and chattered about current events back home. She learned that Jack was involved in mall developments and four American food chains. He was also an investor in a few alcohol labels. She was impressed!

Despite pressure from various business interests, Jack remained calm. He'd never throw a fit over a deal like Pascal did in Cap Estel. Charlotte studied his looks with new curiosity. He was average height and medium build, but his broad shoulders aligned symmetrically with his square jawline, giving him a presence of authority. His skin and hair were the same shade of cappuccino, magnifying his hazel eyes. His deep voice projected a hint of a Southern twang due to his Texas upbringing. Occasionally, she wondered how a relationship with him would feel, but she loyally pushed such thoughts out of her mind to respect Pascal.

Upon finishing their last meeting on Friday afternoon, Jack instructed Charlotte to go home and freshen up so he could treat her to an authentic Parisian dinner at Le Relais de l'Entrecôte. It was renowned for serving the best steak frites in Paris and she was eager to eat there, but seeing Pascal upon his return from Italy was her priority. He surprised her with several loving texts during his trip, and she believed they had a strong chance to make their relationship a success.

Caught between a rock and a hard place, she asked Jack if they could make it a quick meal because she was exhausted from the week. But Jack moved at his own slow pace, while she grew antsy. After a delicious feast, complete with crème brûlée and Sévigné (the most delectable chocolate cake she ever experienced), he ordered another bottle of wine while Charlotte discreetly texted Pascal to please be patient.

Catching Charlotte off guard, Jack asked, "Do you want to get married and have kids someday?" She was used to personal questions from Lorenzo and Marco, who were often too drunk to remember her answers. But from him? It felt odd. Then again, the entire week was strange. She got the vibe that he was interested in her and the wine made her PR skills fuzzy. She attempted to answer without leading him on.

"Of course! What about you?" As soon as she asked, she regretted it.

His face softened as he looked deep into her eyes. "Sometimes I work so much that it's hard to have a relationship...And there's something I never talk about, but I feel like telling you."

Jack was an enigma and Charlotte wanted to keep it that way. Although she cared for him platonically, she was hesitant to cross the line of professionalism. Her heart belonged to Pascal and she feared she was losing focus.

"What is it?" she asked politely.

His head drooped down toward the table. "I was engaged, but my fiancée committed suicide."

Whoa. Charlotte took a second to register the shocking admission before finally responding. "Oh my God. I'm so sorry. What happened?"

Tears welled up in Jack's eyes as he told the story of his college sweetheart who seemed stable and healthy, even getting accepted to a top-notch law school. But after depending upon stimulants to stay awake to study for the bar exam, she became erratic. She battled her addiction until she jumped off of a roof hours before the mailman delivered her exam results. The poor woman had passed the test before she passed away.

Charlotte was moved to tears as Jack's voice cracked. He was in so much pain. It happened twenty years ago, but he'd never gotten over it. The tragedy explained why he was single. He was scarred and afraid to get close to anyone again.

She reached across the table and sympathetically put her hand on his forearm. "Jack, this is so terrible. But you know it wasn't your fault, right? She was sick from the drugs. They tainted her mind. She'd never intentionally leave an amazing guy like you." Empathy flowed through Charlotte's veins and she teared up, thinking of her father's death. Life could be so cruel. He nodded. They sat in silence for a bit until the waiter came by to check on them.

"Charlotte, I keep my private life separate from Angelino's. This conversation stays between us." Jack stiffened up, back into his serious persona.

"Of course." Charlotte returned to PR mode. "You can always count on me." She meant it. She wouldn't even tell Sofia. Her lips were sealed.

He smiled softly. "You're working that PR angle as usual."

"Jack, you know you can trust me, PR or no PR." Charlotte looked him squarely in the eyes.

Jack chuckled and threw his head back, "This is what I mean. You're the ultimate PR woman. That's why I might steal you for another venture when you get sick of Angelino's." He winked at her and this time, she appreciated the gesture.

Although it was an emotional night, Charlotte believed her new bond with Jack would improve her career. She genuinely liked him, and she finally understood his quiet, brooding manner. The tormented guy was shuffling through life with a broken heart.

He insisted on dropping her off at her apartment. She couldn't refuse the ride with the excuse that her sexy future husband was waiting for her, so she reluctantly climbed into his taxi. When they arrived at her stop, Jack patted her on the knee and said he'd wait until she entered the building safely. The knee pat was awkward, but Charlotte didn't dwell on it. She ran past the gate and frantically pulled out her phone to find a text from Pascal. *Darling, it's late. Going to sleep. Let's save our energy for tomorrow. Bisous*

Disappointed, she slid off her heels and started the five-story climb up to the empty apartment. As much as she longed to be in Pascal's arms, she was emotionally drained from her evening with Jack and realized it was best for her to get some beauty sleep to look fresh the next afternoon.

The final days with her French lover were perfect. He was in great spirits and showed her new corners of Paris. They laughed, bonded, and even made future plans. She was to leave Monday morning, and Pascal would meet her in NYC just five days later to spend the weekend there. After he carried her luggage down the treacherous stairs of her French apartment building, he took her to the airport to see her off, holding her hand tenderly all the way to Charles de Gaulle. They hugged and French kissed curbside. It wasn't *au revoir*. Pascal would soon be with her again in the Big Apple.

Chapter 16
NEW YORK CITY

Intense August heat and humidity transformed the city into a frying pan as tempers flared among those stuck in the inferno. The chosen ones fled for the Hamptons or other vacation destinations. Charlotte detested scorching weather, but trudged forward, knowing she'd soon be back in the arms of her man.

The slow month at Angelino's enabled Charlotte to cope with jet lag without it affecting her work performance. Lorenzo, Marco, and Jack rarely stepped foot inside the unwelcoming corporate office crowded with cubicles and filing cabinets, allowing the staff to work independently. Charlotte spent most of her time in the air-conditioned space, chatting and lunching with her coworkers, Melvin being the only exception. He kept to himself in his corner cubicle wearing earphones, watching movies, and occasionally cackling.

Friday finally arrived. Pascal had booked a room at The Dream Hotel, not too far from Charlotte's studio. Relieved that they weren't staying in her little place, she packed a bag for the weekend.

There was just one pressing issue: Charlotte's period was a week late. And she was ecstatic! She'd never admit it to anyone, but an accidental pregnancy with Pascal's baby was a dream come true. She imagined the family they'd create and prayed she wouldn't get her period as she envisioned the precious little child growing inside of her. She gleefully counted the days as she felt the early signs of pregnancy—sore breasts, sleepiness, and increased hunger. She scheduled an appointment with Dr. Radcliff and grinned with satisfaction, imagining her gynecologist's shock when the pregnancy test came back positive.

Pascal was in a jovial mood when he arrived, and they spent two hours in bed before it was time to meet Sofia and Tracy for dinner. Charlotte was excited to introduce him to her friends and hoped that her mature relationship would rub off on Tracy. Her animosity toward the maneater simmered because, with Pascal in her life, she viewed everyone through rose-tinted glasses. The foursome dined at Angelino's SoHo and Charlotte ordered the best dishes for Pascal to try. Much to her disappointment, he wasn't impressed. He took a bite of his truffle ravioli and said, "I'm surprised this chain is so popular. The food is mediocre. Angelino's would never make it in France."

Charlotte reassured him, "*Mon chéri*, I think jet lag has affected your taste buds. Nothing tastes great after a long flight. But try our tiramisu, it's to die for!"

"No, thank you, I already feel like dying," Pascal laughed. Sofia appeared offended while Tracy quickly changed the subject.

"Do you have time to check out the Hamptons?" she asked.

Pascal took a sip of wine. "Tracy, did Charlotte tell you about Cap Estel? When you can go to the south of France, the Hamptons are a major letdown. You can't even swim in that cold, dark water."

Charlotte jumped in and tried to smooth things over. "If he experienced the Hamptons our way, he'd appreciate it. A lot of Europeans don't get it. You have to know the right places."

Pascal laughed and kissed her cheek. "Okay darling, if you say so."

She wrapped her arms around him adoringly, ignoring the irritated glances Sofia and Tracy exchanged. The group headed to Bar and Books for a nightcap. It was one of the few places in the city where Pascal could smoke a cigar while Tracy hunted new prey. Charlotte steered the conversation away from Angelino's for the remainder of the night.

The lovebirds were on their own the rest of the weekend. They braved the heat and walked the Highline, strolled around the Whitney Museum, checked out a Broadway show, and spent plenty of time in bed. Pascal was very critical of New York and his disdain for her city was disconcerting. He complained about traffic and trash on the sidewalks, made comments about New Yorkers being rude, and insisted that Central Park was overrated.

Fortunately, Charlotte was able to impress him with Jean Georges' spectacular waterfront restaurant, The Fulton, in the Seaport. There, they talked about a future together and how to make it work despite the distance. She was ready to quit her job and give up NYC to be with him in Paris. He advocated a slower approach by taking turns visiting each other at least every two weeks, and in six months, they could entertain the idea of her making the move. For the first time in years, Charlotte felt safe, loved, and hopeful about the future with her boyfriend.

Before his flight Monday morning, they ordered room service for breakfast. He suggested mimosas with their meal and then questioned Charlotte's reluctance for a morning cocktail. When he commented on her very minimal alcohol consumption during the entire weekend, she decided to tell him the news.

"I was going to wait until I was sure, but…" She smiled coyly.

"But what?"

"Well…I know you were on the fence about having more kids, but…I think I'm pregnant!"

Pascal's face fell. "Are you serious?"

"I don't know for sure, I'm seeing the doctor on Wednesday, but my period's a week late, so it's a good sign." Charlotte attempted to hug him, but he shook her off.

"Are you crazy?! This isn't good news!" His words knocked the wind out of her and continued, "I told you I don't want any more kids! I already have enough problems with my kids, and I'm too old to have more! I told you this in France! Remember?" His veins thickened on his neck.

Charlotte fought back tears. "I remember you said you'd think about it."

"Well, I thought about it and the answer is NO! God, I hope you're not pregnant. This is horrible." Pascal threw his belongings together, cursing in French.

Charlotte's voice quivered. "I had no idea you'd react this way. For me, it's like a miracle because the doctor said I might not be able to have kids naturally, without IVF."

Pascal lowered his voice and spoke slowly, trying to control his anger, "Charlotte. I thought I made it very clear in Cap Estel that kids aren't in my future."

Charlotte's hurt turned to resentment as she struck back, "No, you didn't make it clear. You said you'd think about having kids and then you flew to New York to visit me and we talked about continuing our relationship long distance and the possibility of me moving to France. And we never use protection, so what am I supposed to think?"

"Fine, you're right. But now that I thought about it, I don't want more kids. Jesus. I hope you're not pregnant." Pascal zipped up his bag. "I have to go. I'm getting to the airport early, so I don't miss my flight." He walked out without a hug or a kiss. Before the door slammed shut, Charlotte had already collapsed on the bed, her body shaking with sobs.

She worked the next few days like a robot, completely numbed from the argument. Convinced it might be her only chance to have a baby, she still prayed she was pregnant and assumed he'd eventually approve. Many guys had freaked out about unexpected kids and ended up loving them unconditionally.

Charlotte woke up feeling anxiously hopeful about her appointment with Dr. Radcliff. But when she used the toilet, she saw dreaded red spots and she knew there was no need to go to the doctor. She cried for over an hour before showing up to the office with bloodshot eyes. Nobody noticed; nobody cared. Ironically, Melvin chose that day to speak to Charlotte. He got in her face and growled, "Where's my red pen?"

He picked the wrong time to antagonize her. She stood up, slammed down her notebook and shouted, "I didn't take your pen, Melvin! You can shove all your pens up your ass!"

She hurled her chair against her desk and grabbed her purse. The entire office sat in stunned silence. As she stormed out she heard Melvin mutter, "Must be that time of the month." Her colleagues erupted into laughter.

In her lonely little studio, Charlotte drank vodka out of the bottle, cried a bit more, and then composed herself when she called Pascal. It was late in France, but he answered on the second ring.

"You'll be happy to know that I'm not pregnant," she said in a quiet monotone.

"Thank God! You really scared me, darling," Pascal said with relief. She didn't respond. "Charlotte, are you still there?"

"Yes, I'm here, but I don't know what we're doing. You're so against having kids with me." Her voice was flat, her emotions numbed by alcohol.

"I know, darling. I've been thinking about it. I really care for you, but I don't want any more children. I'm sorry to disappoint you," he said with sincerity.

Charlotte muted the phone while she sniffled. Pascal continued, "You're a great girl and you deserve to have everything you want in life."

She unmuted the phone, "Thank you. I just wish you'd reconsider—"

"I'm not changing my mind," Pascal interrupted. "You don't understand now, but once you have them and you're my age, you won't want more. I'm sorry, darling, but that's the way it is."

"I have to go." Charlotte hung up and reached for the bottle of vodka. She figured she'd drink herself into a slumber. The phone rang a few times as she dozed off.

Daylight woke her up. She was wearing clothes from the day before and her pillowcase was smeared with eye makeup. Her head throbbed as she dizzily stumbled to the kitchen, grabbed a bottle of water, and crawled back into bed. She emailed Jessica to tell her that she was taking a sick day before calling her lifeline.

Grandma McPherson listened with patience and finally said, "You need to learn that you can't change a man."

"I know, Grandma. You're right. I was too stubborn to believe him when he said he didn't want more kids."

"When a man tells you what he wants, move on if you want something different." Words of wisdom.

With the exception of an agonizing dinner with a vile food critic who brought his cat, berated the waiter, and trash-talked the most popular chefs in the city, Charlotte spent the rest of the summer sequestered in her air-conditioned cubicle where she dedicated excess time to updating the Angelino's investor presentation. Motivated to accomplish as much as possible while the city slowed down, she also created a new social media strategy and organized a holiday promotions calendar.

Pascal texted and called for a few weeks, but she never answered. There was no point in wasting time with a man who didn't want a family with her. She lay awake at night with anxiety, haunted by the fact that the time to marry and have kids was slipping away.

Part 3

FALL

Chapter 17

NEW YORK CITY

September's renewal gave Charlotte hope. Pleasant weather combined with iconic events like Fashion Week, US Open Tennis, New York City Ballet Gala, and the commencement of football season created such excitement that New Yorkers forgot to mourn the end of summer as soon as they were swept into fall. Hamptonites relocated back into Manhattan, kids started school, companies launched new projects, and Angelino's was packed. The city pulsated life and optimism, making it Charlotte's favorite month.

The start of the new season was so busy that she nearly forgot about Pascal. Angelino's SoHo hosted a fashion week after-party for a trendy Norwegian designer that ended at 3 a.m., when those still standing hobbled over to Marco's loft for more drinks. Charlotte's sore dancing feet required flats at the runway shows her friend from *Glamour* invited her to. Although entertaining, they weren't the right places to meet men.

Sofia invited Charlotte to a customer's company box at the US Open. (Angelino's affluent clientele occasionally gifted their favorite GM cash, presents, and access to events.) Some people went to watch tennis, while others, like Charlotte, came for the lobster rolls and the scene. Sofia introduced her to a few men, but she didn't feel a connection. After engaging in polite conversation, she ducked inside the suite to check her emails. She had several new messages, starting with a customer complaining about a mouse spotted at Angelino's Union Square. Another email jumped out at her:

> *Subject: Please read*
>
> *Hi Charlotte,*
>
> *I hope this email finds you well.*
>
> *It's time for us to part ways as I've made several attempts to reach you in the past but to no avail. You seem upset about something, but I still think you're a good person. I wish you all the best and I enjoyed our brief friendship.*
>
> *There is no need to respond and I will no longer contact you.*
>
> *All the best,*
> *Jorge*

Charlotte didn't know what to make of it. The relationship was such old news that she couldn't figure out why he suddenly wanted to put something in writing to officially end things. Searching her mind for answers, she didn't notice Sofia come in to refill her wine glass.

"Do you like anyone here?" Sofia loved playing matchmaker.

"Look at this email from Jorge. Isn't it random?" Charlotte handed her the phone.

After scanning it, Sofia said, "Yeah…It's so weird…Maybe his wife checks his email and he wanted to prove that he ended things with you?"

Charlotte considered this possibility. "Maybe she hacked into his account and saw our messages. Awkward!"

"I don't know, but I'm glad that liar is out of your life. I really want you to meet someone special. I won't rest until you forget about Jorge and move on with a good guy."

"Oh, Jorge is a thing of the past. Don't worry about that," Charlotte said with conviction.

After the match, she was too bothered by Jorge's email to stir about in her empty studio. She opted for a nightcap and hoped for conversation at Angelino's SoHo, determined to forget about the adulterer. When she arrived, she found Ray working and admired his body while he talked to a group of gushing women paying their bill. Charlotte hovered at the far end of the bar and observed him. He had shaved his hair into a short buzz cut, grew out a goatee, and displayed muscles so defined that his tight white Angelino's t-shirt looked like it might rip apart to expose his bare chest. He wore a soldier's dog tags and a medallion of Our Lady of Guadalupe.

He confidently strolled over to her end of the bar. "What's up, Red? What're you drinking?"

"Actually, I'm here on official business. Marco sent me to make sure that you aren't giving those ladies free coffee." Charlotte couldn't resist.

Ray smiled. "Good one, Red. Forgot about that meeting."

"How could you forget? You walked out while Marco was screaming at you. We were all shocked. You became an instant hero." She was still impressed by his behavior at the summer staff meeting.

He looked her straight in the eyes, "They should know not to mess with me. I do what I want."

"But didn't Jessica talk to you? I'm surprised she didn't fire you. She takes human resources very seriously," Charlotte teased.

Ray looked caught off guard. "It's no big deal."

"Apparently not. But there are no secrets at Angelino's." Charlotte slyly looked at the cocktail menu.

Ray squirmed away from the topic by changing the subject. "You should have that menu memorized by now."

"Okay, I'll just do sparkling water with vodka." Charlotte had many since her London trip.

Ray objected. "Boring. You like tequila, right?"

"Yes, but I drank so much wine at the US Open, and I don't know about mixing—"

"You'll be fine," Ray interrupted. "Share a pizza with me. We're closing soon."

During the next hour, Ray tried to impress Charlotte with his cocktail concoctions. As the cleaning crew removed tables and the manager huddled in the corner counting money, Ray leaned into Charlotte's ear and whispered, "Come on, let's get out of here."

He came around the bar, helped her gather her purse, and caught her when she stumbled through the door tipsy and giggling. "Those drinks loosened you up," Ray commented.

"I'm always loose," Charlotte uncharacteristically quipped.

"Good," Ray said as they walked down the street into the comfortably warm night.

After a few minutes, Charlotte asked, "Where are we going?"

"Back to your place."

"No way, I'm not that drunk!" Charlotte laughed, but she could see that she had hurt Ray's feelings. "I didn't mean it like that, it's just that it's late and I have to be in the office tomorrow morning to meet with the new website designer," Charlotte said.

"Cool. Let's take the subway up. You're on 56th, right? It's on my way home." Ray seemed so calm. Charlotte didn't usually take the subway late at night, but she knew she'd be safe with the big, strong bartender. They entered Spring Street Station and Charlotte let out a squeal as a rat scurried past her.

"Relax, Red. It's gone." Ray was nonchalant.

"They're so gross!" Rodents terrified her.

The train arrived with plenty of seats available. They sat next to each other in silence until the subway started moving. Charlotte turned to ask Ray where he lived, but she didn't have a chance to get a word out. He quickly grabbed her and pulled her onto his lap, biting and kissing her neck while running his hand beneath her shirt and fondling her breasts. She was caught off guard, but too turned on to resist as she passionately reciprocated his kisses. He repositioned her to straddle him and she could feel him through his pants, teasing the area between her legs. She pulled her face back to momentarily scan the train. There were people scattered about the car. In the seat across from them, an old lady shook her head in disapproval while the remaining passengers appeared uninterested, as if Ray and Charlotte weren't there. After all, New Yorkers misbehaving was nothing unusual.

"Ray, wait, people can see us." Charlotte was out of breath.

"Shhhh. Nobody cares. Ignore them." Ray seemed turned on by her resistance.

"But—" Charlotte tried to protest.

"Stop it. Nobody's watching." Ray returned his lips to hers and resumed kissing as he slid his hand beneath her skirt and into her underwear. It was too much for intoxicated Charlotte to handle. She wanted to rip his clothes off and have sex with him right then and there. It took every ounce of willpower to avoid public fornication. The 6 Train made several stops between SoHo and Charlotte's exit. Their car had almost completely cleared out and only two people remained, a blind man with a cane and another man who sat leering in the far corner with his hand down his pants. She was vaguely aware but tried not to think about him as she made out with Ray. Just when she couldn't resist him any longer, the subway arrived at her stop. She knew it was a godsend as she jumped out of the subway before Ray had a chance to say anything or follow her. As the train sped off, she turned to see him through the window. He licked his lips and gave her a nod as he disappeared into the tunnel.

The doorman looked surprised to see her stumble in with lipstick smeared across her face, partially hidden by her disheveled hair. "Did you have a good night, Miss Charlotte?"

"Yes, thank you." She scampered off, knowing she looked like a drunken mess. She threw herself on her bed, incredulously reliving the train ride home. Ray was beyond sexy. The way he grabbed her was rough but sensual. Her body was throbbing, and she wished he were in her bed at that very moment.

She grabbed her phone and drunk texted Tracy. *Omg, made out with Ray on the subway, so HOT. Don't tell Sofia!*

The next morning, Charlotte woke up with a heavy head and a filthy taste in her mouth from not brushing her teeth. She grabbed her phone and saw a text Ray had sent five hours earlier. *Got home. Not working tomorrow, let's go to movie*

Charlotte giggled. She wanted another piece of him. She wrote back. *Yes, but I'll meet you there. You're too dangerous on the subway*

Her glee diminished when she read the next text from Tracy. *How much did you drink last night? Ray is not an option. You work together and he's a walking STD. Brunch Saturday?*

Charlotte brushed off Tracy's message and went about her day in the office. However, she couldn't focus on work. Distracted by erotic flashbacks of Ray, she tuned out the loud argument between Melvin, Lorenzo, and Marco. As she stared at her computer screen, she remembered how incredible Ray's body felt: his strong arms, his hands all over her, straddling him in between her legs, his hard—

"Are you okay, Charlotte?" Jack startled her back to reality.

"Oh, hi, Jack. I didn't know you were here." She longed for privacy to fantasize.

"They called me over to break up Lorenzo and Marco's argument with Melvin. My meeting canceled, so it was perfect timing."

"That's great. Glad it worked out." Charlotte used her PR voice and hoped he'd leave soon.

"Are you sure you're okay? You were zoned out, staring at a blank computer screen."

"Um, yeah, that's just because I'm so hungry. Don't worry. I was thinking about what to eat and I just sort of spaced out." Quickly creating diplomatic excuses came naturally to Charlotte.

Jack smiled. "Well, it's good you work for a restaurant group. Come on, let's have lunch and talk about a few things. How about Angelino's Columbus Circle? I need to meet the new manager there."

Charlotte had dug herself into a hole; the last thing she wanted to do was spend lunch with Jack and concentrate on an intellectual conversation. She longed to stay lost in her daydreams but tried to be upbeat and witty during the meal. She ordered a thick, meaty lasagna covered with layers of cheese and crispy focaccia, which she doused in olive oil. Not very healthy, but it would subdue a hangover. Jack opted for a fresh beet salad and a low-calorie tuna carpaccio.

"I don't know how you stay in such good shape when you eat food like that," Jack said while nodding in wonderment as he cut up his salad. Charlotte found it remarkable that he had grown so much closer to her since the Paris trip. In the past, he would've never lunched alone with her or complimented her body. She couldn't figure out his intentions, but she hoped he wouldn't develop feelings for her and cause problems at work.

Ray texted around 3 p.m. *Just woke up, lets meet for movie at 9pm. I'll send address*

Night bartenders in NYC often stayed up until the morning and slept most of the day. They usually took three or four days off a week to let their bodies recover in between shifts. It was a different lifestyle, but the job was lucrative, and many night owls liked working odd hours.

Charlotte was concerned when Ray texted her the address of a movie theater all the way in the Bronx. As she left her apartment, she heeded Tracy's text about Ray, "the walking STD," and grabbed a condom, confident they would end up at his place. She jumped in a taxi instead of the subway.

As the car sped away, leaving her disoriented in a new neighborhood, Charlotte saw Ray turning the corner. He looked delicious in a gray t-shirt, jeans, and a black leather jacket. "Come on. I'll get our tickets."

The theater seemed dodgy and the horror film didn't interest Charlotte, but she went along with Ray like a puppy dog. He felt so amazing the night before that everything else was trivial. The cinema was almost filled to capacity, but Ray found two seats in the back corner.

During the previews, there was a trailer for Wyatt's new movie about a surfer who discovered a secret island developed with sustainable living products, where he falls in love with a mysterious woman who only appears at night. Charlotte had a sad flashback to missing Wyatt in France, but she instantly refocused on Ray as he started giving her a deep neck massage.

Within two minutes of the opening credits, Ray had Charlotte's bra unfastened and gently rubbed her back, stimulating her with every caress. His hand moved forward and electricity shot through her entire body as his fingertips caressed her nipples. Before she realized it, he had her on his lap, straddling him as she had in the subway, while he took her breast in his mouth. Charlotte was on the verge of ecstasy, which succumbed to panic when Ray unbuttoned his jeans and whispered into her ear, "We're going to do it right here."

Before she could respond, a woman seated in front of them turned around to locate the source of the heavy breathing and smooching. "Oh, my gawd!" She tossed a handful of popcorn at them and yelled in her thick Bronx accent, "Whad a whore! Ged a room!"

Jolted back into reality, Charlotte jumped off Ray and refastened her bra. The woman turned around again and glared at her. Humiliated, she grabbed her purse and ran off, as Ray followed her out to the lobby with amusement.

"We can't do that! The subway last night and the theater today?!" Charlotte was beside herself.

Ray grinned. "Come on, you were into it." He grabbed Charlotte's hair to pull her close, but she broke free.

"I don't want to get arrested for indecent exposure. I mean, can we be normal and go somewhere private?"

Ray was nonchalant. "Sure, I live a few blocks away. Let's go."

As she feared, Ray's apartment was a mess. Located on the first floor of a dilapidated building, metal security bars protected the windows and the hallway light flickered as moths swarmed around it. The interior reminded Charlotte of a dormitory room, complete with two twin-sized beds squeezed together to make one. It was small and disorganized. She thought of what Pascal said about needing a woman to organize a home and decided that Ray's place could use a female's touch. She went to use the bathroom and was dismayed to find lingerie hanging to dry above the shower curtain.

She came back to the bedroom and asked, "Whose stuff is in the bathroom?"

"Just a friend," he said as he grabbed her and pulled her onto the bed. They spent the next hour having sex on top of a bedspread with cigarette burns. At times, his moves were sensual, while other times, he used his rough strength to hold her down and command control. It began as purely physical, animal attraction, but when they snuggled during the aftermath, an attachment blossomed.

They stayed up until 6 a.m., talking and eating take-out Chinese food. Ray told her about his cousins in the Dominican Republic who wanted to move to the US and his plans to help them with the documents. He also revealed that his muscular physique was due to his involvement in amateur boxing. After recently winning a Golden Gloves competition, he'd stepped up his workouts in hopes of fighting in tournaments with prize money that he could designate to an immigration lawyer to aid his family.

"If I push hard enough, I'll win fights and make enough to bring them over. I gotta help them get here." Charlotte cuddled up next to him, realizing that she had been too quick to judge the hottie who was so endearingly supportive of his family.

Ray went to sleep "for the night" around 7 a.m. and Charlotte headed to the subway to go home and shower. During the walk, she saw his neighborhood in daylight and decided that it wasn't so bad after all. *Ruff! Ruff!* Sudden ferocious barking from a pit bull behind a chain link fence shattered the serenity and sent her sprinting away in fear.

The next three weeks were all about Ray. Charlotte planned her meetings at Angelino's SoHo and 72nd Street, depending upon where he was working. They spent every night together, sometimes at his place and sometimes at hers. He sought to dominate her, sometimes with light spanking, often pushing the limits with his roughness. He initiated intense make-out sessions on the sidewalk, in the subway, on park benches, in taxis, at diners, and in elevators. In fact, Ray seemed even more aroused whenever their intimacy was in public. One night, he took her into a corner of Angelino's SoHo concealed from security cameras, backed her against the wall, lifted her up, put his hand across her mouth, and stared deep into her eyes while he did the deed right there.

Charlotte was in a trance. She savored the physicality of sex with Ray and she felt empowered by the fact that she became his universe. He reveled in his domination of her. One night he commanded her to undress, call him 'sir,' and give him a foot massage before throwing her on the bed, holding her wrists down, and thrusting aggressively inside her until she blurted out their safe word to make him stop: "Pizza!" He was hooked on her and wanted to see how far he could go with someone who had never played a submissive role, in or out of the bedroom, while she relished the consistency of his attention. There was something invigorating about a man who lusted for her and provided daily intimacy. She felt wanted, needed, and most of all, she didn't feel alone.

Ray was a drug and Charlotte was addicted. She believed she'd unraveled his tough guy demeanor and beneath the tattoos was a deep man who made her feel alive. He expressed his desires about wanting to be a dad when he opened up about growing up fatherless: "I'll be there for my kids to give them what I didn't have." Surprisingly, he used protection religiously, so she knew an unexpected pregnancy would be impossible. But there was a chance they could plan for a future together, and she dreaded the thought of leaving him for the weekend to go to California for a friend's wedding.

* * *

Tracy chased Charlotte for weeks, saying there was something she needed to discuss, and insisted they meet for brunch at Balthazar before her trip. After ordering quiche and mimosas, Charlotte swore Tracy to secrecy before she spilled the story about Ray. She told her everything: the subway make-out session, the movie theater incident, and the marathon sexual encounters.

She smiled as she concluded, "The more I think about it, Ray is husband potential. I shouldn't have been so judgmental."

Tracy listened in stunned silence. Convinced the wacky Californian had completely lost her mind this time, she grasped for appropriate words. She truly feared the publicist was going through some sort of mental crisis.

Charlotte continued, "I know you're not a fan of Ray, but he has a really good side, too. Don't you think it could work?"

Tracy gathered her thoughts. After a tiring week of work, she had to find a way to save her idiotic friend from a sinking ship. Due to their history, she felt obligated to throw Charlotte a life vest. After taking a deep breath, she said, "I think you've been through a lot these past few years with your dad's death, working for those assholes, and a very intense New York lifestyle."

Charlotte frowned. "What does all that have to do with Ray?"

Tracy leaned forward. "Charlotte, Ray is a loser. He sleeps around, he's up all night. I don't care about his tattoos or the Bronx, but he has a criminal record. He's dangerous and imagine if he lost his temper and lashed out at you. Didn't he beat up someone?"

Charlotte crossed her arms. "Fine, you have some points. But I've been so wrong about guys in the past, I just thought I should give someone different a chance. And our chemistry is undeniable."

"It's great that he's a good fuck, but he's just a rebound from Pascal and you need to learn not to fall for random hookups. You're always planning the wedding before the end of the first date. Don't be so desperate!" Tracy narrowed her eyes and asked, "Are you guys at least using condoms?"

"Yes. He always insists," Charlotte said quietly.

Tracy sighed deeply. "Good because I know you weren't with Pascal."

"I guess French guys aren't into protection. Yet Pascal was pissed off when he thought I was pregnant. I don't get it." Charlotte looked forlorn.

"Forget about that frog. He acted like such a superior dick when he was here. Screw him and forget about Ray, too. Maybe you'll meet someone at that wedding you're going to."

Tracy was so turned off by Charlotte's behavior that she decided not to reveal the information she'd intended to share when she'd organized the brunch. Eager to flee another one of the redhead's train wrecks, she made a hasty departure, ditching Charlotte at the table.

Chapter 18

BEVERLY HILLS

F lying across the country provided space Charlotte needed to step out of the Ray avalanche to evaluate their relationship. Tracy's intervention resonated with her as she stared out the airplane window with the sinking realization that she had nothing in common with the bartender besides sex. Ray had no desire to interact within her circle and balked at the invitation to her friend's wedding at The Beverly Hills Hotel. Although plagued by the preparations for over a year, Charlotte had kept the nuptials on the back burner and barely participated, much to the ire of the bride. The weekend had finally arrived and, dateless, Charlotte desperately wanted it to be over.

Growing up in Newport Beach, she'd avoided the stereotypical beach bunnies and instead befriended the most unique girls in class. Her best friend, Sherry, came from a Persian family, spoke Farsi, and ate exotic food like Fesenjoon and ghormeh sabzi. Sherry's palatial abode, full of thick rugs and heavy antiques, starkly contrasted Charlotte's modest, cookie-cutter, Ikea-style home. Sherry's mom adored her daughter's freckled friend and braided her hair while telling her stories about the glory days in Iran when ladies were free to wear the best European designers in public and parties raged all night long.

The girls were inseparable throughout their youth, until high school graduation sent them on different paths: Sherry headed to University of Southern California, while Charlotte attended UCLA. Rival universities, but at least they were both in LA. They vowed to meet once a week, but unfortunately, the commute between USC in Downtown and UCLA on the Westside could take over an hour. As time passed, Sherry became engrossed in her studies and Charlotte was inseparable from her new boyfriend and they only met once a month. Eventually, they skipped the LA meetings and caught up when they were both home for the holidays. After Charlotte moved to New York to attend Columbia graduate school, it was a miracle if they'd see each other once a year. Sherry excelled as an attorney at a firm in Century City, while Charlotte embarked on the publicist path in NYC.

Sherry wasn't on Charlotte's mind at all when she received a text. *Hi Char, it's official! We're in Mykonos, David proposed and I said yes!! Look at the ring!!! It's HUGE!!! Can't wait for you to be a bridesmaid!*

Several pictures of Sherry and the ring followed the text. David appeared in the last photo, but only the back of his head was visible as Sherry hugged him and smiled, victoriously holding up her hand wearing the bling.

Charlotte didn't know much about David except that he was a Beverly Hills native from a prominent Persian-Jewish family. He started dating Sherry after they met at Loyola Law School and his parents had discouraged marriage for religious reasons but, after a decade-long courtship, gave in because they wanted grandchildren.

Charlotte responded. *That's so amazing Sherry!!! Congratulations!!! I can't wait to be your bridesmaid! Tell David he chose a great wife!*

She responded. *Thanks but stop calling me Sherry! I keep telling you, it's Shokoufeh! I'll call you after our trip, and here are more pictures of the ring. It's HUGE!!!!*

Charlotte often forgot that Sherry had reverted back to her birth name after joining a Persian clique at USC. Her childhood teachers couldn't pronounce "Shokoufeh," and so, to blend in with other students, she'd used a Western nickname: Sherry. It stuck with her until college friends inspired her to embrace her heritage. Shokoufeh was a Persian name that meant "blossom." To Charlotte, Sherry (AKA Shokoufeh) had "blossomed" into a bridezilla.

Because she lived on the East Coast, Charlotte was excused from Shokoufeh's pre-wedding requirements: two engagement parties, three bridal showers, a wedding cake tasting luncheon, and a bachelorette party in Las Vegas. She sent a present each time regardless. She also bought the five different bridesmaids outfits required for the wedding weekend. Between the gifts, airfare, and garment expenses, she'd spent nearly $3,000 on the royal nuptials. To add insult to injury, Shokoufeh complained that she wasn't taking her bridesmaid duties seriously and accused her of deliberately skipping *mandatory* weekly bridesmaids conference calls. But Charlotte couldn't participate anyway because the calls were conducted in Farsi as all *nine* of the other bridesmaids were Persian.

During the ride from LAX to the hotel, she received a text. *Hi Charlotte, I hope you had a nice summer. When will you be in LA for that wedding? Wyatt*

She hadn't heard from him since they missed each other in France, but her heart soared with familiar hopefulness. She responded. *I'm here now! Do you have time to meet?*

He replied. *Lunch tomorrow? Noon?*

Yes! Where?

How about il Pastaio?

Charlotte smiled and hurriedly typed. *Great! See you there!*

As she exited her Uber, she remembered that Shokoufeh had scheduled some sort of swimsuit photo session the next afternoon. She groaned aloud as she pulled out the Run of Show for the weekend:

Shokoufeh's Bridesmaids Itinerary

Thursday: 12-5pm Arrivals to Beverly Hills Hotel
5-6pm Glam Squad Available (book in advance)
6-7pm Welcome Cocktails. Attire: Pink Floral Dress
7-10pm Welcome Dinner at Polo Lounge
10pm Midnight DJ and Dancing

Friday: 8am Breakfast delivered to your Bungalow
9am Meet in lobby for transportation to Greystone Manor photo session. Attire: Daisy Sundress with flat sandals, curly hair for stylist to add flowers at the shoot.
11am Lunch on your own at hotel. Spray Tan Services (book in advance)
2pm Swimsuit photo session at pool. Attire: Floral Bikini of your choice with custom Floral Bathing Suit Cover-Up. **You will be photographed with

and without cover-ups, I recommend spray tans.
Hair in high ponytail and bring sunglasses.

Charlotte stopped reading—she'd lucked out! She'd be back at the hotel by 11 a.m. just in time to quickly change, sneak out to meet Wyatt, and return to the pool after lunch around 2 p.m. Perfect!

The evening was a nonstop photo shoot, and to Charlotte's dismay, the other bridesmaids brought their significant others who also served as groomsmen and thus were included in the pictures. Though Charlotte was accustomed to fighting back her insecurities over her pale complexion, she stuck out like a sore thumb as she posed with the bejeweled, olive-skinned prima donnas. She retreated back to her lonely bungalow at the end of the night. (Shokoufeh and David had generously paid for the entire wedding party to stay at the hotel.) Greeted by a bottle of Champagne and "his and hers" gifts, she caressed a pink nightgown with Shokoufeh and David's initials and wedding date embroidered on the sleeve and looked longingly at the navy-blue t-shirt with matching embroidery left for the man she didn't have.

Saddened that she lacked a guy to share the experience with, Charlotte checked her phone to see if Ray had contacted her and he certainly had. He had sent a text. *Miss me?* Along with a picture of his erect penis. Disgusted, Charlotte wished men would realize that women don't want to see photos of their manhood.

The next morning, she woke up excited about her lunch date with Wyatt. She was on time for the photo shoot, wearing the obligatory daisy sundress and flat sandals. The stylist complimented her curly red hair as she adorned yellow flowers on the crown of her head. Unfortunately, Bridezilla wasn't satisfied. She insisted that her flower crown consist of *white* daisies only. The clock ticked while a special wreath was created for Shokoufeh, and Charlotte grew increasingly nervous. 11:00 a.m., 11:15 a.m., 11:30 a.m. and they were still shooting! She needed to escape and meet Wyatt.

Everyone, even the stylist, spoke Farsi as the shoot droned on and Charlotte broke into a sweat. She silently thanked God when an event planner from Greystone Manor appeared and told them that they needed to vacate the premises to give the next crew access to the property.

After the last pose, the girls shuffled to chauffeured SUVs while Charlotte made a mad dash around the corner to order a Lyft. She was late to il Pastaio and felt like a fool for keeping the Hollywood legend waiting as she texted him that she was on her way. She told the driver to speed up as her mind raced. Still embarrassed from her behavior in Mumbai, she wondered if she should explain the cause of her dramatic exit. She tried to calm herself during the ride and almost forgot to text the bride. She wrote that she had to run an errand and would skip the spray tan, meeting them later at the pool. Shokoufeh instantly responded. *Ok, but don't be late.*

Wyatt was incognito in a Dodgers baseball cap and dark sunglasses. Charlotte didn't recognize him at first when the hostess led her to his table in the patio. Once he flashed his lopsided grin, she awkwardly leaned in to give him a hug as he rose to reciprocate. His blissfully strong arms melted her until he retreated to his seat.

"I'm so sorry I'm late! How are you?" she asked as she plopped down.

He studied her carefully and slowly said, "I'm good. Where were you?"

"Don't ask." Charlotte sighed and rolled her eyes. "I'm a bridesmaid and I'm coming from one of many photo sessions." She quickly tried to change topic.

"Is there a daisy theme at the wedding?" he asked.

Charlotte's eyes grew wide. "It's a flower theme all weekend, but how did you know?"

Wyatt smiled. "Because you have daisies all over your hair and on your dress."

Charlotte blushed, realizing that she had rushed from the shoot without removing the flowers scattered throughout her mane.

"Don't worry. It looks cute."

Wyatt flustered Charlotte who smiled shyly. It was the first compliment she heard from him in a long time. The moment was interrupted by a waiter rattling off specials. Wyatt opted for the vegetarian lasagna while Charlotte chose the grilled salmon, and they enjoyed a delicious meal and chatted throughout. Toward the end, Wyatt told Charlotte that he decided to make a life change and he wanted to discuss it with her. Her sleep-deprived mind was so consumed by wedding fever that, for a split second, she fantasized he'd tell her that he was ready to settle down. Sexy Ray was quickly forgotten, as her crush on Wyatt had never really died.

"What is it?" She sweetened her voice. "I'm happy to discuss anything with you."

Wyatt reached into his pocket. "I've decided that life is too short to live alone."

Charlotte felt lightheaded at the idea that he might propose. After all, he was so unconventional, it really could happen. But instead of a ring, he pulled out his phone. Charlotte cocked her head in curiosity.

"I'm going to get a dog!"

Charlotte hid her disappointment. "Oh. That's so sweet."

"Yes! And I thought you could help me pick out the breed. I don't want one too big, so I narrowed it down to a bichon or cocker spaniel. Here's pictures of two rescues my assistant found at the animal shelter. Take a look." Wyatt handed Charlotte his phone.

"I think you should meet both of them and see which one you bond with," Charlotte commented as she wistfully studied the adorable pups and wished he had a stronger bond with her.

"That's a great idea. I'm so glad I asked you." Wyatt was as happy as a lark.

He gave her a ride to the hotel in his Tesla. She halfheartedly listened to his excited chatter about his latest film, feeling down knowing that she was still in the friend zone. Hiding her emotions, she conversed lightly and gave him an idea for a film about dogs lifting people out of depression. He loved the concept of incorporating man's best friend into a movie and decided to consider her idea. It wasn't until they said their platonic goodbyes that she realized she was fifteen minutes late to the photo session. She bolted directly to the pool to face a mob of angry Persians.

Shokoufeh was furious. "Charlotte! What took you so long? We're all waiting! And why aren't you in your bikini and cover-up? Didn't you read the Run of Show?"

"I'm so sorry—"

"Sorry doesn't cut it! Go to your bungalow, get on your bathing suit, put your hair in a ponytail, and get back here now." Shokoufeh was enraged.

Charlotte sprinted to the bungalow, changed her clothes, and ran back to the pool, blinding hotel guests with her bright white skin in dire need of a spray tan. She was met with angry glares, followed by hysteria once the bridal posse discovered she'd forgotten her sunglasses. The photographer took pity on her and loaned her his glasses. They were too big for her head, but she had to make do.

Completely ostracized for the rest of the day, the bridesmaids gave Charlotte the silent treatment and she suspected they were gossiping about her in Farsi. To make matters worse, one of their boyfriends squeezed her knee under the table during the rehearsal dinner speeches. Charlotte winced and looked at him with disgust, but he just winked and stared at her breasts for a moment. His name was Reza. He was a cheesy cornball who wore ostentatious clothes, flashy gold jewelry, and bragged about his Ferrari. His parents had forced him to become a doctor, but he was convinced that his true calling in life was to be a DJ. He used rapper slang and was a self-proclaimed "Baller Ambassador." His heavy cologne made Charlotte gag and she couldn't remember the name of his nasty, superficial girlfriend whose lifelong dream was to be an Instagram influencer.

As the night wore on, Charlotte's loneliness intensified. While the crowd danced to Persian music, she snuck off to the bathroom to check her phone. She emerged twenty minutes later and bumped into Reza standing by the door.

"Finally, you come out," he said.

"Do you need something?"

He moved in closer, backing her into the wall. "Yeah, a kiss."

"What's wrong with you?" She shoved him away. "Your girlfriend is in the other room."

"She's dancing. We won't get caught." He leaned in.

Charlotte ducked away. "I'd rather spend the rest of my life celibate than touch you."

She ditched the party and retreated to her bungalow to pop Champagne and take a big swig. She yanked open the door to the minibar and downed a mini vodka bottle. Agitated about being a prisoner at the wedding, frustrated that Wyatt kept her in the friend zone, upset that nasty Reza thought he had a chance with her, irritated she'd wasted time with Ray, disturbed she didn't have a boyfriend, and terrified that her eggs might die before she found a sucker to marry her, she finished off a second vodka, tossed the bottle on the floor, and passed out.

Daylight woke Charlotte and she rolled over, still wearing her dress. Alcohol bottles surrounded her and she had a massive headache. She vaguely remembered that she had to put on the blue floral dress and prepare for the wedding day brunch photo session, but her blood pressure skyrocketed when she realized it was starting in five minutes. She rushed around, left last night's eye makeup on, brushed her teeth, applied lipstick, and made it down to the dining area fifteen minutes late. Everyone was already seated. She heard a bridesmaid snark, "The New Yorker should learn how to use an alarm." Charlotte pretended not to notice and avoided eye contact with Reza, who sat directly across from her.

Later that day, Charlotte forwent the bridesmaids' glam squad, insisting to Shokoufeh that it would be more efficient to doll up on her own and meet in the bridal suite just before the photo session. Charlotte zipped up her purple floral dress and examined her appearance in the mirror. Satisfied with her reflection, she gave herself a pep talk to be on her best behavior for Shokoufeh's big day, and she even decided to leave her phone in her room during the wedding. Before heading out, she took one last look at it and nearly collapsed in shock when she read a text from Sofia. *You won't believe it, Ray got the blonde hostess at Angelino's SoHo pregnant! And she's keeping the kid!*

Frozen with nausea, Charlotte leaned against the wall to steady herself as tears welled up in her eyes. Her phone pinged with a message from Bridezilla. *Don't be late this time!*

That was it. Charlotte yanked open the minibar, grabbed two mini whiskey bottles since there was no more vodka, and downed both of them. It wasn't until she swayed over to the bridal suite that she remembered she hated whiskey. She had to keep her chin up, be strong, and get through the wedding. She'd be a team player for the bride, her oldest friend.

In the bridal suite, four photographers snapped away as Charlotte did her best to act the part of the glowing bridesmaid. She pretended it was a PR job and smiled her way through the photo session, complimenting her fellow bridesmaids and gushing over the bride. Shokoufeh's mom leaned into Charlotte and whispered, "Don't worry, honey, your day will come. You'll get married someday."

Charlotte fought back tears as Shokoufeh's father held up his glass to make a toast. "Can I have everyone's attention?" The room fell silent. "I'm so proud of my daughter. She worked hard her entire life to get good grades and have a good career. We named her Shokoufeh because we knew she'd blossom into a beautiful flower. She's the light of my world and she'll become a wife tonight, but she'll always be my daughter." He wiped a tear from his eye, hugged the bride, and said, "I'll always love my beautiful Shokoufeh."

Bridesmaids tearfully clapped and cheered, photographers snapped away, and Charlotte slumped into a nearby chair, burdened with grief, knowing that her father would miss out on her future wedding. To respect her friend, Charlotte managed to pull herself together. She stood up straight for the traditional Persian ceremony, posed for endless pictures, sat still during speeches at dinner, whirled with the bridesmaids on the dance floor—and then things became fuzzy.

A slight buzzing noise woke Charlotte and she adjusted her eyes to daylight while she pieced together how the wedding had ended. She remembered drinking wine and tequila shots, but she had no recollection of anything afterward. She sought to uncover the source of the noise. It sounded like a phone vibrating, but her phone didn't make that beep. She sat up, discovered a man lying next to her, and jumped out of bed.

Heart pounding, she quickly came to her senses and realized she was still fully clothed in the bridesmaid dress, so it was unlikely she'd had sex with the stranger. He was fully dressed in a tuxedo and passed out on top of the bedspread, facedown. Charlotte tiptoed to the other side of the bed and softly said, "Hello?" No response. She repeated herself a little louder a few times until the mystery man finally rolled over. It was Reza.

"Oh my God! What are you doing here?" Charlotte was repulsed.

Reza rubbed his eyes and held his head up for a moment until he finally said, "Shit. Fairuza is going to be pissed. Get me some aspirin. My head's killing me."

Charlotte grabbed a pillow and smashed it against his face. "Get your own damn aspirin! Seriously, how the hell did you end up in my room?"

"You were throwing yourself at me all night and begged me to come back with you. Don't fake amnesia. Crap, my head is about to explode." He could hardly sit up.

"Think of a good story and leave. Your girlfriend is probably looking for you." Charlotte worried she'd gotten herself in another mess with the Persian crew. She hesitated but needed to know. "Did we hook up or anything like that last night?"

He laughed. "You tried all night, begging me for sex." Charlotte grimaced before he continued, "But I'm a gentleman and couldn't do it while you were so wasted."

Charlotte let out a sigh of relief. "Okay. Thank you, I guess. I really don't remember anything after we danced in circles."

"But we did make out a lot. You were wild, kissing me non-stop. I couldn't break free." Reza winked. "How long are you in LA? We should hang out again before you go back."

Charlotte was beside herself. "Yeah, right, Reza. I highly doubt I was kissing you all night. Must've been in your dreams. I'm leaving today to see my family in Orange County and then back to New York, so good luck with your girlfriend."

Reza was smug. "Baby, your lipstick's all over my shirt. Think whatever you want, but you were hot last night. You kept begging me for more."

"I'm not having this conversation with you. Go back to your girlfriend and tell her that you were drunk and took an Uber home. It's already 9 a.m. and everyone's probably awake. Your phone has been vibrating. Please get out. Now."

Reza finally left as Charlotte found her phone and smiled at a text. *Hi Charlotte, thanks for the advice at lunch. It's official, I'm the proud papa of a Bichon! Sending pics soon. Wyatt*

Then a group text from Shokoufeh started at 3 a.m. *Ladies, have you seen Reza? Fairuza can't find him and she's very worried.*

Charlotte went pale as she read down the text chain from the others.

I saw him going into the bathroom around midnight. I hope he's ok!

Oh no, did David check with the groomsmen?

He's the love of my life, we have to find him! (from Fairuza)

Did someone look in the pool? What if he drowned or something???

Yes, David texted all the groomsmen, nobody saw him.

I'm so drunk! I have no idea, best wedding ever Shokoufeh!

Ladies, we can't sleep until we find Reza!!! For real!!

Her sense of dread intensifying, she read down the chain, painfully aware that she was the only bridesmaid who hadn't commented. There were a few responses in the morning when people woke up. With a foggy mind, Charlotte entered the chain. *Just waking up! I hope he is ok.... Maybe drank too much and took Uber home?*

Then Charlotte noticed a different text chain from David that included both bridesmaids and groomsmen. It consisted of similar messages until Charlotte read one that sent a chill down her spine. *I'm working with hotel security to find out what happened to Reza. They're reviewing the cameras now, if he left the hotel, we'll be able to see what time.*

Fairuza responded. *Thank you so much David, I can't stop crying, I'm so scared. I called his parents and they haven't heard from him. Call me as soon as you know. If anyone else hears anything, please tell me!*

Charlotte's jaw dropped as she imagined them looking at security footage and discovering Reza walking to her bungalow and leaving in the morning. Overcome with stress, she knew her text would make her look guilty once the footage revealed that he was with her.

She squeezed out of her bridesmaid dress and washed her face while trying to clear her mind. She swore off alcohol, thinking about what a mess she caused. She heard her phone buzz in the other room, and she found a private text from Shokoufeh. *Charlotte, I'm speechless!!! The cameras show Reza and you going to your bungalow last night and him leaving this morning. Seriously?? Fairuza has been with him for 5 years! Why would you go after her man??? So messed up! And why didn't you tell us that he is ok??? I'm so shocked, you've changed so much and everyone could see how jealous you've been of me since I got engaged. Maybe if you stop whoring around and going after other people's guys, you'd have your own man!*

It was followed by one more text. *It's best for you to skip the departure photo session. I don't want Fairuza to be uncomfortable.*

Charlotte put the phone down. She was shaking. A buzz alerted her that there was a new message in David's group text. *We found Reza! Don't worry everyone and thanks again.*

Someone responded. *Good! Where was he?*

The phone rang and it was Lorenzo with a work emergency. "*Ciao! Carlotta! Come stai?* We have a big journalist from *Departures Magazine* coming tonight. I text you her number with the reservation time and tell everyone at Angelino's Park Avenue to treat her nice-uh!"

After speaking to the manager and arranging dinner for the journalist, Charlotte responded to Shokoufeh's text. She typed with rage. *I'm not jealous of you, Sherry. You're so ungrateful! I bent over backwards for you and spent thousands of dollars on YOUR big day and I don't remember ever hearing you say THANK YOU. As for Reza, I'd never want that superficial hairball. I don't know how he ended up in my bungalow. He was probably so drunk that he followed me back, he's a cheater and a player. But nothing happened between us! He's disgusting and tell your friend that she got herself a real winner.*

Charlotte tossed the phone on the bed and then wondered if she was too harsh on the text. She quickly had a startling fear; she looked at her phone again and her eyes nearly popped out of her head. She'd accidently sent her message to David's group text chain for the entire bridal party, not just Shokoufeh. She buried her head in her hands, completely mortified.

A few minutes later, the buzz from her phone sent her blood pressure skyrocketing. It was from Fairuza. *Charlotte, get your facts straight! Reza is safe with me now and he said you were so drunk he had to carry you back to your bungalow. He feels sorry for you because you're the only single girl in the group and he wanted to protect you. He's a good guy which really makes me wonder why you said such insulting things about someone who just wanted to help you. You're welcome and please don't respond. You've caused us enough grief!*

Chapter 19

MOSCOW

Back in New York, Angelino's was bustling, leaving Charlotte little time to dwell on Shokoufeh's wedding drama. Instead, she navigated a busy work agenda. She completely ignored Ray and managed to schedule meetings away from his bar. Wyatt occasionally texted pictures of his new bichon. She was always ecstatic to hear from him and she even named the pup: Starlet.

Angelino's Moscow was due to open on Halloween. Charlotte would miss the parties in NYC, but she was starting to outgrow costumes and she looked forward to her first trip to Russia. The pre-launch work had been especially challenging because their PR team barely spoke English. In one instance, it wasn't until the end of the long marketing strategy session via Skype that Charlotte realized she'd referenced the wrong PowerPoint presentation the entire time. It was an extremely frustrating situation exacerbated by the fact that her Russian colleagues took forever to make a statement.

Trouble started at the Aeroflot lounge before Charlotte could greet anyone from the team. Marco snapped at her, "My phone is broken! Find out where I can get a new battery in Moscow. I can't believe this shit!"

"No problem. I'll ask the Russian PR team. They'll know where to go." She sent an email and hoped to receive a solution by the time they landed in Moscow.

"*Ciao! Carlotta!*" Lorenzo was happier than usual. "I invite cute girls and gave them your number. Help them when they arrive to Moscow tomorrow. They stay in our hotel-uh."

"How many are coming, and which nights will they be there?" Charlotte hid her annoyance about being responsible for Lorenzo's harem.

"Just four-uh! You know them. Natalya, Alina, Olga, and Svetlana."

They were nice girls from the NYC model scene, but Charlotte didn't understand why Lorenzo needed to import Russian girls to an opening in Russia. It was a meaningless task to add to her heavy workload.

For the first time ever, Charlotte's assigned seat was next to Jack. He seemed oddly happy about it while she was perturbed. She'd hoped to catch up on sleep and watch movies during the nine-hour flight to Moscow, not talk about work with her boss. Nevertheless, she smiled and pretended to be thrilled with the situation.

"Maybe we should have a vodka toast after take-off," Jack joked.

Charlotte had avoided alcohol since Shokoufeh's wedding. "I might have a little sip of wine, but no hard liquor for me," she replied innocently. "Besides, I never drink on the job." It wasn't entirely true, but she tried to project a good girl image.

"You're not really on the job until we land in Moscow and you have to help Marco with his phone. Good luck with that, by the way."

"Well, I'd rather do that than coordinate Lorenzo's model brigade. It's complicated dealing with a group of women. Maybe now is a good time for me to mention the raise I've been seeking," she said with an eye roll.

"Don't talk to them about it during a work trip. If it goes bad, you won't have an escape."

"That's true, but I still don't understand why I have to go through them instead of you."

Jack sighed. "Because they think of you as their assistant, so you need to deal with them first. You can involve me if they don't give you what you want. But at least start with them."

Charlotte hated playing games and was often confused between the "family business" style of Angelino's, paired with Jack's more serious corporate mentality. She desperately wanted to have the discussion with Lorenzo and Marco, but they always avoided the topic in New York. Something had to change soon. It was already October and she still needed a man and a raise. Time was running out!

After they passed through passport control, two cars waited for the group and Charlotte begrudgingly escorted Marco to a telecom store instead of going to the hotel with the others. The phone shop was dingy and everything was written in Cyrillic. Charlotte used the language of smiles and hand gestures to explain the problem to the clerks while Marco barked in English and Italian to replace the battery. Miraculously, they fixed it, but they refused to take Marco's credit cards and he wasn't carrying any rubles. He finally handed the shopkeeper a $100 bill. The Russian took a puff from his cigarette, blew out the smoke, and shook his head "*niet.*" When Marco offered an additional Benjamin, he quickly snatched the money and flashed a toothless smile while nodding his head "yes." Charlotte knew Marco got ripped off, but she was eager to leave the store and freshen up before dinner.

The hotel was eerily reminiscent of a Soviet Union-era bunker. The large black block building was dotted with square windows. The lobby was drab with 1970s furnishings and Charlotte's room was big, square, and heavy. There was a phone on each side of the bed, the old-fashioned kind with a curly cord connecting the handset to the base. It was perhaps the result of watching too many spy movies, but she had an uneasy feeling that the room was bugged. Hoping there were no hidden cameras in the bathroom, she quickly showered before meeting the Angelino's group in the lobby. They all agreed that the hotel had an awful vibe. Lorenzo insisted the franchisee would upgrade the group.

Dinner with the Angelino's team and the Russian franchisee, a young real estate tycoon Marco had befriended on a yacht in Capri, occurred at 02 Lounge, located on the top floor of the Ritz Carlton. Sparkling city views stunned Charlotte, who once again felt grateful for the opportunities her job gave her. She was a long way from California.

"Please, we need a different hotel. Where we stay is so sad-uh," Lorenzo begged with a sorrowful face. The Russian nodded his head "yes." Lorenzo was satisfied and then he launched into stories about white truffles.

Charlotte was unsure how much the franchisee comprehended. But she was starting to tire and quietly chewed her food without saying much besides, "Moscow is so beautiful. I'm glad you brought Angelino's here."

She nearly dozed off during the ride back to the hotel and much to her dismay, Jack invited her to join him for a nightcap. Because a true PR professional never turned down an invitation from the boss, Charlotte obliged and headed to the lobby bar with him while the rest of the crew retired to their rooms for a good night's sleep. Jack ordered two vodka tonics "in the spirit of Russia" and pulled out a chair for her.

"Russia looks good on you," Jack said in a cheerful voice.

"Oh, thank you. I'm a mess from jet lag."

"Nonsense, you always look good." Jack smiled as he gazed into her eyes.

Charlotte didn't know how to respond to his flirtation. "Oh, you're so sweet," she said, and quickly wished she'd avoided the term of endearment.

"Well, I'm not sure if anyone ever called me 'sweet' before. I guess I should say 'thank you.'" Jack's smile widened as he stared even deeper into her eyes.

Desperate to spin the conversation a different direction, Charlotte tried to think of something else to say. "What do people usually call you?"

"Well, some think I'm this strict guy who only cares about business and profits. Others think I'm aloof or uncaring. I like that you called me 'sweet.'" He kept his eyes on her while he took a sip of his drink.

"Not to change the subject, but I feel like our hotel rooms are bugged." Charlotte gave him a serious look and hoped it wasn't obvious that she was indeed trying to change the subject.

"Bugged? Like KGB spies?" Jack asked incredulously.

"Yes! I totally get that vibe and I heard it's very common in Russia for American executives to be taped by Soviet officials."

Jack smiled. "Do you want me to go to your room with you to check for recording devices?"

Charlotte thought for a second before rebutting, "That'd be pointless because their equipment is so good, we'd never find it. They can plant recording devices in the ceiling that are invisible to the naked eye."

Jack took another sip of his drink and transformed back into his usual serious self. "Charlotte, that era is over. There are no more Soviets. They're called Russians and they encourage international business. Bringing a company like Angelino's to Moscow helps their politicians fulfill economic goals."

"Good point. I never thought of it like that before," Charlotte said with feigned interest. Satisfied to halt the flirting, she kept him focused on his Russia lecture by asking intelligent questions.

After Jack's twenty-minute dialogue about Russian geo-economics, they decided to end the night and get some sleep. Charlotte thought about him while she brushed her teeth. He was smart, polite, and had a nice build, but she never had feelings for him in the past. She wondered if she should consider him as a potential suitor or if perhaps the vodka was impairing her judgment.

The next morning, as the Angelino's team began eating their breakfast in the gloomy cafeteria, Lorenzo broke the silence. "Guys, I think this hotel is bugged."

"That's what I told Jack!" Charlotte felt vindicated and hoped Lorenzo's comment would add credibility to her assertion the night before. Marco and Jack argued that they were paranoid, and the subject was dropped by the time they finished their meal.

Angelino's Moscow was a site to behold. It looked as if a Czarina decorated it. The rooms were crowded with candelabras, stately antique tables, oversized cushioned chairs, and gold-framed mirrors while chubby baby Angelinos gazed from celestial murals on the ceiling. The appearance was totally off-brand, yet Charlotte walked around the space in awe as she took pictures with her phone to send to Sofia for her amusement.

Lorenzo, Marco, and Jack were huddled in the center of the main dining room when Charlotte joined their conversation after her photography stint. They were furious that the restaurant didn't resemble traditional Angelino's locations. "But *Carlotta,* why you didn't tell them to make it look like Angelino's?" Lorenzo demanded.

Incredulous that she was being blamed for the debacle, she growled, "Lorenzo, their PR team doesn't speak English. I forwarded all the renderings and images they sent me to you, Marco, and Jack. It isn't my place to tell the investor to change things. I assumed you were fine with everything because you never said anything to the contrary."

"I never saw these emails! Why not call me and text me and tell me that they are fucking up-uh?" Lorenzo demanded.

Jack jumped in. "Lorenzo, she sent us the emails and she can't control how they build the restaurant. Her job is to work with their PR team to organize your interviews, branding, and messaging to the press."

Charlotte was grateful and relieved that Jack defended her. He was usually on her side, but now he was more supportive than ever.

Lorenzo wouldn't let it go. "No! She talks to them but doesn't warn us they did this!"

"I sent you guys everything. I can't help it if you don't respond. I don't have an assistant, I'm handling a lot on my own, and when I send information to the three owners and nobody responds, I assume everything is fine."

"Show me! You never send nothing!" Lorenzo was furious.

Marco joined the lynching. "Yeah, I didn't get anything from you. Why didn't you tell us?"

Charlotte frantically searched her phone for emails she sent seven months earlier containing the renderings and interior design specs. "I'm trying to find it, but I don't have cell reception." Her heart raced as she moved around the room to find cellular coverage.

Lorenzo continued on, "Because you never send! My phone works fine-uh."

"Then give me your phone and I'll check your in-box." Charlotte snatched it from his hand. As she searched "Moscow" and reviewed the March section, she had a flashback of the breakup with Jorge that happened the same month. She suddenly feared she never sent the emails because she was too busy crying over the dirtbag.

"Wait, why doesn't your email box go back past March twenty-fifth?" Charlotte was in panic mode and thought she was losing her mind.

"My phone broke and they don't put the old emails on new phones. But you never send-uh!" Lorenzo stomped his foot while Charlotte hoped he missed the email when his phone was out of service. She usually followed up with texts and phone calls, but she slacked off while she grieved over Jorge.

"It's right here, guys. I was cc'd on an email with the renderings and interior shots on March sixteenth and it looks like…yep, she even followed up on March nineteenth because you didn't respond. I was in Argentina and figured you guys had it under control." Jack held up his phone to show them the emails. He saved the day!

"But nobody said nothing to me-uh!" Lorenzo fumed.

It was Jack's turn to get mad. "You were sent two emails that I have right here, and knowing Charlotte, she also called and texted you. I'm not responsible for the design of the locations. I'm busy overseeing the finances and franchise deals. You guys need to take accountability for your responsibilities. If you didn't get Charlotte's emails and messages for whatever reason, I'd expect you to ask her for copies of the renderings and show some concern about what this place looks like. I won't do it all. We have a partnership and now here we are, standing in Angelino's Moscow, which looks ridiculously more suited for Czars of a bygone era than our target customers," Jack scowled. "Stop placing the blame on your PR girl and do your goddamn job!"

Silence fell over the stunned group as Jack glared at Marco and Lorenzo. Charlotte had never seen Jack lose his temper and she was intrigued. In fact, for the first time ever, she thought he looked sexy. Very sexy. It felt good to have a strong man on her side.

"Mr. Lorenzo," the Russian GM broke the ice, to everyone's relief. "We still need to build kitchen. Come, I show you."

"My God-uh!" Lorenzo ran off with the GM, eager to escape Jack's wrath, while Marco slumped into a chair and got on a video chat with his sons in the US. The chef and the restaurateur often avoided accountability by making a quick exit.

Charlotte stood next to her new hero and thanked him directly. "That was nice of you to stick up for me." She hoped her voice had just the right tone of flirtation mixed with gratitude.

"I know it's not your fault and you tried to tell them, but when it's an issue this big, please speak directly to me about it." Jack didn't hide his irritation.

Taken aback by his criticism, Charlotte quipped, "Well, you were cc'd on those emails too. I don't have time to chase you guys when you don't bother checking emails. It's bad enough that I have to constantly call and text Lorenzo and Marco because they don't use computers and their phones are always messed up. Quite frankly, I don't get paid enough."

She turned and stormed off. Jack was no longer sexy to her.

The day was full of frustrations and stress. The interpreter was fluent in Russian and Italian, but not English, leaving Charlotte struggling to communicate with the PR team she hadn't been able to understand for months. Meanwhile, the pizza chef traveling on a later flight was denied entry and detained at the airport. Charlotte had to work with the franchisee's assistant, another non-English speaker, to provide the correct documents for his visa. Worst of all, the kitchen still needed to be built. Charlotte toured the large, empty room in shock. There were pipes and wires, but nothing else. No ovens, no refrigerators, not even a sink. The opening party was two days away. It'd be impossible. Her head spun at the thought of rescheduling everything.

That evening, they were supposed to host the Italian consul general to Moscow at Angelino's. Instead, Charlotte had to book the group at a different Italian restaurant. The Russian never followed through with his promise to upgrade the hotel, so after only twenty minutes to get ready in the poorly lit bunker, the group set off for dinner. Marco apologized profusely in Italian for the change of venue to the empathetic consul general, who explained that business matters were handled unconventionally in Moscow and not to worry because the franchisee had ample connections to launch the restaurant.

During the meal, Lorenzo amused the group with his food analysis and proudly showed the table a video collage created by his daughter of every pizza variety at Angelino's. The consul general brought his stunning Russian wife, who shared fascinating stories about her childhood during the communist era. She spoke excellent English and Charlotte chatted at length with her while the others spoke Italian.

There was just one gloomy aspect of the evening: the tension between Charlotte and Jack. She ignored him and avoided eye contact. When they returned to the hotel, he awkwardly asked Charlotte what she was going to do for the rest of the night.

"I'll be in my room working on emails and then hopefully get some sleep. It's been a long and *disappointing* day." While entering the elevator, she said, "But the models Lorenzo flew in from New York should arrive at the hotel shortly. I'm sure they'll have a late night out if you're looking for company."

* * *

The elevator doors shut, and Jack stood alone, feeling emptier than the lobby.

He realized he had been too hard on Charlotte earlier, but he didn't know how to apologize, and he learned that it's best not to draw the ire of the redhead. Her demeanor had turned cold, stubborn, and downright cruel.

Jack had always admired Charlotte's dedication to the company and, behind the scenes, warned Marco and Lorenzo not to drive their skilled employee away from Angelino's. He wasn't sure of his intentions with his attractive, amusing, hardworking subordinate, and he'd be lying if he said he'd never imagined the taste of her lips and what her body would feel like pressed against his in bed. However, he also found her overemotional and temperamental. Whenever she complained about Lorenzo and Marco being too dramatic, he had to stop himself from telling her to look in the mirror. The more he thought about it, the more he realized that her anger toward him over one little comment was uncalled for. Such oversensitivity followed by vengeance convinced Jack that her bad attitude was the reason why she was thirty-five and still single. He stomped off to find Lorenzo and Marco to join them for the night.

At breakfast the next morning, Jack watched Charlotte survey the mischievous group. "Late night, guys?" she asked.

"It was the best-uh!" Lorenzo energetically chimed. "Girls! Girls! Girls!"

"Gee, so sorry I missed that," Charlotte said sarcastically.

"Nobody sleep alone!" Lorenzo laughed and Marco joined him.

Jack caught Charlotte's eye for the first time since their argument. "Oh, how interesting," she said flatly. Jack turned red and began to say something, then stopped.

Lorenzo spoke about how he bedded the most beautiful girl in the universe. Then he described the gorgeous blonde Marco met and, before he could reference Jack, Charlotte jumped up and excused herself. "I need to answer emails. I'll be in the lobby whenever you're ready to go."

Jack watched with mixed emotions as Charlotte rushed off. She wore her heart on her sleeve and he could tell that she was hurt by the idea that he brought a woman back to his room. To the contrary, he barely spoke to anyone at the noisy club and he sat alone most of the night, wishing he was somewhere with her, having a meaningful conversation like those they had in Paris. He often thought of their time together in France because it was there that he noticed something special about her. She seemed relaxed and happy, very different than her normal anxiously performed balancing act at Angelino's. He believed he was the source of her refreshed glow while they ventured around the city, and he was deeply moved by her caring reaction and gentle caresses when he told her about his fiancée's suicide. Jack never opened up to anyone about it before, but he had felt comfortable with her that evening. He craved her touch again.

On the flip side, starting an office romance would cause a headache. Although many employees dated each other, it was strictly against company policy, as Jessica liked to remind everyone whenever she lifted her head out of her human resources manuals. Besides, Charlotte was steady in her career but so unpredictable in her dating life, and a relationship with her would surely end in disaster. She had erratically stormed off after he'd made a legitimate criticism and then punished him at dinner by not even acknowledging him as she pretended to be completely engrossed in the consul general's wife. Charlotte usually wasn't so childish and unprofessional during work trips, and he suspected her odd behavior stemmed from the flirtation that had been brewing. Jack knew what he had to do.

* * *

Charlotte worked hard throughout the day with the Russian PR team and dealt with a crisis in NYC involving a manager who forced a group of spoiled teenagers on the Upper East Side to tip 20 percent on their bill. Waiters had a habit of illegally adding tips when they assumed young customers or tourists would forget. Her mind kept wandering back to Jack and her eyes constantly darted around the restaurant to see if he had arrived, but he never showed up.

Finally, around 5 p.m., she tried to get information from Marco when she casually asked, "Do you know if Jack is coming to dinner tonight? I haven't seen him since breakfast."

"Why do you need him? What's wrong?" Marco asked.

"Nothing's wrong. I just wondered who'd be at dinner tonight, so I can get a head count. I assume he's coming?" Charlotte tried to sound nonchalant.

"No, he texted me that he is going to London for two nights and he'll be back for the opening now that we moved it to Friday."

"Why did he go to London? And why Friday? When did they change the opening? I need to be prepared." Charlotte felt sad about Jack and stressed about work.

"How the fuck do you think we can open without a kitchen? They need more time to build it out."

"Okay, but I wish I would've known." Charlotte hated his nasty attitude.

"We talked about it at breakfast, but you ran away. You're supposed to stay with us instead of leaving the group." Marco glared at her. "What's wrong with you lately? You didn't warn us about the design of this place, and I hear you're always drinking at the bar when Ray's working. Your work performance is slipping."

Mortified by the reference to Ray, Charlotte went on the offensive. "We established yesterday that I sent you guys all the info for this place, but you chose not to respond. And I wish I had free time to hang out at the bar, but I'm swamped with work, which is why I rushed to the lobby this morning to get cell reception to respond to an urgent email." As fear set in that she screwed things up with Jack, she couldn't stop herself from asking, "But do you know why Jack went to London?"

Marco's irritation grew stronger as he snapped, "Hopefully he's going to get laid. He was such a pain in the ass last night, didn't talk to anyone. He sat there looking depressed until he finally left. I'm glad he's gone. He'll be back for the opening. Forget about Jack. I told you to always answer to me."

He stormed off, leaving Charlotte to absorb the news. She realized her tantrum toward Jack was unacceptable and wished she could take it back. Of course he didn't sleep with any girls from the club; he was too sophisticated for such behavior. The thought of him in London made her miss him even more.

The rest of the night was torture for Charlotte. She dined with the Italians and the Russian girls from NYC but tuned them out as she fixated on what was happening between her and Jack. She reminisced about Paris and the effort he made to spend time with her while she had been engrossed in a French playboy who didn't want more kids. She had missed a great opportunity to really get to know Jack.

With only one driver for the group, Charlotte was trapped in a club until nearly 3 a.m. Miserable the entire time, she yearned to be at the hotel drinking vodka with Jack. She wistfully thought of his offer just a few nights prior to check her room for spy devices.

At the end of the night, she yawned in the elevator as Marco informed her that they'd meet for breakfast at 8 a.m. and then go sightseeing. This was his typical behavior when they went abroad for openings—party all night and work or play the next day on just a few hours of sleep. It was a challenging schedule for Charlotte to keep up.

She was completely fatigued at breakfast. Lorenzo was still asleep while she embarked with "Energizer Bunny" Marco. Just like in Tokyo, he wanted to see it all. The franchisee's assistant sent a driver and English-speaking tour guide.

They started at The Pushkin Museum of Fine Arts and she found it remarkable that a man as rough as Marco adored all the great masterpieces. He "oohed" and "aahed" over Picasso, Van Gogh, and Renoir paintings. She smiled and contemplated the way Italians loved beauty in any form—women, clothes, cars, food, and art. They appreciated everything beautiful.

After stopping outside the nearby Cathedral of Christ the Savior to take a few pictures of the magnificent architecture, they headed to Gorky Park for lunch. Charlotte's feet became tired as she tried to keep up with Marco, who raced ahead to see the rowboats on the lake. She was relieved when they finally sat down at a café to eat.

It was already mid-afternoon, and they were expected at Angelino's by 5 p.m. for a training meeting, leaving them time for just one more destination: Red Square. Charlotte was eager to see the place she'd learned about throughout her education. Located in the center of Moscow, it housed some of the country's most significant sites. The interpreter took pictures of Charlotte and Marco in front of the Kremlin, Lenin's Mausoleum, and the enormous GUM department store composed of medieval Russian architecture with elements of British-style steel framework and glass.

The high point of Red Square was the wondrous Saint Basil's Cathedral. Resembling colorful staggered layers of flames, the edifice was made up of eight churches surrounding the core. Although secularized during the communist era, the grandiose radiance of the buildings looked like a divine miracle to Charlotte. She couldn't fathom how they'd constructed something so incredible nearly five hundred years ago.

Marco suggested they walk over to the Kazan Cathedral—built in the 1600s, destroyed by communists in the 1930s, and rebuilt in the 1990s—to say a prayer. It was smaller than Saint Basil's Cathedral but still exquisite with its soaring gold-plated domes adorned with crosses, set upon a brightly painted aqua blue, white, and peach structure. Charlotte asked the interpreter if there were any customs they should respect. They were informed that, as Catholics, they could enter the Russian Orthodox Church, but it was best to stay toward the back to observe and pray in silence.

Slowly passing through the heavy doors of Kazan Cathedral was like being transported back in time. Ornate gold crosses hung from the ceiling, incense filled the room with clouds of smoke, candles flickered, and worn icons stared intently into the past. A priest kept his back to worshipers while he faced a heavy gold-plated alter and chanted prayers in Russian. The authenticity of the environment mesmerized Charlotte.

Marco nudged her out of her stupor. "What's wrong with you? Cover your head," he whispered loudly with contempt. Charlotte glanced around and noticed the women wearing scarves over their hair. Yet, there she was, with her thick red locks exposed. She ripped the scarf from her neck and tried to wrap her head, but it was too narrow to cover her tresses. Marco rolled his eyes and took his scarf from his neck and thrust it at her.

Startled back into reality, Charlotte felt like a fish out of water and hovered in the back while Marco roamed around the church. Almost everything was visible from her vantage point near the rear door. She watched men and women pray while she wondered about their daily lives, and if they had to hide their faith during the communist era. She silently gave thanks for the freedoms she had known her entire life.

Back at Angelino's, they attempted to share highlights of the tour with Lorenzo, but he was annoyed that Marco and Charlotte whittled away most of the day.

"There isn't much I can do now that the opening is delayed," Charlotte said. "Tomorrow you'll have interviews and an interior photo shoot. I'm actually working around the clock with the time difference in New York—" Lorenzo ran off to yell at the Russian chef while she was midsentence.

The Angelino's Moscow grand opening couldn't come soon enough for Charlotte. When the day finally arrived, she performed her duties as usual while trying to observe Jack, who barely muttered hello as he took a quick tour of the space. He spent the remainder of the night in the corner on his phone, not speaking to anyone, and hardly cracking a smile during photo ops. The event was so crowded that she often lost track of him for long periods.

The kitchen, with the exception of the pizza oven, had been miraculously completed in time for the opening. With it haphazardly strewn together, and not up to Lorenzo's standards, they were at least able to cook pasta and prepare food for the guests.

At one point, the models from Lorenzo's entourage grabbed Charlotte and dragged her into a picture in front of the Step and Repeat. She stood straight and posed with the beauties, and when it was time to disperse, she turned to gather her purse from the ground. *Bam!* Charlotte's high heel snagged the red carpet, sending her crashing to the floor. Her left knee and elbow broke her fall as she hit the ground, leaving bits of bloody flesh exposed. Within seconds, two of the franchisee's bodyguards lifted her up and whisked her to a private room, where first aid was administered by a third Russian man who appeared out of thin air. She was alone with them and felt completely abandoned by Jack. The men didn't speak English, leaving a helpless Charlotte repeating "*spasiba*," "thank you" in Russian.

Nearly half an hour later, she hobbled out of the private room, complete with a bandaged knee and elbow. A few of the models asked if she was all right. Loud popping noises made it impossible to talk and they rushed outside to watch a spectacular firework show organized by the Russian team. More extravagant than any 4th of July she'd ever witnessed, the night was set alight with beautiful sparks. At one point "Angelino's" was spelled out in lights as Lorenzo and Marco shouted, "Viva Angelino's!" She scanned the crowd for Jack and spotted him far off to the side, standing alone, expressionless, staring at the sky. He looked moody and somewhat depressed. Typical.

On the flight home, Jack sat far away from Charlotte. It baffled her that she missed him when just a week earlier she'd been annoyed when he was seated next to her. As they flew across the Atlantic Ocean back to NYC, she decided that maybe she got caught up in the idea of being with him and found it bizarre that she'd suddenly have feelings for him after ten years. Chalking it up to fatigue and, quite frankly, her desperation to find a mate, she decided to stick with her gut and forget about Jack as a love interest. Besides, he was clearly back in business mode and wanted nothing to do with her after she got just a tiny bit upset with him. His crankiness was so unappealing that she resolved to thoroughly relinquish any romantic thoughts of him.

Chapter 20

NEW YORK CITY

Charlotte, the hopeful romantic, repeatedly ignored Sofia's suggestion of online dating until finally concluding that technology might be the only way to find a suitor. She went out with a few guys she met on dating apps, but there was no connection, and as she'd predicted, corresponding with several strangers on the internet was frustratingly time-consuming. The worst part was coming across profiles from fellow employees at Angelino's, knowing that they saw her profile. She cringed thinking of the probable gossip and jokes at her expense. The final straw was receiving an online "wink" from Ray. She deleted all dating apps right then and there.

Her love interests had drifted away. Jorge was ancient history, Eric happily married. Pascal had given up texting her, Jack barely acknowledged her at work, and she'd read somewhere that Wyatt was filming a movie in Vietnam. The only guy she still heard from, unfortunately, was Ray. He texted her inappropriate pictures and vulgar messages like: *I want to eat you.* Charlotte was so thoroughly disgusted and perplexed that she ever had anything to do with him—she ran to a therapist to figure out if she was mentally ill.

The session didn't help, as she was told what she already knew deep down. "You're not insane. You're just desperate to get married and have kids, which is why you unwittingly fell for incompatible Ray." The therapist lacked solutions and Charlotte canceled the follow-up appointment to avoid wasting another $300.

There was another man who remained consistent in her life: Marco. Texts, emails, and calls all hours of the night constantly unnerved her. His newest girlfriend tried to give Charlotte some of her personal projects to manage. Normally, she'd complain to Jack about it, but he was hardly speaking to her, so she vented to Jessica, who assured her that she was allowed to ignore her without any employment repercussions.

Charlotte worked tirelessly on the new website design, which needed to be completely revamped to bring it from 2010 to the modern day. She struggled to get all parties aligned, and it was no easy task, as Lorenzo and Marco were notorious for disagreeing and arguing about every aspect of any project. Trapped in the middle, her mind often drifted while they cursed each other out in Italian. Stuck inside a deep malaise and not knowing how to meet her relationship and career goals, Charlotte's anxiety had reached a breaking point. Her ovaries buried themselves in despair.

Chapter 21

ANGELINO'S FALL STAFF MEETING

Angelino's fall quarterly meeting took place in mid-November before some staff departed for Thanksgiving vacation. Most of the employees were born abroad and eagerly filled in for those who wanted to spend the American holiday with their families. The true battle over shifts occurred during Christmas and New Year's.

Charlotte planned to stay local and save her vacation days for December travels. It felt surprisingly good to avoid airports for an entire month. She improved her body by eating healthy, exercising after work, and getting ample sleep. Her gut was shrinking as her social life slowed down considerably. November had been unusually rainy and cold, allowing Charlotte to spend many nights in her cozy studio with the heater turned up while binge-watching different Netflix series. She dreaded gearing up for the rain in the morning, venturing out of her warm dwellings, and catching a crosstown bus to the staff meeting.

Forlorn faces wandered through the doors of the flagship, weather weary. Puddles from excess water sliding off umbrellas and raincoats formed across the floor. Jessica shook her head in disapproval as she took roll. She'd contact the missing workers later and give them a stern warning. Ironically, she never took disciplinary action against those who missed staff meetings, but most employees didn't want to chance it.

Jack barely acknowledged Charlotte when she said hello. His rebukes since Russia stung, but she'd moved on. Ray was punctual and she managed to avoid his gaze, allowing her thoughts to wander elsewhere. Bored by the meeting, Charlotte yawned as Jessica rambled about the new fingerprint policy to clock in for each shift. Melvin lashed out about managers who bought new chairs to replace those that were broken instead of fixing them. And then, it was Charlotte's turn.

"Hopefully, customers won't fall out of inadequately 'fixed' chairs and sue us…" Charlotte couldn't resist taking a jab at Melvin under her breath before she continued. "As many of you know, Angelino's Moscow is now open for business! It's a beautiful space, decorated differently than traditional Angelino's, but it fits in with the local Russian style. If you haven't already seen it online, please check the email I sent with the opening party video. You can also find it on Angelino's Facebook, Instagram, Twitter, and YouTube channel. The opening was a huge success, complete with live music and fireworks. But when we first arrived, the kitchen wasn't quite finished. It was a challenge, but the Russian and New York teams rallied together and triumphed over adversity by pushing the opening party back just a few days and completing the kitchen at a rapid pace. It took true teamwork to make it happen and it's a reminder that when you work closely with your colleagues, we can create magic together! I hope you'll encourage your customers to visit Angelino's Moscow. Our next international opening will be in Melbourne, sometime in the spring if construction is completed on time. Keep checking our social media, and of course, I'll email info when it's available."

Charlotte sat down with a smile and snuck a glance at Jack. He was, as always, sharply dressed in suit pants and a button-up shirt. He only wore a tie for important meetings and opening parties. His skin was slightly tanned, and his head was neatly covered with thick, brown hair. Charlotte sought reasons why things didn't work out with him, but before she completely lost herself in soul searching, she refocused on Lorenzo who rattled on about Thanksgiving specials, followed by Marco who spoke about erecting canvas vestibules in time for the winter cold.

"So just make sure you have them up by the end of next week," Marco concluded. "Is there anything else, Lorenzo?"

Charlotte was in disbelief. It was the first time they didn't have a lynching prepared. Just when she thought it would be a new record, she noticed Lorenzo's scowl.

"Yes! I'm so pissed off-uh!" Lorenzo exclaimed. Marco looked as perplexed as the rest of the staff, not sure what he was upset about. Lorenzo turned to Marco. "We hire your nephew Gianni to work at Angelino's Columbus Circle and now he's dating our hostess at Union Square! My God-uh! We could get sued for sexual harassment!"

Marco was stunned. "What are you talking about?"

Lorenzo looked out to the staff. "Gianni! I see you! We give you a job-uh! But look what you did! This girl can go crazy and sue!"

Everyone else, except Melvin, felt bad for Gianni. He was a nice kid from Tuscany and barely spoke English. His *tio* Marco employed him at Angelino's and he didn't deserve this admonishment.

"Stand up-uh!" Lorenzo demanded. Gianni rose, hanging his crimson red face in shame. "You're fired! Get out-uh!"

Marco stood by, helpless, as poor Gianni gathered his coat and umbrella and stumbled out of the room. Lorenzo wasn't finished; he looked around the room and continued. "So many of you fuck each other! We can get sued! Do you want to keep fucking and get fired?!"

Reality descended upon the staff as they squirmed in their seats and kept their gaze to the floor. Charlotte accidently made eye contact with smug Ray and quickly lowered her head. Humiliated, she wanted to crawl under the table. Lorenzo informed them that security cameras were stationed in every restaurant and through company gossip "everyone knows who is fucking who." Charlotte glanced over at Jessica who stared down at her notebook. Then, she looked back at Ray who crossed his arms defiantly against his chest, wearing a big smirk on his face. He winked at Charlotte and she turned away, silently praying that nobody on the corporate panel, especially Jack, saw his gesture. Petrified that Lorenzo might know about her and Ray, she feared he'd yell at her next. The degradation would be unbearable!

Charlotte knew romances flourished among employees at Angelino's, just like any other restaurant group. Some couples even got married and had children after meeting at Angelino's. Lorenzo's wife had been a sommelier for the company, and he was known to carry on affairs over the years with bartenders and waitresses. It was shockingly hypocritical that he reprimanded Gianni and scolded the entire Angelino's workforce about sexual relationships.

Jack finally intervened. "Lorenzo, we get the point. Jessica, quickly remind us about the official dating policy."

Everyone turned toward Jessica who appeared flustered. She cleared her throat and quietly said, "We're not allowed to date or have sexual relations with coworkers and anyone violating this policy can be fired immediately." She looked down at her lap.

Ray beamed with satisfaction, and Charlotte knew the troublemaker was untouchable because he'd slept with Jessica.

Jack adjourned the meeting and the crowd bolted for the door, seeming eager to escape before being called out for their misbehavior. Charlotte, one of the last to exit because she was coming from the head table, overheard Marco shout at Lorenzo, "What the fuck is wrong with you?! He's my nephew!"

The office was particularly quiet that day. It was as if everyone who harbored guilt for dating a coworker thought that maintaining a low profile was the best way to avoid Gianni's fate. Charlotte and Jessica kept to themselves, and even Melvin was silent. Charlotte wondered if he was ever bearable enough to attract a poor, helpless new hire who didn't realize that he was a monster. The heart was a peculiar organ. Or perhaps it was other body parts that provoked so many inexplicable workplace romances.

Chapter 22

WHITE PLAINS

Family separation on Thanksgiving was emotionally challenging for Charlotte. Sofia took pity on the popular PR girl who paradoxically found herself alone and invited her to White Plains to spend the holiday weekend with her new boyfriend, Jason, who she'd met online at the end of the summer. Sofia believed that a woman in her thirties should know exactly what she wanted, and she was convinced that her new beau was "the one." Charlotte was ashamed that during the last year she had mistakenly declared two men, Jorge and Pascal, to be "the one." Her brief relations with Eric and Ray didn't help matters. At least the failed romances taught her not to jump into relationships, or bed, without due diligence. Inspired by Sofia, she was on a mission to seal the deal with a good man and although there were bound to be some landmines, she resolved to march forward through the dating battlefield with determination.

White Plains, located in Westchester County, was about an hour drive from NYC. Although many residents commuted to Manhattan daily, there was a city center robust with businesses surrounded by suburbs. Jason's family lived a short distance from town in a cozy two-story home complete with a white picket fence and a tire swing hanging from a large oak tree in the front yard. He belonged to a tight Irish-American clan with five kids and two dogs.

Charlotte was grateful for the invite, but she felt like a third wheel as she sat in the back seat during the drive. By the time they pulled into the driveway, she was overwhelmed with guilt. "Guys, I just realized that maybe I shouldn't crash your family holiday."

"Don't be absurd!" Jason was animated. "My family's so big, nobody will notice one extra person. Besides, with your red hair, everyone will assume you're a cousin from Ireland we haven't seen for a long time." He laughed and Sofia turned around in the front seat to give her a giddy wink.

Sofia had told Charlotte that Jason was the nicest guy she'd ever met. He volunteered as a fireman in college and skipped graduate school to earn money to help his parents put his younger siblings through school. In his mid-thirties and doing very well at a hedge fund, he still found time to assist the Special Olympics with fundraising and participate in an annual marathon to support a cancer charity.

Sofia chimed in, "I'm glad you're here. It'll take pressure off me while I meet his *entire* family."

"Are you crazy? There's no pressure. They're going to love you!" Jason locked eyes with the pretty brunette and smiled sheepishly.

"Um, maybe focus on the road." Charlotte hated to interrupt the lovebirds but preferred to avoid a car crash.

Jason turned to face forward and laughed, "I can drive up here blindfolded. I grew up in this house." He reached over and took

Sofia's hand in his. Charlotte was impressed by their mutual affection. Maybe he really was "the one" for Sofia.

The house was packed with at least forty people, all different ages. Jason's parents and grandmother welcomed Charlotte with open arms, and she attempted to chat with as many of the other guests as possible. It felt good to talk about California and life in general without having to pitch Angelino's to this new crowd. She assumed many of them had gone to the restaurants in NYC, but she steered clear of the subject. She was curious about everyone else's occupation. Throughout the night, she met a fireman, a doctor, two teachers, a policeman, an artist, a flight attendant, a graphic designer, a bar owner, and a few full-time moms. Unable to identify Jason's siblings from his cousins, she guesstimated that there were at least twenty kids running around, all of them oozing cuteness.

If Sofia had warned Charlotte that there'd be such a large group, she would've brought more than just one bottle of wine to give to Jason's parents. The tribe was so big that they used three rooms for dinner. Food was displayed buffet style in the kitchen. The next room held two long tables with space for twelve people at each, and the last room had four smaller tables set up for the children. A few grown-ups, moonlighting as saints, volunteered to eat in the kids' room to supervise and prevent food fights.

Charlotte couldn't speak to Sofia as they sat on opposite ends of the table, but her heart was warmed by her friend's happy glow. She discreetly observed the scene while she talked to others because she knew Sofia would expect a full report when they were back in the city. The plan was to spend two nights at Jason's family home and then he'd drive them back to Manhattan.

At the end of the meal, many guests helped put their dishes in the kitchen. Jason, his mother, and two of his sisters asked the crowd to return to their seats and enjoy a drink while they prepared dessert. Eventually, they came out and placed a ramekin topped with a lid in front of each adult guest.

"Inside is our family's traditional chocolate cake. Don't lift your lids yet, we're going to have a toast first," Jason said, as he darted through the room, making sure everyone had their dessert and spoons to eat it with. The kids were summoned to the adults' room to hear the toast and he asked everyone to stand so that they could see each other. Charlotte obliged, although she was starting to feel a bit tipsy from all the wine.

A cousin held his phone up to record the toast. Jason cleared his throat and banged a fork against a wine glass, "Can everyone hear me? Do you have your dessert?" A chorus of "yes" echoed throughout the crowd and one of his sisters appeared from nowhere and placed a sealed ramekin in front of Sofia.

"Now I do," Sofia smiled.

Jason took a second to smile at her and continued, "Good, we can start. I'd just like to say that Thanksgiving is a time to be thankful, and on behalf of my parents and my brother and my sisters, we're so happy that you all joined us. We're especially grateful to have my grandma here. She just celebrated her ninetieth birthday and she still has more energy than all of us combined."

A few people broke into applause and Charlotte sensed love vibrating throughout the room.

"But there's another reason why this Thanksgiving is so special," Jason continued. "This year, we have my girlfriend Sofia with us." He turned and gave her a doting gaze, sending a sweet blush across her face.

"I hope you had a chance to meet her, but if you haven't yet, you will soon. She's the smartest, kindest, warmest woman I've ever known—who I'm not related to," Jason joked. "So, Sofia, as our special guest this year, we decided that you should be the first person to enjoy your dessert. We won't start until you do," Jason said as he gestured toward the table.

Sofia was taken aback but quipped, "Thank you for the honor. I always say yes to chocolate!" She lifted the lid on her dessert and gasped, "Wait, what?"

Jason fell to one knee. "I hope you don't mind that I put a ring in there instead of cake." Everyone echoed her gasp and a few spectators reached for their phones to take pictures.

Sofia was speechless as she choked out, "Oh my gosh."

Jason continued anxiously, "Sofia, you make me so happy and I hope you'll spend the rest of your life with me and marry me."

Sofia started crying. "Of course!"

Jason stood up and hugged her while camera flashes flickered. Charlotte wept with emotion and a group toward the back of the room chanted, "Show us the ring! Show us the ring!"

The new fiancée slipped it on her ring finger and held it up for everyone to see. Another round of flashes flickered. The women were flushed and teary-eyed while the kids watched with bewilderment.

When the guests calmed down, Charlotte made her way over to Sofia and Jason and gave them each a big hug. "Congratulations! I'm so happy for you guys!"

Sofia was over the moon. "Thank you so much! I'm so glad you're here for this!"

Jason cut in, "I knew Sofia would want one of her best friends to witness the proposal."

"Oh my gosh, it was good that I came. Thank you!" Charlotte said, truly thrilled for them.

"Char, we're going to go in the other room and call my parents. Jason said he asked my dad for my hand in marriage a few weeks ago and we need to let them know what happened." Sofia shed tears of joy as she headed away for privacy with her fiancé.

Charlotte watched them leave and then bolted to the nearest bathroom, where she locked the door and let out tears. The thought of Jason asking Sofia's dad for permission to propose pained her heart and made her think of her own father being denied this patriarchal rite of passage. She missed him terribly on holidays like Thanksgiving. Equally painful was the fear that nobody would ever propose to her. Shokoufeh and now Sofia. Everyone was getting married while Charlotte didn't even have a boyfriend.

After a good cry, Charlotte refreshed her makeup and sauntered back into the adult dining room. Nobody noticed her. Everyone was drinking, chatting, and laughing. Charlotte dug into her cake, convinced every bite would fatten her gut for eternity and she'd never be thin again. She took a big swig of wine and looked around the room with the realization that all the adults were coupled up. With the exception of Jason's grandmother, Charlotte was the only woman without a man.

She leaned over to the lady next to her and asked, "Are you going to eat your cake?" The woman had been deep in conversation.

"No, I'm one of the few people on the planet who doesn't like chocolate. It's all yours." She chuckled as she slid it over to Charlotte.

After finishing two desserts, Charlotte was ready to go home to break down and cry in private. But she was far out in the countryside, without any taxis, subways, buses, or even Ubers to bring her back to her little studio on 56th Street. She was stuck pretending to be fine while making conversation with Jason's seemingly perfect family.

Around midnight, people filtered out and those sleeping in the house retreated. Charlotte braced herself for Sofia's euphoria. They'd planned to sleep in the bunk beds in Jason's childhood room because his religious parents prohibited him from sharing a room with his girlfriend.

To her disappointment, she learned that because they got engaged, Jason and Sofia were allowed to sleep together in the guest room. Charlotte would sleep in his room, but she wouldn't be alone. She was assigned the top bunk while Jason's seven-year-old twin nieces slept on the bottom bunk and three nephews ages five to ten years old slept on the floor with sleeping bags.

Charlotte pretended to be a good sport, but she was beyond annoyed. While Sofia snuggled with her new fiancé, she was stuck with other people's kids, as if she was destined to forever be the babysitter instead of a mother. What were they doing up so late anyway?

The children, amped up on sugar, giggled profusely. They tossed stuffed animals at each other after lights out. Charlotte tried to calm them and even recited a bedtime prayer. They listened dutifully until she finished the last line: "'And if I die before I wake, I pray the Lord my soul to take.'"

At last they were quiet until one little boy sniveled, "But why did you say, 'if I die'? I don't wanna die."

In the middle of the dark White Plains night, Charlotte put on her PR cap and said, "No, sweetheart. It's supposed to be, 'And guide me through the dark of night so I may see the morning light.'"

"But that's not what you said," one of the twins chimed in.

"But that's what I meant," Charlotte growled through gritted teeth.

"I'm scared," one of the boys whimpered.

Charlotte softened her tone. "Everyone needs to relax. We had a really fun Thanksgiving and Uncle Jason got engaged to my best friend! Let's think about where the wedding will be. I bet you'll all be there. You might even be in it."

"Really? I love weddings! Like Cinderella," said one of the twins.

"Yep. Cinderella. She's lucky she didn't live in New York," Charlotte said with sarcasm.

"What do you mean?" one of the little boys asked.

Charlotte sighed. "What I mean is that it's time for us to go to sleep. Let's all play the quiet game. Think happy thoughts so you'll have happy dreams."

It was silent for about three minutes and just as Charlotte was dozing off, one of the boys broke the silence. "I'm scared. I want my mom." He sniffled.

Charlotte sat up. "But she's probably already asleep. Is there anything I can do to make you feel better?"

"Can I sleep up there with you?" he asked.

The last thing she wanted was a child tossing and turning next to her in a tiny bunk bed, but she had no choice. "Yes, be careful climbing up."

Worse than predicted, she was kicked and shoved until daylight by the little rascal who twisted as if he battled dragons in his dreams. She cuddled and soothed him, but every time she drifted off, he bumped into her again. At one point, he nearly pushed her off the bed.

The next morning, Charlotte helped the grateful moms get her little roommates dressed and composed herself for breakfast. Jason's sisters prepared a big buffet of sausage, eggs, potatoes, bagels, and fruit. He draped his arm over Sofia's shoulders while they happily munched on food. Charlotte looked around the room and was touched by such a loving family, but she didn't belong there. She was an outsider, merely observing. Unable to bear another sleepless night, she made an excuse to take a train back to the city in the afternoon. They protested and tried to convince her to stay, but Charlotte was a PR professional and she presented the situation in a proper manner so they wouldn't feel guilty about her early departure.

On the train back to Manhattan, Charlotte watched trees whiz by with the realization that she was more lost than ever. By the time the skyscrapers approached, she couldn't inhale the excitement Gotham usually sparked. Instead, she felt alone and confused. She wondered where her life was headed, and as she moved closer to the center of the city, she was convinced that she was going in the wrong direction.

Part 4

WINTER

Chapter 23

NEW YORK CITY

For most New Yorkers, December was truly magical. The winter month meant the season's first snowfall, crowds gathered at the Christmas tree lighting at Rockefeller Center, holiday window displays along Fifth Avenue spread cheer, and jovial office parties completed the year. Unfortunately, Charlotte lacked time to enjoy the festivities because she was busy prepping for the Angelino's Miami opening, planning the company Christmas party, and reining in Sofia who'd morphed into another bridezilla.

Sofia asked her to be her maid of honor under the pretense that it would be a small wedding. Still suffering from PTSD caused by Shokoufeh's nuptials, Charlotte was tempted to decline but couldn't deny her most loyal friend. She later worried she'd made a huge mistake when Sofia asked her to reserve five days to help with dress shopping, bridal registries, and shower planning. The bride-to-be wasn't a procrastinator and insisted on quickly organizing two engagement parties in both NYC and her native Chicago. She even considered two separate ceremonies so neither family would be forced to travel for the event, but Charlotte convinced her to book just one destination wedding.

Another daunting task was organizing Angelino's company Christmas party. Charlotte was expected to team up with Jessica to create the big bash. There were logistical challenges because the restaurants were open 365 days a year. No matter which time was chosen, some employees would be on duty, serving customers. With no other solution, they usually rented a deserted nightclub in a central location from 2 p.m. until 8 p.m. to enable people to stop by before or after their shifts. Lorenzo and Marco loved to party and had specific requests like strippers dressed as Santa's Helpers, fake tattoo stations, and photo booths.

Charlotte set her personal life aside to focus on completing tasks before heading to California for Christmas. She worried that by putting work first she might end up like so many New York women married to their careers. While feeling a bit gloomy during a particularly chilly morning, Charlotte received a surprising text as she warmed up in the bus heading to work. *Hope all is well, will you please get my cousin Brigham a part time waiter job at Angelino's? Great kid. Thank you, Wyatt*

Without hesitation, she suggested he come to Sofia's location on Fifth Avenue around 4 p.m. They usually needed more waiters during the holidays due to throngs of tourists combined with employee vacations and she'd do anything to please Wyatt. Charlotte devised a scheme to meet the young buck and nonchalantly extract intel about her mysterious "friend."

Angelino's was buzzing when she arrived and Sofia stood next to the hostess stand, busy mitigating a dispute between two customers who'd spilled wine on each other and argued over dry cleaning reimbursement. "Brigham's waiting for you on the second floor," Sofia said hurriedly as she kept her attention on the irate Upper Eastsiders.

Charlotte zipped up the stairs with exhilaration; she couldn't wait to meet Wyatt's cousin! But when she arrived on the second floor, the tables were occupied by a few families, a Euro couple on the brink of intoxication, an African American guy who sat alone reading the menu, and three schoolgirls giggling over their post study session pizza and Diet Cokes. She paced back and forth, wondering if Brigham was in the men's room. The lone customer scoped her out, but she gracefully ignored his gaze until he finally waved his hand at her. "Charlotte?"

"Yes, can I help you?" she said with her plastic PR smile.

"I hope so! I'm Brigham!" He stood up with an eager grin and extended his hand.

She noticed a résumé peeking out from beneath the menu. "Oh, I was looking for you! Nice to meet you!"

"I'm not sure if Wyatt told you that I'm adopted, but that's why I'm a few shades darker than the other Ashcrofts." His smile and twinkling eyes gave the nineteen-year-old a special warmth that would surely please Angelino's customers.

Charlotte pulled out a chair and sat down across from him. "Oh, I hardly notice skin tone because our lighting is so dim." Worried that she sounded awkward, she quickly absorbed the news and wished Wyatt would have told her that his cousin was adopted to spare her confusion. "But I know you're not here to talk about your ethnicity." With another offbeat comment, she grew nervous that she was making a bad impression.

"You can ask me anything. Wyatt said he's known you for so many years that you feel like family."

"He did? He said I'm like family?" Charlotte leaned in closer.

"Yeah, he said you guys met at one of his premieres in LA and you were 'refreshingly different' compared to the Hollywood crowd he works with."

"'Refreshingly different?'" Charlotte blushed. "What else did he say?"

"Um…I mean, he just said you're a great person and pretty much run the show at Angelino's, so hopefully you can find a place for me here. I have experience as a server in Utah—this is my résumé—and I moved to New York a couple months ago to attend John Jay College. I live a few subway stops from here."

Charlotte took his résumé and pretended to scan it, but she wanted to turn the topic back to Wyatt. "This looks great, we'll hire you! Sofia is the GM and Jessica in HR just needs to process your paperwork."

"Really?" Brigham looked surprised.

"Absolutely. We always need extra staff this time of year and I'm sure Sofia will keep you on board after the holidays since you're only part-time." Charlotte tucked his résumé in a folder. "Can you stay for a coffee so we can chat a bit? I've never been to Utah, I'm so curious to hear about it."

Brigham was obliged to remain seated and make small talk about his state until Charlotte stealthily maneuvered the conversation to grammar school, leading to the topic of childhood and family. He opened up easily. "I got really lucky. My parents saved my life when they adopted me from an orphanage in Somalia. That's why I decided to go to John Jay College. They have a good criminal justice program and I want to do something to benefit the community and pay it forward."

Charlotte listened with interest. "Have you ever been back to your native country?"

"No, but I was hoping to be assigned there for my mission when I'm twenty-two. I'm not sure yet because I don't get to choose where I go."

Charlotte realized that Wyatt must have skipped his Mormon mission while he rebelled in Hollywood. She mentioned it to Brigham who laughed and said, "My cousin is completely unorthodox, but we love him. He's a hero back home to my entire family, and there's a lot of us."

"Were you guys close growing up?" Finally, she could get some info on Wyatt.

"Not really, because he's thirty years older me. He didn't come around very often, and he had a falling out with my uncle…." Brigham looked away, deep in thought.

"Over what? Wyatt hasn't told me much about his family."

"His dad was pretty rough. Everyone was scared of him. He was a Jack Mormon, meaning that he drank alcohol, but it made him very angry. I rarely saw him, and I was pretty young when he died."

"Died? What happened?"

"Drunk driving. He hit another car head on. Killed himself and the other lady driver."

Charlotte's blood froze. Wyatt also lost his father to drunk driving. However, his father was the aggressor and took another person's life. She once told Wyatt about her father and assumed that his extreme look of discomfort stemmed from the unpleasant nature of the topic. Perhaps he felt ashamed that his own father was a culprit in a different drunk driving incident.

"Nobody talks much about it." Brigham shook his head.

"Right. I suppose some things are better left unsaid. But I'm glad you had a happy childhood," she said briskly to hide her shock.

"Yeah, I love my parents. I'm so lucky they picked me. When kids at school bullied me because I'm dark, my dad used to say that I'm extra special because most parents take whatever they get, but they flew across the world and chose me to be their son. My mom says that it was love at first sight."

His endearing attitude melted Charlotte's heart. Wyatt's aunt and uncle sounded like saints.

After Brigham left, Sofia slid into his seat. "How did it go? Sorry, I was slammed earlier and only got to meet him for a minute."

"No worries, but you have to hire him." Charlotte stared in the distance, replaying their conversation in her mind.

Sofia was taken aback. "Can you at least give me a chance to review his résumé and interview him? I'm sure he's fine, but—"

"Can you believe Wyatt's aunt and uncle found him in a Somali orphanage? They totally changed his life." The magnitude of meeting the college student was setting in. He might not even be alive if it wasn't for Wyatt's family.

Sofia nodded. "A couple in my building adopted a little girl from China. She was nearly starving to death when they met her. Now she's ten and one of the smartest kids in her school. It's amazing how many lives are changed through adoption. Jason and I already talked about having a baby and adopting a second one."

Charlotte had an epiphany. "I've been so busy trying to find a guy while my eggs are still viable, but I never even thought about adoption before."

"Oh, it's such a great thing. You should totally do it. And it's a good back-up plan if you can't conceive naturally and you don't want to give birth on your own."

"On my own?"

"Like with a sperm donor. It seems like more and more career women are opting for that these days."

Another light flipped on in Charlotte's head. "I shouldn't be so stressed out about finding a man to conceive with when I can adopt or do it on my own."

"That's what me and Tracy tried to tell you…"

Charlotte exhaled a sigh of relief. "You're so right. I never thought of it that way before."

Sofia shrugged. "Better late than never."

Contemplating alternative options for parenting, Charlotte felt refreshed by the idea of alleviating the pressures of time. The bus ride home gave her a chance to Google adoption and donor sperm laws, but first, Charlotte smiled as she texted Wyatt. *It was great meeting Brigham. He's hired!*

Chapter 24

MIAMI

Relieved to leave chilly gray weather and fly into the Florida sunshine, Charlotte eagerly anticipated the Angelino's Miami opening. Upon exiting the airport, the Angelino's team shed their winter coats to bask in the warmth, their moods elated as they drove past the bright art deco buildings along Collins Avenue and into the Delano's circular driveway. The chic hotel lobby was packed with a cosmopolitan jet set as Art Basel was due to begin in a few days. It was a great time to launch Angelino's in the Miami Design District because the city was packed with so many New Yorkers familiar with the brand—it was sure to open with a splash.

Charlotte enjoyed working with the Miami PR team, and if all went well, there would be more Angelino's locations in the Magic City. Opening preparations flowed smoothly, thanks in large part to the partners who already ran several successful restaurants in Florida. It was only a few months behind schedule (better than two years, like Angelino's Melbourne); the licenses were secured, the staff trained, and construction completed. The last thing left to do was finish the outside paint job and throw the opening party. But something went horribly wrong. It was evident when Charlotte exited the gleaming white hotel shower and saw several missed calls, texts, and emails from the local PR team.

She quickly dialed the head of the agency, Sara, who answered on the first ring and shrieked, "You won't believe it!"

"What's wrong?" Charlotte's heart pounded.

"They painted over the memorial mural for Cuban Carlos 2K!" Sara squealed.

PR professionals often pretended to know what was going on even when they were clueless, but Charlotte couldn't fake it this time. "I'm so sorry, Sara, but…I'm confused, who's Cuban Carlo?"

"It's Cuban Carlos 2K and he's a huge deal out here!" She was hysterical and took a few deep breaths. "He was a hero, a truly unique individual. He fled Cuba and came to Miami, dirt poor, but he had such talent as a graffiti artist that he made it big. He was loved in the art world and the club scene. When a guy from Havana murdered a Haitian immigrant, Cuban Carlos 2K stepped in and brokered peace between the two communities to avoid all-out war. When he died a few years ago, after a courageous battle with lung cancer, a Haitian American artist named Skippy painted a beautiful mural to honor him. It was at the rear of the Angelino's building when the old Caribbean restaurant was there. People made pilgrimages and left flowers and candles; it was like a shrine. You couldn't see it from the street, but everyone knew it was back there."

"Oh no." Charlotte was mortified. "But why did they paint over the mural if it was in the back of the building?"

"We don't know why! The GM just told me that the owners wanted the entire wall white. Why didn't they ask me? I would've warned them not to paint over it! The community is outraged. Skippy sent me a text and said he is crying too much to even talk about it and he already posted messages on his Instagram, calling for a boycott of Angelino's." Sara almost seemed glad that Angelino's would suffer for committing such an unforgivable offense.

"Sara, I'm so sorry. Lorenzo and Marco will be furious when I tell them. This was a huge mistake. Maybe Skippy can paint a new tribute and we'll make it visible to our customers? Would something like that work?" Charlotte eagerly sought a solution.

"Highly unlikely. He's devastated. I can't believe you never talked to me about it."

"Oh my gosh, I wish I could've stopped it, but I had no idea. Can you give me a second to tell Lorenzo and Marco what's going on?" Charlotte assumed they'd suggest a solution.

She called Lorenzo, but he didn't answer, so she tried Marco, who picked up on the third ring. "We're at the pool bar having drinks. Come down."

"But Marco, something horrible happened. There was a mural at the restaurant for a famous Cuban guy—"

"I know, we heard about it. We don't want a fucking mural on the restaurant. We painted over it. My other line's ringing," Marco said as he hung up.

Charlotte sat on the bed, stunned. She tried Lorenzo again.

"*Carlotta! Come stai?*"

"There's a big problem at the restaurant with a mural that was painted—"

Lorenzo interrupted, "Marco told me, but it's gone-uh. Too late to do anything, don't worry. Come down for mojitos! We see you soon-uh!"

Charlotte paced around the room a few times before calling Sara back. She was sick of lying for Marco and Lorenzo to make them look good and she was so disgusted by their disregard for the activist's life that she decided to tell the truth. "Hi, Sara. I'm so sorry but Lorenzo and Marco don't seem to understand the importance of the mural. I don't know what else to say except that if you come up with any solutions, I'll try my best to convince them to support it."

Sara's demeanor changed sharply; she spoke as if she was addressing an enemy instead of a colleague. "There's no need for that, Charlotte. The damage is done, and I hope you know that voodoo is still practiced in these parts. There will be a price to pay. I'll see you tomorrow at the 9 a.m. meeting." *Click.*

Perplexed, Charlotte stared at her phone for a moment before sending an apologetic text to Sara. It went unanswered.

Once the hysteria over the mural died down, the opening was a huge success. There was the blogger lunch, media interviews, and, of course, the pasta ribbon cutting ceremony featuring the mayor and Italian consul general. The party was packed with a gorgeous international crowd and glamorous Miamians. Charlotte endured a spray tan for the occasion in the hopes of blending in with the local bronzed goddesses sipping mojitos. She noticed the sculpted bodies of Miami women and mused that LA women were the only group that could compare.

Although Tracy had RSVP'd to attend the Angelino's Miami opening party, she was a no-show and didn't respond to texts.

Charlotte was disappointed but not surprised. She figured the sex addict had met a new guy and blown off Angelino's without hesitation. In better days, the two friends would've shared a hotel room and hit all the Basel events together. But times had changed. They barely spoke and Tracy's disregard for Charlotte's launch was another nail in the coffin of their friendship.

Fortunately, Charlotte knew people in Miami who invited her out after the opening and the fun lasted until 5 a.m., when she left a yacht party in the Miami Beach Marina. Watching the sunrise after a night of partying was oddly gratifying, but the novelty wore off when she was sitting in a meeting only four hours later with Lorenzo, Marco, Jack, and the restaurant franchisees. Since Miami was less expensive than the Big Apple and Angelino's needed to compete with local restaurants, an excruciatingly long discussion ensued about menu pricing. Ultimately, the men agreed to lower the prices in Miami. Charlotte was frustrated it took so long to reach such an obvious conclusion.

The first day of lunch service at Angelino's Miami flowed nicely, besides a few minor hiccups in the kitchen: Lorenzo was up in arms about the unflattering plating of the beef carpaccio and complained that the tuna tartare had a bit too much lemon zest. Charlotte and Sara were pleased with the lunch crowd and the positive blog reviews populating the internet.

"Maybe Skippy got over the destroyed mural and decided not to curse us after all," Charlotte joked to Sara, who shot her a dirty look. Quickly realizing that her comment was insensitive, Charlotte transformed into PR mode and offered solutions. "I'm sorry, I didn't mean it like that. I feel bad about the mural and I thought maybe we could look around the building to find a place where Skippy can replicate it and add something more. Like, 'no matter what happens, you'll never be forgotten.' We can twist it into a new positive, with themes of perseverance. You know, like, 'They can't tear us down! We'll rise again!'"

The more Charlotte talked, the more Sara warmed up to the idea of creating a big PR initiative around rectifying the "accidental" destruction of Skippy's tribute to Cuban Carlos 2K. The unveiling of the new mural would be a huge press opportunity and they could even add a charitable element like feeding the homeless with pizzas from Angelino's during the event—a gesture that would make Cuban Carlos 2K proud!

Sara's forgiveness provided Charlotte with a huge sense of relief. They agreed to embark on the project together and Sara promised to talk to Skippy. If he gave the green light, Charlotte would get Marco and Lorenzo on board. She'd already concocted a plan: Ask Skippy to wait and repaint the mural during the summer while the Italians were soaking up sun in the Mediterranean, then covertly pull off the PR stunt.

Angelino's was expanding so quickly that locations were going rogue without any discipline. Not only did Angelino's Moscow look like a palace, but also Charlotte heard through the grapevine that they served borscht and removed pizza from the menu because they'd never installed the proper oven. In Mumbai, they offered naan bread instead of focaccia, and in Greenwich, the franchisee's wife placed huge floral arrangements throughout Angelino's, completely changing the ambiance and covering the murals. Meanwhile, the Tokyo location was now offering pizza by the slice, something Angelino's NYC prohibited because it was a proper restaurant, not a pizzeria. The list went on and on.

Perhaps it was the optimistic sunshine that caused Charlotte's lapse in judgment, or maybe it was the excitement of teaming up with Sara to right a wrong, but she decided to ignore Jack and Sofia's advice and when she was alone with Lorenzo and Marco during the ride back to the Delano, she said, "Guys, I've been trying to get time with you in New York to talk about my pay situation and possibly getting a raise after ten years at Angelino's." Her gut told her to stop as they were just a block from the hotel and the irritated glares from her bosses confirmed her intuition. Yet, she continued. "So, I wanted to know if, by next year, I can get a raise so I'll make at least $100,000 like other PR women with my position."

Looking for an escape, Lorenzo turned his neck to stare out the window while Marco scowled at her.

"Here we are!" The driver broke the silence.

"Yes, *Carlotta,* we pay for you. Don't worry." Lorenzo slid out of the car. Marco gave her a disapproving glance and then followed Lorenzo.

Charlotte jogged up the front steps to catch up with them. "So this means I can get the raise?"

Lorenzo's phone chimed, and he answered it on the first ring while Marco mumbled something about going to the bathroom and ducked down the hall. Lorenzo walked away, talking excitedly, leaving Charlotte alone in the hotel lobby. She texted Jack. *I asked them for a raise, $100K. Lorenzo told me not to worry and they'll pay for me. Do you think that's a yes? Will you talk to them?*

The relationship between Jack and Charlotte had been strained since Moscow, but she believed he remained an ally. Sofia told her a rumor that he was dating an airline stewardess he met while flying to a conference. Charlotte feared she let a good one get away, but she also knew it would be nearly impossible to date anyone at Angelino's without gossipmongers wreaking havoc.

Jack responded. *I'll talk to them when we're back in NYC.*

During the first dinner service at Angelino's Miami, Charlotte wondered if it was her imagination or if Lorenzo and Marco were avoiding her. They went to Sara with press issues and barely acknowledged Charlotte when she introduced them to important guests. There was tension in the air, and toward the end of the night, they left without inviting her to their next party destination or even saying goodbye.

Tracy, her former partner in crime, was still missing. Charlotte had other options and she checked out a few gallery parties and went to a magazine event at SLS Hotel. She hung out with a group from NYC and danced until 2 a.m. An acquaintance was also staying at the Delano, and they walked back together, barefoot, carrying their high heels and laughing about all the characters hanging around South Beach.

Checking her phone before passing out asleep, she thought she might see a text from Tracy. Instead, Wyatt sent her a picture with Brigham at Angelino's Fifth Avenue and a message. *Thanks for giving my cousin a chance. He's working hard.*

Charlotte studied Wyatt's face in the picture. Kindness resonated in his grin and he looked especially at ease towering over Brigham. His proud stance gave him a paternal quality, exemplified by his height. His attitude made his thin body appear physically stronger than she had noticed before, while his broad shoulders squared off his frame. Drifting asleep, she hugged her pillow and imagined his arms wrapped around her.

The next morning, her dreamy state dissipated with the unsettling discovery that Lorenzo and Marco had taken a car to the airport without her, while Jack had left the night before for Dallas. Charlotte jumped in a taxi and dreaded giving Melvin the receipt for reimbursement, but she wouldn't need to bother if her raise began soon. When she found them at the gate, she played cool and acted natural. "You guys left without me. Is everything okay?"

Marco responded, "Yeah. We checked out a new location near Bal Harbor. We wanted to let you sleep." A rather odd comment because he never seemed to care about waking Charlotte for even the slightest work queries.

"Oh, thank you. How was the location?"

"It was okay. Listen, Charlotte, we can't pay you $100,000. Melvin will never allow it. He says you don't do anything important for the company. In fact, he's pressuring us to lower the amount you get paid," Marco said nonchalantly.

She tried her best to hide her anger, but it was impossible. "What does Melvin have to do with it? He says *I* don't do anything important? Seriously? He hides in his cubicle watching porn all day while his assistant does all the work!" She wanted to punch something.

"*Carlotta*, calm down, it's ok-uh." Lorenzo never liked to see a woman upset.

But she couldn't control herself as indignant tears flowed. "I work so hard for Angelino's and I do so many things that you don't even realize! It's so unfair that I'm not paid as much as PR women who do half as much as me!" Charlotte shrieked.

Marco looked at Lorenzo and rolled his eyes. "We'll try to work something out. Maybe Jack can talk to Melvin and we can raise you from $75K to $85K, but there's no way we can go higher than that."

Charlotte raged on, "Why does Melvin matter? Jessica could be involved because she's in charge of HR, but not your idiot accountant! He hates me, he has a personal vendetta against me, always accusing me of stealing office supplies. He's a freak and he doesn't own the company. You can make the decision about my salary, not that moron!"

Lorenzo looked around nervously at the crowd witnessing Charlotte's breakdown. It was time to board. "*Tesoro*, please don't be so upset. Angelino's has no money for you. The mayor made us raise minimum wage and now we have to pay health insurance for everybody. I'm so sorry." He shook his head with feigned sadness.

Charlotte knew he was lying. Lorenzo and Marco made millions of dollars. They had vacation homes in the Hamptons, Vail, and Italy, along with significant real estate holdings throughout the city. Angelino's was a gold mine, and with every new opening Charlotte slaved away for, they received a hefty franchise fee, management fee, and made a fortune with royalties. Angelino's could afford to pay her $100,000; Lorenzo and Marco simply refused because they didn't believe that women deserved significant salaries. To confirm her suspicions, Lorenzo once told her that he'd avoided giving her certain projects because, eventually, she'd get married and leave them. Ten years later, she was still at Angelino's and her salary hadn't gone up, not even by a dollar.

Composing herself as they boarded, Charlotte made one final plea. "Angelino's opened over twenty new locations since I started, and my workload, along with your profits, has increased dramatically. Yet my salary remains the same. The math doesn't add up."

She stormed off and thanked God her seat was a few rows behind them. She watched the duo during the flight, laughing and drinking wine. They were in their own world, two peas in a pod, and she'd never be treated fairly in their kingdom. When the plane landed at JFK, she zipped past them without a word and jumped in a taxi.

Charlotte heard her phone chime and expected an apology text from Lorenzo or Marco. Shivering from the arctic blast, she wrapped her coat around herself and realized Tracy sent the message. *Hey, was caught up in Miami. How was your opening? Any hot guys?*

She tossed the phone aside and stared out the window at the dreary scenery. Everything looked bleak. After ten years, she couldn't get a sufficient raise from Angelino's. She'd most definitely submit her taxi receipt to Melvin.

Chapter 25

NEWPORT BEACH

After weeks of silent treatment from Lorenzo and Marco, even during the Christmas party, Charlotte landed with great relief at John Wayne Airport in Orange County. She was thrilled to be far away from Angelino's, even if her phone was constantly buzzing. It felt good to be home.

Although Newport Beach was known for its affluence, Charlotte's family resided in San Joaquin Hills, the more modest section of the city. Her father worked tirelessly to provide for his family and had managed to pay off the house before his death. Her mother continued living there alone, until her boyfriend eventually moved in. The presence of a new male in their childhood home, full of cherished memories, was uncomfortable for Charlotte and her sisters. Their parents had planned a five-year age gap between each child and Charlotte often noticed an emotional disconnect from her sisters as they were at different phases in their lives. The youngest attended law school while her middle sister recently moved into a condo in nearby Irvine with her boyfriend of four years.

One thing the siblings agreed on was that their mom's new boyfriend, an anthropology professor at University of California Irvine, was a nice guy, but he couldn't take the place of their beloved father. Charlotte's residency in New York removed her from the daily reminders her sisters experienced. However, the distance prevented her from mourning thoroughly, and her family expressed concern that her emotional outbursts were caused by the grief she'd never come to terms with. Until her father's death, Charlotte had been an overachiever, a true role model. But now, she was thirty-five, single, childless, overworked, and underpaid. Her family, especially her mother, urged her to pull her life together.

After Charlotte unpacked, the group met at their favorite childhood dinner spot, The Old Spaghetti Factory. The two-story family-style restaurant, showcasing an antique train car in the middle of the ground floor, lacked the glamour of Angelino's, but she savored the relaxed casual atmosphere and laughter with her family. At one point, she noticed that she was the only woman in the family without a man. Even her mother had bounced back from losing her husband. She casually observed how happy they seemed with their significant others. They reaped the stability, comfort, and affection that companions provide, while all she had to show for her love life over the past year was married Jorge, party boy Eric, non-committal Pascal, man whore Ray, and some dudes she met online whose names were long since forgotten. Unsure of how to categorize Jack, she decided if there was no kissing involved, it didn't qualify as "dating."

Charlotte's sisters departed with their men after dinner, while she retreated to her childhood home as third wheel to her mom and her boyfriend. Her adolescent bedroom reeked with eeriness. Gone were her posters of Bono, Anthony Kiedis, and Eddie Vedder, yet the furniture remained the same and bouquets from her dried flower collection still hung on the walls. Charlotte sat on her old bed, flooded with memories that made her eyes water. Her phone vibrated with a new text message. *Hi Charlotte, Are you in California for Christmas? Wyatt*

She responded. *Hi! I arrived today. Where are you spending xmas?*

Wyatt replied. *I'm in LA but flying to Vancouver on Christmas because we resume shooting on Dec. 26th. Not much of a holiday.*

Charlotte typed with excitement. *There's plenty of room at my house if you want to cruise down to OC tomorrow to celebrate Christmas Eve.*

She knew he wouldn't come but thought it was a nice gesture to invite him. Poor guy. So much fame and success, but no family to share it with.

Wyatt didn't hesitate. *What time?*

Charlotte giggled as she typed. *Everyone arrives by 2pm to hang out, play games, dinner at 5pm, watch sports, snacks around 10pm and then midnight mass. McPherson Family tradition. Join us!*

He responded. *Thank you. Text me your address and I'll be there at 2pm. Sorry I can't stay for church.*

Charlotte sat stunned. Wyatt was going to spend Christmas Eve with her and her family! She drifted asleep with the satisfaction of knowing that she wouldn't be pitied the next day because she'd finally have a "date" to introduce to her family. A good one!

She lay wide-awake at 4 a.m. Her insomnia was partly due to jet lag, but excitement about Wyatt coming to her house made her giddy. She fantasized about how the day would play out, and she planned to warn her family to treat him like a normal guy, not a Hollywood legend.

Wyatt was always punctual and Charlotte's heart pounded against her chest when the doorbell rang right on time. It was sunny and seventy-five degrees, typical Southern California holiday weather, but when she opened the door, Wyatt stood there wearing a suit and tie and holding Starlet. Charlotte realized she should have warned him that her family was casual, and the other men would be in jeans and t-shirts.

"You made it!" She pushed her nervousness aside and hugged him affectionately. "And you're so sweet to wear a suit! Mom has been begging the guys to dress up for Christmas and now you'll be a good role model. She'll love you for it!"

Wyatt smiled and put Starlet down so he could proudly retrieve a large box on the ground. It was wrapped beautifully in silver paper with a big red velvet bow. "This is for your mom. It's sort of a gift for the entire family."

"Thank you so much! Come in. Everyone wants to meet you and Starlet will love my mom's dogs." Charlotte ushered them inside.

After her family got over the initial shock of meeting Wyatt Ashcroft, they hit it off with him. They complimented his movies and he described his latest passion project—a television series about plants coming to life to torture people who abuse the environment. They were impressed and excited to hear the inside scoop. His gift for her mother turned out to be a fancy mint green Cuisinart Classic Drink Mixer to make milkshakes. Charlotte winced with embarrassment as her uncle joked about spiking the shakes with vodka or Bailey's Irish Cream.

Her family's fixation on alcohol caused a bit of tension throughout the day. She never realized how much they drank until she included Wyatt, her teetotaler love interest, in their Christmas celebration. Beers while watching football, tequila shots before playing basketball in the backyard, spiked apple cider while waiting for dinner, wine with the meal, brandy to accompany dessert—they drank nonstop. To make matters worse, her drunk uncle repeatedly nudged her in front of Wyatt and asked, "Why aren't you drinking, Char? What's the matter with you?" Resisting the urge to tape his mouth shut, she quickly changed the subject.

When it was time to eat dinner, the group had grown to seventeen people. The dining room table had initially been set for eight people on each side until they added a chair for Wyatt at the head of the table, flanking him with Charlotte and her mom's boyfriend. It seemed like a good idea until everyone sat down, and Wyatt became the main attraction.

Trays of traditional Christmas food, including turkey, mashed potatoes, stuffing, gravy, green beans, buttermilk rolls, cranberry sauce, and salad, covered the table and Charlotte's mom had graciously prepared a vegetarian platter for Wyatt. Glasses all around were filled with wine, while Charlotte and Wyatt drank non-alcoholic sparkling cider with the kids. Like a typical Orange County family, they said a prayer before the meal and Charlotte referenced her dad in Heaven. The drunk uncle chimed in, "Or as I like to say: Dear God, rub a dub dub, thanks for the grub!" He burst out laughing while the others lifted their utensils to eat.

Charlotte's middle sister jumped up suddenly, startling the group before food reached their mouths. She grabbed her boyfriend's hand and pulled him up next to her as she squealed, "We have something exciting to tell everyone! We're getting married!" She threw her arms around him and kissed him on the lips. Charlotte, her mother, and youngest sister exchanged shocked glances, although the couple had dated for years and recently moved in together.

Wyatt leaned toward Charlotte and joked, "Maybe I should have brought a camera crew to record all this action." She smiled closed-lipped and tried to hide her annoyance that her younger sibling was engaged before she was.

"And there's more!" Charlotte's jubilant sister continued, "We're expecting a baby!" She gleefully threw her arms around her fiancé.

Congratulatory remarks echoed throughout the table. Charlotte and her youngest sister sat stunned, while their mother cried for joy. "I'm going to be a grandma! A dream come true!" Her boyfriend put his arm around her and squeezed her.

Charlotte plastered on another fake smile while the empty hole inside her expanded. Her ovaries were on the verge of quitting, yet her little sister was carrying a child. Feeling like a complete failure, she struggled to fight back tears until a hand touched her arm. It was Wyatt. "Hey, are you okay?"

"Yes, I'm fine. Thank you so much. I just feel bad that my dad isn't alive to witness my sister so happy." Charlotte didn't mention her fears and jealousy. Wyatt took her hand under the table and gave it a compassionate squeeze. It was exactly what she needed.

Dinner transpired pleasantly while Wyatt bonded with her mother's boyfriend, falling into a deep philosophical conversation about anthropology beyond Charlotte's comprehension. After the meal, she yearned to break free from her family as they grew louder with each drink. She wondered if she was as boisterous as they were when she consumed alcohol.

She invited Wyatt on a walk around the neighborhood with Starlet and her mother's two dachshunds. As the five of them set off, Charlotte's mood lifted. Wyatt seemed more relaxed since he'd adopted his dog. He asked her questions about her childhood and life in Newport Beach, and they chatted about how the warm winters in Southern California compared to the East Coast. Then, Wyatt grew serious. "Charlotte, are you happy?"

"I'm really happy that you're here today, that's for sure."

"No, I mean, are you happy with your life? Working at Angelino's and living in New York," he pressed her.

"It's interesting you should ask because when I come home to Orange County, I feel like this is a more fulfilling existence. It's all about family and healthy lifestyle here, although you can see that my family might drink too much." Charlotte shrugged.

"Sometimes I picture you in a more wholesome environment than living in New York and working for those Italians." Wyatt was pensive. "You don't seem like a true New Yorker."

Charlotte stopped in her tracks, confused. Contrary to what Wyatt had said, she believed she was a quintessential New Yorker. She was stylish, career-driven, cultured, and read the news every morning before her family in California even woke up. She worked hard to get on the right guest lists, attend fabulous dinner parties, and travel around the world as a respected publicist.

"But what do mean?"

"I don't mean it in a bad way. To be honest, I just think you're capable of so much more than working for a restaurant group," Wyatt said.

"Well, it might be meaningless to you, but it's a multi-million-dollar company that employs over a thousand people and gives customers a place to create their happiest memories—birthday parties, dates, family meals. It all happens at Angelino's and I'm proud of what I do," Charlotte said defiantly.

Wyatt, who she knew notoriously avoided emotional confrontations, said, "Okay, I just want you to be happy and I see that you have a lot of potential. You alluded to making a change when we spoke in India. Maybe you'd be more fulfilled putting your talent and energy into a cause that you believe in or working for a nonprofit. You could even start your own PR firm and have your own clients."

Charlotte snapped, "But I do volunteer at my dog charity and what would fulfill me is having a family and getting married like all my friends and now my little sister. Instead, I have to deal with a bunch of noncommittal losers." She instantly regretted her words.

Wyatt looked uncomfortable. "Okay, well I have to head home soon. We should turn around."

She swiftly attempted damage control. "I'm sorry. That came out wrong. I had some bad luck dating this year and I'm still recovering." After ten years of friendship, she figured she might as well cut the PR act.

"I assumed that was the case. I don't know why any guy would blow it with you. You're a catch." He stared up at the sky pensively. It was the biggest compliment he'd ever given her, and it was in his unique style. Dusk had fallen and the streetlight shed a warm glow on Wyatt. She smiled and said, "Thank you. You're a good catch yourself. Why haven't you ever gotten married?"

Wyatt sighed. "That's the big question the press always asks. I don't like to answer it, so they call me a loner. But, have you seen the dating pool in LA? I attract actresses who want to use me for fame. They have no depth and many of them are on drugs. But I was so naïve when I first started in show biz. I fell hard and had my heart broken when I was a nobody. And when I became somebody, the girls who used to reject me would do anything to be with me. I can see through their act."

"Yeah, I never trusted actresses. I've heard all about the casting couch."

"There are some good ones," he said. "But most of them are married, and I'd never go near a married woman."

Charlotte felt a pang of guilt as she was reminded of Jorge. "Of course not."

"That's one of the reasons why I always liked you." Wyatt gingerly moved a strand of hair from Charlotte's face and tucked it behind her ear.

As she tried desperately to decipher what Wyatt meant, he looked at her intently and she thought he might lean in and kiss her. Instead, one of her mother's dogs barked and lunged toward a squirrel. Yanked out of the trance with Wyatt, Charlotte's arm jerked forward before she could reel the pup back in. They retreated back toward the house in silence as she tried to think of a way to rekindle their conversation. "Wyatt, um, what were you saying back there? A reason that you always liked me?"

He burst out laughing. "You're so funny! That's the point, I like you because you're genuine and not an actress trying to use me to get a part in a movie."

Charlotte smiled, but she was still perplexed. Did he like her as more than a friend? She hesitated for a moment and then summoned her courage. "Do you think you'll ever get married? Do you want a family?"

"Absolutely. I just need to meet the right girl. Someone like you." He looked up at the stars.

Charlotte wore her heart on her sleeve. "Yeah, I feel the same way, like I need to meet someone like you. But here we are.... We already met."

Disregarding her comment, Wyatt sighed, "It's getting late, I need to go home. Thank you for including me today. Your family is very nice."

"Thank you so much for coming. Everyone thinks you're great," Charlotte quietly responded.

Every time she got close to Wyatt, he seemed oblivious to her insinuations. But before she knew what was happening, he embraced her. He felt steady and he smelled clean, like Dove soap mixed with a hint of a smoky wood scent. She melted into his arms as their bodies became one.

"Hey, you two!" They jumped apart as Charlotte's drunk uncle startled them. "What're you doing out here? We're making margaritas with that machine you brought. It blends the ice just right!"

Charlotte was mortified. Wyatt's gift was meant for milkshakes, not cocktails. Her family looked like a bunch of alcoholics!

"We'll be in soon. Here, take my mom's dogs back to her," Charlotte handed him the leashes and shooed him inside.

She turned toward Wyatt. "I'm sorry about him. He's a good guy, just a little drunk tonight."

Wyatt laughed, "Don't worry, every family has a wacky uncle. He seems alright."

Charlotte was pleasantly surprised by Wyatt's empathy. She moved toward him and said, "Where were we?"

He ducked her embrace and nervously took a few steps backward. "I better hit the road. I have an early flight tomorrow." He whisked Starlet to his car and waved goodbye. "Thanks again, and Merry Christmas."

Charlotte watched his car speed away and felt a piece of her heart leave with him. None of the guys she fell for in the past made her feel the warmth and compassion that Wyatt gave her with his embrace. She stood on the sidewalk long after he was gone, thinking about him and wondering if they were meant to be together. If so, why was it taking so long? After ten years of over-analyzing the smallest signs of hope, his unpredictable behavior and long absences repeatedly forced her to give up. Eventually, he always came back, renewing her hope, and tonight felt magical but tomorrow was uncertain.

* * *

A few days later, Charlotte visited Grandma McPherson before joining her mom for lunch at Fashion Island, the crown jewel of Newport Beach. The outdoor shopping center housed several restaurants, department stores, upscale boutiques, fountains, and breezy ocean views that attracted shoppers from all over Orange County. They strolled peacefully along until Charlotte's mother cried out, "Sherry! Sweetheart! How are you?"

Charlotte froze in her tracks and discovered Shokoufeh and David. Her mom hugged the new bride as she shrieked, "Mrs.

McPherson! It's so good to see you! I go by my real name now, Shokoufeh, but it's okay."

"Yes, I heard about the name change, but you'll always be my little Sherry. You were like a fourth daughter to me! And this must be your handsome new husband?" Charlotte's mom fawned over David.

"Yep, I'm the lucky guy. It's nice to meet you." David flashed his toothy grin and extended his hand.

Charlotte managed to squeeze out a meager, "Hi…How are you guys?"

To Charlotte's dismay, Shokoufeh grabbed her arm and led her aside, telling the others, "We just need a moment alone." Charlotte's mom gleefully chatted with David.

"Char, I feel so bad about everything that went down at my wedding. In retrospect, I was a little demanding with the schedule and whatnot. But you just can't imagine how much stress I was under because you never had a wedding and I really wanted to prove myself to David's family. Everything had to be perfect."

"It's okay, Sherry—I mean Shokoufeh," Charlotte said, planning to run away ASAP.

Shokoufeh tightened her grip on Charlotte's arm. "No, it's not okay. You're my best friend in the entire world and I've been asking David what I should do to make amends to you. He told me to call you to wish you a happy New Year, but now you're right here. I can't believe it." She choked back tears as she spoke.

"Don't cry, it's—"

"Let me finish," Shokoufeh interrupted. "It turns out you were right about Reza! He's a lying scumbag! He cheated on Fairuza and broke her heart. It's been nearly a month and she can barely get out of bed, she's so depressed. He dumped her for a blonde wannabe model. Can you imagine? He's disgraced his entire family. And, you won't believe it, David told me that in the security footage, it looked like Reza was sort of stalking you at the wedding. What a creepy weirdo! And it caused such a big fight between us. I feel so horrible," she said as she wiped away a tear.

Although vindicated, Charlotte was cautious. She'd forgive Shokoufeh, but it would take time to heal. She embraced her and graciously said, "It's okay. I know I wasn't a perfect bridesmaid, so I take some of the blame, too."

"That's very true, you were extremely difficult, but I want to move past all of it." Shokoufeh broke into a smile. "And I have some amazing news for you…I'm pregnant!"

Charlotte was taken aback. "Already?"

Shokoufeh was jubilant. "Yes! Can you believe it? It happened on our honeymoon and it's such a relief! I was worried I'd have to do IVF because I'm already thirty-six. My doctor freaked me out, but Mother Nature gave us a baby the old-fashioned way!" She hugged stunned Charlotte before turning toward David and raising her voice. "Babe, I told Char about the baby. She's so excited!"

Charlotte plastered on her PR smile. "I'm so happy for you, Shokoufeh."

"Thanks! The baby is almost three months, so we're starting to tell people that I'm pregnant and we'll wait until about the seventh month before we have the baby showers, and of course, I want you to be involved with all of them!"

Charlotte remained quiet for the rest of the day as her mom chattered about all the good holiday news—engagements and babies. Family and friends moved forward with their lives, leaving the publicist trapped in a ten-year time warp of living, eating, breathing Angelino's and only coming up for air during failed romances. The Orange County reality check shook her to the core. Her hometown fostered a family-centric environment where single, childless Charlotte felt like a complete outcast.

Chapter 26

ASPEN

"I t's so unbelievably gorgeous here!" Gentle snowflakes descended upon Charlotte's hair as she climbed out of a small aircraft, down the passenger loading stairs, and onto the quaint Aspen airport tarmac before waltzing into a white winter wonderland. A popular holiday destination, the charming Colorado town attracted jetsetters with its pristine slopes, trendy shops, and glitzy après ski options. Jason and his colleagues rented a cabin to ring in the New Year with their significant others and Charlotte and Tracy had agreed to split the fee for the remaining bedroom. Charlotte was hesitant because she hadn't seen Tracy since her frenemy had chewed her out over Ray and ditched her at Balthazar. She now frequented a new nail salon and dreaded the idea of spending New Year's together. But, eager to see what all the Aspen hype was about, she finally had an affordable opportunity, with her share of the room only costing $400 for three nights. She couldn't say no.

Much to Sofia's displeasure, Tracy canceled three days before the trip. Charlotte wasn't surprised after her disappearing act in

Miami, but it was too late to invite another friend to join them. Fortunately, Jason's colleague who booked the rental generously covered the lodgings fee that Tracy reneged on. Charlotte was annoyed to be a third wheel, yet again, but happy to be in Aspen. She sent Wyatt a picture of the fluffy snow with an early New Year's greeting, but he didn't reply, as he was often non-responsive while filming his next masterpiece.

After settling into the cabin, Jason rushed off to meet his buddies on the slopes, while Sofia and Charlotte caught up at Little Nell's. The five-star hotel was a popular hangout, conveniently located on the edge of town and at the base of the mountain. They found seats at the property's Ajax Tavern and ordered hot toddies and truffle french fries.

"It feels so good to be here. Thank you so much for including me, I really appreciate it," Charlotte said.

Sofia smiled. "Of course! But I feel bad that Tracy flaked. I thought you two would roam around man hunting."

"She totally vanished in Miami during the Angelino's opening. I really don't feel close to her anymore. Maybe it's better she didn't come, but I don't want to intrude on you and your fiancé."

"Don't worry, you're invited everywhere with us. We're getting married! I have the rest of my life with him." Sofia was kind and welcoming as usual.

"What's Tracy doing these days?" Charlotte asked.

Sofia shrugged. "I have no idea, we barely talk. When I text her, it takes three days for her to respond. I started going to a new nail salon."

"Me too! She totally ghosted both of us!" Charlotte was surprised Tracy had blown off sweetheart Sofia too. They both shrugged and sipped their drinks.

"Have you heard anymore from Lorenzo and Marco about your raise?" Sofia asked.

"No, they disappeared like Tracy. Maybe they're all hanging out somewhere," Charlotte laughed. "But, seriously, I've been gone from New York for a week and I'm so far removed from Angelino's. What's been going on?"

Sofia loved to gossip. "Apparently, Jessica's secretly interviewing with another restaurant group."

"Are you sure? I can't believe it!" Charlotte was shocked.

"Yes, because she knows she'll get paid more anywhere else. She's been with Angelino's for five years and never gotten a raise. Besides, she hates working with Melvin. I don't know how anyone could stomach him." Sofia shook her head in disgust.

"Jessica's strict, like most HR people, but she's good at her job. Angelino's needs to pay competitive wages, or risk losing the best employees," Charlotte declared and started thinking more seriously about an exit strategy.

"You're right."

"Jack should really get involved and make sure the best talent stays with the company. Speaking of Jack, is he still dating that flight attendant?" Even though Wyatt consumed Charlotte's thoughts, she was a little curious about Jack.

"Yeah, they're still together. Jack's cleaning lady told Marco's cleaning lady that he was taking his *girlfriend* to Hawaii for New Year's." Sofia's friendship with everyone affiliated with Angelino's gave her access to all sorts of insider info.

"Don't remind me, I have to go to Hawaii with Marco in February to look at a location. Lorenzo isn't going, which means I'll be stuck alone with him the entire time." Charlotte dreaded the trip.

Sofia teased, "But Marco's single again. It could be a romantic trip for you two." Charlotte shot her a stern look. Sofia laughed. "Hey, at least you'll escape the bad weather and get some sunshine."

Charlotte nodded in agreement.

The two city slickers toasted by clinking their glasses and then surveyed the room. Everyone appeared fit in their ski clothes. Women wore cashmere sweaters and tight pants, while men appeared taller in their ski trousers, showing off toned arms in snug, long-sleeved shirts. Charlotte liked the rugged look of these mountain men.

"Did you hear about Ray and the hostess?" Sofia asked.

Charlotte gulped and quickly played nonchalant. "Yeah, you told me she's pregnant."

"No, I can't believe you didn't hear what happened! She made up the entire story because she's so obsessed with him. She tried to trap him with the baby, but he found out the truth after he moved her into his apartment."

"Really? Did he freak out when he caught her lying?" The drama Ray constantly attracted left Charlotte in disbelief.

"No, the opposite happened! He thinks it's sweet that she loves him enough to fake a pregnancy. They're still living together, and he wants to marry her. He tattooed her name across the back of his neck and I'm sure she'll really be pregnant soon."

"He's such a player. It'd be a nightmare to be in a relationship with him." Charlotte changed the subject as she fumed to herself that even Ray was growing up and considering marriage. It was time to get on the bandwagon. The sentiment was magnified as Sofia unzipped her tote bag to reveal a pile of bridal magazines for the two to peruse.

The next few days were anticlimactic after the special Christmas Eve Charlotte had shared with Wyatt. The group was congenial, but it consisted of four couples and herself. She was the third, fifth, seventh, and, sometimes, ninth wheel. They skied, shopped, ate dinner at Casa Tua, cooked at home one night, and rang in the New Year at the exclusive Caribou Club—an extremely awkward evening for single Charlotte. At midnight, everyone kissed their significant others while she sipped a drink and tried to look busy on her phone. Many couples in the club appeared odd to her, several old men sported young, fake-breasted women wearing flashy designer clothes. Jason explained that these were Hollywood couples who flocked to Aspen for the holidays. Charlotte wondered if Wyatt would wait a few more decades to get married and then choose a juvenile, plastic bimbo.

In honor of a new year, Charlotte was re-energized to achieve her goals. She used the entire flight back to NYC, including a stopover in Denver, to ponder her next moves. She planned to find a matchmaker and she'd set up a meeting with Jack to discuss her raise. It was time to make things happen!

Chapter 27

NEW YORK CITY

Charlotte's first challenge in the new year crept in unexpectedly after she dragged her suitcase into her studio and discovered two huge water bugs, eerily resembling cockroaches, prancing around her bathtub. She frantically called the doorman who informed her that the super wouldn't return until the next day. Taking a deep breath, she pulled on snow boots and plastic gloves, grabbed two paper bags from underneath the kitchen sink, and threw them over the evil bastards. She jumped on top of the bags, stomping and yelling until she was sure they were both dead. But she was wrong. They darted to the other side of the tub, waving their tentacles defiantly to taunt her. She channeled her Viking heritage and waged full-scale war against the sons of bitches, chasing them around the basin until she cornered each one and smeared them into oblivion. Afterward, she sank down onto the floor and wiped the sweat from her forehead. She'd done it. Charlotte had defeated the pests and she vowed to also clinch relationship and career victories. She'd ride this winning streak!

However, it started as a quiet ride in January, the most miserable month in NYC, when Christmas joy and New Year's excitement dissipated. New Yorkers reluctantly returned from vacations and the city braced itself for another long, harsh winter.

To stay focused on her goals, Charlotte had scheduled a meeting with a reputable matchmaker she found online. When she arrived at a small studio office filled with binders and plastic plants, she found an old lady puffing on a vape. She ripped Charlotte from head to toe in a scruffy voice. "Honey, don't wear your hair curly, men prefer straight. Is your polish chipped? Keep those nails flawless to get a guy. And make sure you're exercising enough. You've a decent figure, but some Spanx could help push in that gut. Always wear heels and don't tell guys your real age. We'll knock a few years off. My clients are in their forties and fifties and they want girls in their twenties so they can have some fun and not be pressured to have a baby."

The meeting was so bad that Charlotte was surprised the matchmaker set her up with someone just three days later. He was an Argentinean diplomat who worked at the United Nations. Dinner was fascinating as they had a great conversation over steaks at Rue 57, but there was no spark for Charlotte. A week later, she was set up with a real estate broker who lived between Phoenix and New York and unloaded as if she was his therapist. He went on a diatribe about his ruthless ex-wife who stole his money and snatched his two young sons. She managed to duck out before dessert.

A week later, the matchmaker arranged a date with a finance guy who lived near Wall Street and graciously trekked all the way uptown to take her to dinner at MR CHOW on 57th Street, just a few blocks from her apartment. He was forty years old, had never been married, and recently moved back to NYC from Hong Kong. They talked endlessly until a waiter politely asked them to leave to allow the restaurant to close for the night.

Charlotte excitedly called the matchmaker the next day and blurted out, "The date went great! I really like him!"

"Sorry, honey. He said you're nice, but there's just no chemistry. He's a picky one. You're the sixth girl I've introduced him to this month. I'll call you if I find anyone else for you." She coughed before hanging up.

Charlotte concluded that men pay matchmakers to get dates with great women. Matchmakers work for the *men*. They don't care about the woman's needs or wants. Instead, they cater to their paying clients.

Back to the drawing board. Charlotte refocused her energy away from the matchmaker. Around that time, she read an article in a fashion magazine about one's true love sometimes being a friend who is often overlooked, speculating on the right time to transition from friendship into romance: "Is Your Best Bud Really Your True Love?" The title led Charlotte to evaluate her male "friends." The only real men with potential were Jack, who was no longer an option due to his new relationship, and Wyatt. Deep down, she believed Wyatt was her true love, but he clearly didn't share those feelings. Or maybe he did? She was baffled. There were a few cordial text exchanges since New Year's, but nothing substantial to give her hope. Yet, he still dominated her thoughts.

Midway through the month, Jack finally found time to meet with Charlotte at Angelino's Union Square. She arrived first and reserved a corner booth to allow them to speak privately over coffee. When he slid in, he appeared bronzed and chipper.

"You look so happy, Jack." Charlotte didn't hide her astonishment.

"Thanks! Things are great! How about you?" Even his voice sounded more upbeat. Charlotte again feared she'd missed her chance with a good catch, but quickly reminded herself that it would've been complicated.

"Well, as I mentioned, Lorenzo and Marco decided to only raise me up to $85,000 and that just isn't enough in today's marketplace. Can you convince them to at least pay me $100,000, which is still lower than what I should get?" She looked at him intently.

Jack took a deep breath. "Some things are happening that I can't discuss. But everything might change drastically soon and your negotiations with Lorenzo and Marco will be pointless."

Charlotte leaned closer to him and lowered her voice. "That's very cryptic. Can you explain?"

"No, not now. It's a legal issue. Just hang tight for a little longer."

"Um, okay. I guess. If you say so." The mystery frustrated Charlotte.

"Sorry to dash, but I'm off to a meeting all the way uptown." Jack ducked out of the booth and left Charlotte alone as the waitress placed two cappuccinos on the table.

Later that night, during a painful dinner with another abusive food critic, Charlotte continued to ponder what Jack was alluding to. Her imagination ran wild with images of the Italians getting arrested, or maybe there was an amazing job offer from Jack at a different company. The critic sent his salmon back for the second time, catching Charlotte's attention. He was such a bitter bastard who tortured the staff while slinging veiled insults about her appearance. As he asked Chef Lorenzo to prepare a special take-out meal for his doorman, she stopped herself from rolling her eyes. Fortunately, food critics were losing power as customer-generated Yelp reviews and social media were much more relevant to Angelino's success.

The most boring month of the year aggravated Charlotte, who spent her days locked in the office and wasted away many evenings home alone. The meeting with Jack only added confusion to her unfulfilled life. She wallowed in restlessness until an unexpected text at the end of the month gave her hope. *In NYC tonight for opening of vegetarian restaurant I invested in. Would you like to join? Wyatt*

He texted her an address with a green heart emoticon and explained the restaurant used a symbol instead of a name. With scarcely an hour to make it home from the office, change clothes, and catch a subway down to the East Village, Charlotte managed to arrive just a few minutes late. She weaved through lush shrubbery, searching for Wyatt, until a waiter guided her to his table in a dark corner.

"I want to avoid the crowd," he explained as Charlotte took the seat next him. "How do you like the place?"

"It's beautiful, they did a great job with the interior. I feel like I'm in a garden."

Wyatt smiled. "I thought you'd like it. I wanted you to see it since you're in the industry."

"Thanks for thinking of me." Charlotte murmured as she noticed the contrast of Wyatt's suit and tie among all the downtown hipsters in ripped jeans and sweaters. Just like Christmas Eve dinner, he treated the occasion with a sense of formality.

"My pleasure. They're going to bring us a plate of food to try. What do you think of the name?"

"It's a bit confusing, you need to use words and not just a green heart emoticon. Your customers won't be able to find it on the internet."

"Think outside of the box, Charlotte! With only sixty-five seats, we'll be packed with locals every night and our food costs are low because we don't serve seafood and meats. We'll make a profit off liquor and wine sales while showing customers that a vegetarian lifestyle is feasible." Wyatt spoke passionately until he was interrupted by a server who presented them with a tasty assortment of hummus with pita, crispy tandoori cauliflower, tomato quinoa salad, eggplant parmigiana, and roasted vegetable tarts.

Charlotte devoured the food while he explained how eating less meat cuts down on greenhouse gas emissions and gives the planet a chance to breathe.

"This tastes so good, it'll motivate anyone who eats here," Charlotte said between bites. "But what about your parties? You always serve meat."

"Good question." He thought for a moment. "I suppose I'm trying to please my meat-eating guests like you."

She stopped chewing and gave him a guilty look. "Well, I can't resist your spreads, but why don't you tell your caterer to work with this chef next time? Your guests will learn to appreciate meatless meals. You should include a vegetarian cookbook in a gift bag for them to take when they leave."

"That's a great idea…" Wyatt looked at Charlotte with appreciation. "Do you want a ride back uptown? I have a driver outside." She accepted his invitation without hesitation.

Stone cold sober from abstaining from wine out of respect to Wyatt, she felt a bit nervous but relaxed after he instructed the driver to play the soundtrack from his latest movie. "It takes place in the 19th century, the horse-drawn carriage days. Imagine how different transportation was."

"We should take one of those carriage rides in Central Park!" Charlotte's face flushed with excitement as her words spilled out. "Have you ever done it before? It's close to my apartment."

* * *

Motivated by Charlotte's spontaneity and not ready for the night to end, Wyatt instructed his driver to flag down a carriage and pay for a half-hour ride. They climbed inside and the coachman tucked a blanket over the two before commanding his horse to trot.

"This is a side of New York I've never seen before." Wyatt tried to converse normally, but Charlotte's warm body pressed against him, sending electricity up his spine.

She shivered and snuggled deeper into him. "It's great, but so cold. I need your body heat. I hope I'm not smooshing you."

"Uh, no, you're fine. I mean, it's fine." Wyatt fought back the urge to pull her closer and take her mouth in his. Challenged by desire, he worried that making a pass at her would jeopardize their friendship and he couldn't risk losing her. The kind soul who understood him, the green eyes that pierced him with hope, and the delicate hand that held his at Mel's Diner so many years earlier resonated deep within him, but she kept him in the friend zone.

Was she too paralyzed from suffering to share her love, or was he simply imagining their connection? Vibration from the bouncing carriage, her soothing breath, and the warmth from her flesh overwhelmed him.

* * *

Convinced she overstepped his boundaries, Charlotte inched away from Wyatt. To camouflage the awkwardness, she chatted about something nonpartisan. "Brigham is popular at Angelino's. You were right about him being a very hard worker. Everyone loves him."

Wyatt responded cordially, "Yeah, he's great. Thanks again for getting the job. I don't see him often, but I try to help out when I can."

"That's so nice of you. His adoption story really touched me. It made me want to consider adopting. He says your aunt and uncle saved his life."

"He told you about that? It's rather personal for a job interview."

Charlotte's maternal instincts defended the innocent college kid. "Well, it isn't his fault. I sort of inquired about his childhood."

"Did he say anything about me and my childhood?" Wyatt looked concerned.

"Not much, but he did mention your father passed away. I had no idea. I would've at least offered condolences." Charlotte saw Wyatt stiffen and realized that she should have avoided the subject.

"Here we are folks! Right back where we started. I'll help you step down." The coachman held the carriage door open and raised his palm upward. Charlotte clasped his hand and jumped out. She turned to face Wyatt, who climbed out after her.

"Did he tell you how my dad died?" He glared into her eyes, giving her no wiggle room except to tell the truth.

"Yes, he did," she answered softly.

He embraced her and whispered in her ear, "I'm so sorry."

Charlotte fought back tears. "But it wasn't your fault. There's nothing for you to apologize about." His hug felt safe until he abruptly snapped out of it.

"I have to go. I'll walk to my hotel and the driver will take you to your apartment."

Perplexed, Charlotte responded, "But it's too cold to walk. Take your driver and I'll jump in a taxi."

Wyatt was already several feet away. He turned around to face her one last time. "Promise me that we'll never talk about my dad again. Promise?"

"Of course. As you wish." A moment later, Charlotte watched him through the car window as she rode past him. It looked like he was crying.

She couldn't relate to the anger he felt toward his father, but she recognized that they both suffered because of their dads. His was abusive, while hers was angelic. But both had left their children in a state of despair. Charlotte's bond with the Hollywood mogul was deeper than she initially imagined. Although the evening had brought them significantly closer, she vowed to keep her promise and never bring up Wyatt's father again.

Chapter 28

HONOLULU

Scouting new Angelino's locations in Hawaii granted Charlotte a reprieve from New York's bone-chilling February weather, but she dreaded catering to her high-maintenance boss. Melvin booked Marco's ticket in business class while putting her in economy for the eleven-hour flight. Ironically, foreign franchise owners treated her better than her employer. Dealing with Marco on her own would be worse than the flight. He had moments of pleasantness, for sure, but those were outweighed by the drama guaranteed to erupt. There was always a crisis when traveling with the temperamental diva.

Charlotte's mind drifted down treacherous memory lane, recalling hardships she'd endured at the hands of Marco during business trips. There was the time he forgot his passport in a Sao Paulo hotel, forcing them to miss their flight and spend the night in a noisy Brazilian airport. Equally annoying was when he lost his phone in Montreal during a snowstorm and dragged Charlotte on a citywide manhunt before she discovered it in his jacket pocket with the sound set to silent. Even worse was the hysteria he caused in Beirut while she was in a deep sleep before her afternoon flight back to New York. Her hotel room phone rang incessantly at 5 a.m. until she groggily answered to hear Marco's screams commanding her to run to his room immediately. Half asleep, she'd grabbed her key and sprinted through the hotel barefoot, wearing only her tiny pink silk nightgown. When she'd arrived, he was cursing at the safe and a bellhop ran in shortly after her.

"I forgot the fucking combination! I don't know what's in there! I have to leave for Ibiza!" He'd grabbed the porter's arm and commanded, "Unlock it and give her everything!" Unsure if he understood English, Marco also shouted at the perplexed hotel worker in Italian before bolting out the door while Charlotte stood forlorn in her little nightie, wiping sleep from her eyes and wondering if it was all a bad dream. When the security guard arrived, he gave her a look of disdain implying she was Marco's girlfriend or, even worse, a prostitute. They whisked open the safe and... Viola! Nothing. It was completely empty. Charlotte wanted to strangle Marco, but he was already off to Spain. She prayed there wouldn't be drama in Hawaii, but she knew something unsettling was inevitable.

Upon landing in Honolulu, Marco instructed the taxi driver to turn up the music as he grabbed Charlotte and kissed her cheek, "Feel the sunshine! We're in Hawaii, baby!"

She laughed and leaned her head out the window, letting the warm tropical breeze caress her face. They pulled up to the Royal Hawaiian, a grandiose pink "palace" standing proud next to the Pacific Ocean. Couples on romantic getaways swarmed the lobby as Charlotte and Marco accepted coconut shells filled with juice that they sipped through straws while they waited at the check-in line. When it was finally their turn, Marco slapped down his driver's license and credit card in front of the tanned clerk.

"Thank you for your patience, Mr. Giovannetti, and welcome to the Royal Hawaiian! We have you booked in a beautiful suite in the historic wing. We hope you'll make special memories with your lady," he winked at Charlotte.

"No, we're not staying together. There's a room booked under Charlotte McPherson." She pulled out her ID and showed it to the clerk.

"Um…We don't have a separate room for you. We have you booked with Mr. Giovannetti. The reservation was made two weeks ago and reserved with a credit card from a Mr. Melvin Brown."

Convinced that he intentionally booked them in the same room to cause problems, Charlotte clenched her fist in anger. Marco laughed and said, "But she doesn't want to stay with me, I tried before. Just give her a different room."

"Um…I wish I could Mr. Giovannetti, but we're completely sold out. The only other option available is the Queen Ka'ahumanu suite. It has two separate bedrooms and one living area. It's very nice."

"Okay, let's do that," Marco said. "I'm ready for a swim in the ocean."

The suite was fabulously spacious, with waterfront views and elegantly decorated with Asian furnishings. There were plenty of areas to lounge around, a wet bar, three bathrooms, and of course, two bedrooms.

"Aloha!" Marco yelled as they entered the space. "Viva Angelino's Honolulu! Look at this place! Let's throw a party here!"

The suite impressed Charlotte, but she was uncomfortable staying there with Marco. Without physical boundaries between their rooms, she worried he'd treat her like a servant. She also worried co-workers at Angelino's would find out they'd shared a suite, giving gossipmongers a field day.

Marco ran off to the beach while Charlotte stayed in the room to catch up on work and prep for their dinner with potential franchisees. Her phone chimed with a new text, stopping her in her tracks. *Hi Charlotte, wrapped up my project in Vancouver, back in LA. Would you like to check out the Oscars tomorrow? Let me know and I'll get your plane tix. Wyatt*

After reading the text three times and realizing that Wyatt was asking her to be his date for the Academy Awards, Charlotte burst into tears. It would've been a dream come true if she weren't stuck in Hawaii with Marco. She composed several different responses before finally settling on one. *Hi Wyatt! I'd LOVE to go with you, but I'm in Hawaii for Angelino's. I can't leave until day after tomorrow. I wish I would've known. I'm so sorry to miss it! Thank you so much for inviting me!*

There was a fifteen-minute pause before he answered. *It's ok. You're always busy.*

She texted Sofia who told her to join Wyatt on the most important night in his industry. He wasn't nominated for an award, but it would still be an experience of a lifetime. Anxiety overwhelmed Charlotte. There was no way to escape Marco and their Hawaii meetings. She was stuck and devastated.

Charlotte replied. *I'm never too busy for you! If I had known a few days ago, I could've gotten out of this work trip. But we just arrived in Hawaii. I'm so sorry...I hope we can see each other soon?*

Wyatt didn't answer.

Dinner with a local Hawaiian businessman and two of his partners from China took place at Roy's Waikiki, a popular contemporary restaurant with local fusion cuisine. Everyone except Charlotte had a great time. Marco was the happiest he'd been in months. He befriended a hostess who promised to check out his suite later. Under normal circumstances, Charlotte would've enjoyed sipping Mai Tai cocktails with a group of men. But her mind was elsewhere. Incredulous she was missing the Oscars with Wyatt for her job at Angelino's, she pondered the sacrifices she made and bitterly remembered their refusal to pay her six figures.

"Charlotte, he's asking about the famous rapper who got engaged at Angelino's. What's his name again?" Marco interrupted her thoughts.

She kicked into PR mode. "We've actually had countless engagements at Angelino's over the years. A man recently reserved a specific table at Angelino's Park Avenue because it was the same spot where he had his first date with the woman he was about to propose to. She was clueless when the hostess sat them there, but he'd cued the waiter to bring Champagne and roses right after they placed their order. He popped the question and she said 'yes'! It was so sweet!" Charlotte smiled at the memory.

"Yeah, yeah but get back to the rapper and the reality star!" Marco turned to the men at the table and continued, "This girl keeps her head in the clouds." They chuckled and returned their attention to her. Forced to listen to Marco's belittling remarks instead of attending the Academy Awards with Wyatt, Charlotte was tempted to drown herself in her drink.

That night, she tossed restlessly, and when she was finally falling asleep, she heard Marco and the hostess enter the suite. He put on music, launched into a loud monologue about himself, and then they had sex. Charlotte buried her head in her pillow to block out the moans.

* * *

The sunrise brought new hope. Charlotte strolled along the beach in the morning to inhale fresh air and seek a new outlook on things. She sat on the sand and watched the aqua waves rise up, teasing her toes before retreating backward into the ocean. Her mind drifted as she soul searched to try to understand why she was still single. Although grateful for her blessings, she deeply believed humans weren't designed to be alone; everyone needed a companion on life's journey. Adam and Eve, Will and Kate, Bonnie and Clyde—the world revolves around partners. She heeded her grandmother's advice and thought about the lessons she'd learned after each failed relationship. *Eric taught me not to rush into things, Pascal showed me that I can't change a man, and Ray made me realize that amazing sex isn't a strong enough bond when I have nothing in common with the guy. Jack had potential before I blew it, but I care so much more about Wyatt anyway...*

Charlotte reminisced about her late-night milkshake with Wyatt ten years earlier. She acknowledged their undeniable chemistry and realized they needed more time together. Unsure of how to accomplish more personal interactions due to his last-minute planning and her demanding work travels, she remembered their adventures in Mumbai, the way he'd held her on Christmas Eve, and how after their carriage ride, she'd longed to comfort him.

At the end of scouting locations throughout the day, primarily at the upscale Ala Moana Center and the historic themed King's Village Shopping Center, the Angelino's group dined at Tommy Bahama Bar and Grill. Charlotte tucked away her phone to avoid the constant Oscars updates on her newsfeed and wanted to bury her head in the sand when Marco suggested they host an Oscar's screening party in their suite with "all the girls." She tried to talk him out of it, using the time difference as an excuse, but he figured out a way to make it work with a tape delay. She was ultimately stuck watching it with him and his groupies.

By 2 a.m., the party calmed down and Charlotte said goodnight to Marco and the three remaining floozies while they embarked on a game of strip poker. She dozed off into a deep slumber until she was awakened by screaming and pounding on her locked door. She jumped up and flung it open to find Marco holding a woman's dress around his hand and blood dripping down his forearm.

"My God! What happened?" Charlotte was shocked.

"The fucking Champagne bottle! I sliced my hand when I sabered it!" Marco was hysterical.

Charlotte's heart raced, "Okay, keep putting pressure on your hand." She ran for her phone and called 911 and then grabbed the hotel phone to call the front desk.

The hotel operator answered first. "Good morning, Mrs. Giovannetti. How may I assist you?"

"We have an emergency, my boss cut his hand open. There's a lot of blood, please send someone quick! I can't get through to 911!" Charlotte was panicking.

She put pressure on Marco's hand as his blood soiled her nightgown. Out of the corner of her eye, she noticed two naked girls passed out on the couch and another in her bra and panties, perched on a chair, wide-eyed and smoking a cigarette. Within a few moments, a hotel worker arrived with a first aid kit and wrapped Marco's hand with gauze. Then three paramedics burst through the door with a stretcher. They quickly surveyed the naked girls in the room and gave Charlotte a puzzled look while Marco screamed deliriously, "My hand! My hand! My God! My hand!"

Two paramedics helped him onto a stretcher, while the other turned to Charlotte. "Ma'am, we need to know if your husband took any drugs. We have Narcan if he needs it. We have to get him stabilized."

"I don't think he took anything. He's not into drugs, he's probably just drunk. I was asleep when it happened. Maybe she knows what's going on." Charlotte motioned to the smoker.

The paramedic turned to the girl. "Miss, we need your help. She doesn't know what her husband took, did you see him do any drugs?"

"He's married?" She turned to Charlotte. "He told me that you're just a bitch who works for him."

Charlotte glared at Marco on the stretcher with an oxygen mask. "A 'bitch?' That's how you describe me? You can deal with your damn hand yourself!"

"No!" Marco's eyes widened as he screamed, "Don't leave me! I'm sorry, I didn't mean it! Please, come with me!" His shouting woke the two girls on the couch. One of them noticed the blood-stained dress Marco had used to bandage his hand. As she covered herself with a pillow and inquired about her clothes, two hotel security guards walked in, looking perplexed by the scene.

"Which one of you is Mrs. Giovannetti?" a guard asked.

"Not me!" Charlotte answered. "Sorry to run, but we're going to the hospital." Off they went.

Eleven hours later, Charlotte sat dazed at the airport. Completely shell-shocked, she fantasized about shooting Marco if she heard him tell the story to one more person. He called all his friends and family and enthusiastically described how he cut himself on a Champagne bottle when he "impressed the hot girls" by using a decorative sword to saber the cork off the top, "like they do in the movies." For him, it was a badge of honor. He made himself look like a big stud, never mentioning Charlotte's heroics, triaging his hand and calling for urgent medical attention. When they had returned to the hotel, he needed her to help him button his shirt, tie his shoes, and carry his bags. In the car, she had to buckle his seatbelt, twist open the water bottle cap, and dig around his tote to find his phone charger—he required her to do everything for him that he couldn't do with just one hand.

It was going to be a long journey back to New York, and because of the medical emergency, Marco secured Charlotte an upgrade to business class to sit next to him and care for him during the entire ten-hour flight home. She fastened his seat belt, cut his food, and read aloud the titles of the entire list of airplane movies to him (twice) before he chose one to watch. When he finally fell asleep, she glared at him and stopped herself from smacking him only because she feared he'd wake up with more demands. Utterly sleep-deprived, Charlotte stared out the window and reflected on the hours they'd spent in the hospital, the bloodstained nightgown she'd trashed after a sympathetic nurse gave her scrubs to wear, and the screams from Marco as they put thirty-two stitches in his hand. She looked absently at the clouds, expressionless, too tired to cry.

Suddenly, she burst into laughter—crazy uncontrollable giggles that made her entire body shake. She reflected back to when they'd rushed out of the hotel to make the flight and Marco told her to check out for them with his corporate credit card while he was on the phone. Charlotte's eyes nearly popped out of her head when she saw the bill. They hadn't realized that their Queen Ka'ahumanu Suite was $9,500 a night, plus taxes and incidentals, and she decided to keep the discovery quiet to avoid another outburst from Marco. Flying somewhere over the Midwest, she remembered the outrageous bill and imagined Melvin's enraged reaction when he'd receive the $24,739 charge for their two-night stay in Hawaii. Hysterical tears of glee streamed down her face as she envisioned smugly gifting him a framed picture of the Hawaiian beach.

Chapter 29

NEW YORK CITY

Taking advantage of her day off after the Hawaii trip, Charlotte slept late and answered emails from bed. Sofia was dying to hear the juicy details about Marco's accident, and she promised to meet for dinner that night at their "secret" Lebanese restaurant, ilili, a place where they could dine without the prying eyes of coworkers.

Charlotte and Sofia laughed hysterically over the drama in Hawaii and they cracked up at the thought of Melvin's reaction when he'd received the hotel bill. They ate an incredible meal and savored every bite of the warak enab (stuffed grape leaves) before calling it a night.

Wyatt crept back into Charlotte's thoughts during the taxi ride home, but she brushed them aside, with no idea when she'd hear from him again. She unpacked and finished off a bottle of wine from Marco's family vineyard. As she settled into bed, she realized it was only 10 p.m., but she was tipsy and tired. As she was about to drift into dreamland, she noticed a flashing light signifying a new text from Sofia. *Important. Call me.*

Sofia answered on the first ring. "I'm with Jason so I can't talk long."

"Of course. What's going on?" Charlotte inquired.

"Well," Sofia took a deep breath. "I was going through Jason's Facebook and it turns out he's friends with Jorge."

"Gross. How do they know each other?"

"It's such a small world. Jorge was Jason's first boss after college. He even went to his wedding," Sofia said apologetically.

"That's so weird. Let's talk about it tomorrow—"

"Wait, there's something else," Sofia hesitated. "Maybe I should tell you in person."

"Just tell me. I'm totally over Jorge, don't worry." Charlotte was frustrated.

"Okay, here goes. Tracy's been secretly dating Jorge. He left his wife and now they're engaged." Sofia dropped the bomb.

Charlotte jumped out of bed, stumbling into the nightstand. "What? There's NO way! It's impossible!" She winced and rubbed her knee.

"I'm so sorry. I was completely shocked myself. Are you okay?"

"No, I'm not okay," Charlotte's voice cracked. "This can't be right. How does Jason know?"

Sofia took another deep breath. "When we started dating, he mentioned that his old boss moved to Atlanta and eventually left his wife for some evil home-wrecker in New York. Jason suspected the girl of using him to finance her business. I heard the saga, but never thought he was talking about Jorge and Tracy. I mean, what are the odds?"

"But how can you be sure?" Charlotte paced around her studio, slightly limping from her injured knee.

"Char, it's all over Jorge's Facebook. He started posting pictures with her this week, but several were taken a long time ago. Apparently, they made the rounds at Art Basel and there's some from Jamaica over the summer and they spent New Year's in St. Barth's. I can send you screenshots. She's tagged in his photos. Didn't you see them?"

"No. I hate *Fake*-book. I hardly ever look at it." Charlotte grabbed her laptop. "I'm checking now…. Wait, I can't even find Tracy…. Oh. My. God. She blocked me."

It was confirmed. Guilty as charged. Everything suddenly made sense: Tracy's defense of Jorge last spring, her disappearing act over the summer, her distancing herself from Charlotte and Sofia, her flakiness during Art Basel, and the New Year's trip cancelation. Charlotte dropped the phone. *Wow. After a ten-year friendship, this is what she stooped to. Maybe she was banging Jorge the entire time I was with him!*

Charlotte leaped up and grabbed a picture of the two of them from the surprise 30th birthday party Tracy had organized for her. She studied the "Best Friends Forever" engraving along the bottom of the silver frame and then hurled it against the wall as hard as she could. The glass cover smashed, sending pieces across the floor. She staggered into the bathroom sobbing uncontrollably, pounding her fists into the wall. Completely distraught, she yanked open the medicine cabinet, searching for something to calm her nerves, and found her last Xanax. She stared at it for a moment. Suddenly, an epiphany washed over her hysteria, giving her the startling revelation that a pill couldn't solve her problems. It never did. She flushed the drug down the toilet and chucked the empty bottle into the trash.

After a long hot shower, Charlotte wrapped herself in a robe and put on flip flops to avoid stepping on glass. She swept up the shards near the wall, dropped her robe on the floor, and crawled into bed naked. She left the lights on and watched the room sway back and forth. Eventually, she picked up her phone and saw missed calls and worried texts from Sofia. She wrote her back. *Thank you for your friendship. Talk tomorrow*

Then, she thought of the most honest, gentle, and humble man she ever met. She impulsively sent him a text. *Hi Wyatt, something bad happened with two people I once trusted. It made me think about how much I care for you and wish we could spend more time together. Maybe even date exclusively. The truth is… I fell for you during our first milkshake, but I never knew how to tell you. I love you.*

Charlotte woke up eight hours later in a fog. She checked her phone and read with horror the late-night text she'd sent to Wyatt. She wasn't sure what was worse, the possibility of him suspecting that she messaged him while intoxicated or the fact that she'd exposed raw emotions likely to push him away. She texted Sofia to ask her to talk in person. Sofia's response sent her into a tailspin. *Absolutely! After the staff meeting, see you in twenty minutes. xo*

The staff meeting! Charlotte jumped out of bed, threw on a black sweater dress, pulled her hair back into a ponytail, and popped a piece of gum into her mouth. Forgetting to lock the door, she bolted out of her apartment, down the hall, and into the street to hail a cab.

Chapter 30

ANGELINO'S WINTER STAFF MEETING

W hile plastering on lipstick during the bumpy taxi ride, Charlotte scrambled to answer emails and texts on her phone. Every time her phone buzzed, she prayed it was a response from Wyatt. Instead, it was work messages.

Late to the staff meeting for the first time in her career, she burst through the door and heaved out a sigh of relief when she saw that Lorenzo and Marco were absent from the head table. The meeting never started without them and Charlotte assumed she'd get away with being fifteen minutes tardy.

Jack gave her an icy scowl. "Thanks for finally joining us."

"I'm so sorry, you wouldn't believe the traffic! Must've been an accident or something," she pathetically fibbed.

Jack rose to speak. "I want everyone's attention. Lorenzo and Marco won't be joining us today, so we'll go ahead and start now that Charlotte's here." The staff exchanged confused glances; something strange was happening. Jessica looked just as perplexed as Charlotte felt. Sofia caught her eye and shrugged to show that she didn't know what was going on either.

"Some of you know that I'm the majority shareholder of Angelino's Restaurant Group and after over twenty years, I've decided to sell my shares to a fund that manages several successful restaurant chains." Jack paused as gasps and murmurs of panic spread across the room. "They'll set the rules and improve things that aren't working. But I want to assure you that your jobs are safe. Angelino's will remain open and operating at full capacity. For those of you up here on the panel, there'll be changes that we'll discuss in private." He looked at Charlotte, Jessica, and Melvin who sat in stunned silence. Jack continued, "As for Lorenzo and Marco, their role is to be determined. They still have a sizable share of Angelino's and they're the faces of the brand, so we expect them to stay on board. They chose not to be at the meeting today while they devise a strategy to work together."

Jack stopped and looked around the room, almost choking up. "You're all truly unique individuals and I've always appreciated your diligence and dedication. I assure you that I worked behind the scenes to create a productive environment at Angelino's to allow you to enjoy your jobs. When I was going through hard times, it was consoling to know that I could walk into any Angelino's and encounter friendliness with my meal. Thank you."

Ray, of all people, stood up and clapped. Soon the entire staff was on their feet, applauding and cheering for Jack. His face flushed with embarrassment as he motioned everyone to sit down. "Thank you. That's not necessary, but I do appreciate it. You're all dismissed. Go and make your customers happy. That's how we do it at Angelino's!"

Several employees rushed to Jack and told him that they'd miss working for him. Meanwhile, Charlotte and her two corporate co-workers remained frozen in their seats. After the others filed out, Jack lowered his voice and addressed the executive panel. "I'm sorry you guys had to find out this way. Lorenzo and Marco are unhappy and looking into legal options. I have the right to sell and it's time for me to do that. The group taking over my shares already has a central accounting division, public relations team, and a human resources department, and they might streamline your positions." Charlotte and Jessica tried to catch their breaths while Melvin nearly choked. "I have to run to an appointment, but I'll text you each individually with a time to meet. Charlotte, keep this quiet. The new parent company will publish an official press release next week when more details are sorted out."

The group sat speechless after he departed. Charlotte was incensed that a different company, one she'd never heard of, would release a statement on behalf of Angelino's without consulting her. She finally pulled out her phone that had been vibrating through-out the meeting. Her eyes expanded as she frantically read through messages and blurted out, "Oh my God!" Her startled colleagues turned to look at her. "Angelino's Miami burned down!"

Chapter 31

NEW YORK CITY

Sara answered on the first ring. "I warned you about the mural! You guys dug your own grave!"

"But Sara, I thought we came up with a good plan to rectify all that. Was it arson? What started the fire? Was anyone hurt?" Charlotte trembled.

"No, everyone's okay. But apparently a stove was *accidentally* left on overnight and it caused a gas line to ignite a fire. I guess your plan was too late. It wasn't a good idea to cross Skippy and disrespect Cuban Carlos 2K." Sara sounded vindicated that the place burned down.

"Listen, Sara, I'm truly sorry about the mural. We came up with a good solution but now the building is gone and so is the chance to recreate the memorial to Carlos."

Charlotte hung up and stomped toward the office to track down her bosses and draft a press release about the fire. But her calls to Lorenzo and Marco went unanswered. She anchored down in her cubicle and wondered if she'd lose her job and if Jack would have the decency to help her.

The office was thick with tension as Jessica typed on her computer incessantly (Charlotte guessed she was sending follow-up emails to companies she covertly interviewed with in the past), while Melvin huddled in his cubicle, whispering into the phone, presumably plotting his next move or perhaps revealing where the bodies were hidden to an accomplice on the other line. Meanwhile, assistants silently shuffled papers, most likely attempting to look useful for fear that their roles risked elimination by the new owners.

Charlotte activated her company computer and was greeted by a screensaver picture of Starlet. In the photograph, the adorable pup slept on a pillow at Wyatt's house. She zoned out while staring at it, wishing she were there getting a desperately needed hug from Wyatt. She wondered what advice he'd give her if they spoke, which they might not ever do again, thanks to her stupid text.

Her mind flashed back to the warm December night on the street in front of her childhood home in California. It was there that Wyatt told her exactly what he thought she should do—start her own PR firm. She could work for a cause and help others. She had the skills, the contacts, and the passion to strategically utilize her PR experience for a greater good. It was just a matter of figuring out the best path to take. She spent the next few hours web surfing and discovered encouraging resources like the Small Business Development Center created to help female entrepreneurs. With the right planning, she could take on a few corporate clients and also do pro bono work for nonprofits like a drunk driving prevention group, in honor of her late father. She'd find a way to incorporate charities with paying accounts. With ideas brewing, she researched until the end of the day, not noticing that she was the last person remaining in the office until all the other lights went out.

She sat in her chair and looked around the quiet room, reflecting on the good times and bad times with a company that she devoted her prime years to. She was proud of what she'd accomplished but ashamed that she allowed them to underpay her. Memories of her boss's shenanigans, Melvin's abuse, endless travels, and the missed opportunity to go to the Oscars with Wyatt during the Hawaii melee flooded her mind. Jack was jumping ship and he didn't even have the decency to warn her in advance. He could've advocated for her over the years and increased her salary, but it wasn't a priority for him. He made insinuations in France that he'd help her with her career, but it was no coincidence that his concern for her diminished once he hooked up with the flight attendant. She'd never get paid what she deserved, and the new shareholders would most likely dissolve her role to use their PR team. It was time to say goodbye to Angelino's.

With mixed emotions she typed and printed a letter:

Dear Jack, Marco, Lorenzo and Jessica,

I hereby resign my position as Public Relations Director of Angelino's Restaurant Group. It has been an honor to work as an integral part of the team over the last ten years as we have expanded throughout the world. I wish you and the company all the best.

Sincerely,
Charlotte McPherson

She placed the letter on Jessica's desk and stared at it, contemplating if she should go through with the resignation. As she rotated her neck to get the kinks out, the screensaver on Melvin's computer monitor caught her eye. It was a staff photo from the Christmas party. With a sense of nostalgia, she moved toward his cubicle for a better look. Sofia radiated beauty in a festive red dress, her arm happily draped around Jessica's shoulders. There was Marco, Jack, Lorenzo, and a few hostesses who'd jumped into the shot. Melvin's arms were folded across his chest, but he displayed a grin. Ray had photobombed the pic with a goofy expression. And there she was… Charlotte did a double take and inched closer to the screen. Melvin had photoshopped a pig's nose over her face.

There was her answer.

She scribbled on a Post-it note and slapped it onto his chair: *Hey Mel, I borrowed your stapler! xo Char*

She snatched his beloved stapler, shoved it in the furthest corner of her bottom desk drawer, and covered it with old magazines. Then, she downloaded important files onto a USB flash drive, grabbed her coat and personal belongings, and stormed out. Free at last! The weight of the world was lifted from her shoulders as she inhaled icy air, filling her lungs with anticipation of a positive change. She confidently strode down the street with her arm raised to hail a cab.

By the time she settled into a taxi, Charlotte felt like a confident woman instead of a naïve tool exploited by a restaurant group. She caught her reflection in the rearview mirror and realized that even her appearance had matured since she began her tenure at Angelino's. Her face exuded knowledge and experience. She took pride in her strong countenance.

Determined to think with her brain instead of her heart, she walked down the long hallway to her apartment, where the door remained unlocked from her morning mad dash. She'd stopped worrying about her love life and pondered the ramifications of resigning from Angelino's. Sofia would be heartbroken and the thought of not seeing particular colleagues saddened her. But she could visit anytime and leave generous tips with the money she'd make from her new endeavor. It was a season for change.

She tossed her coat aside and sat on her bed to take off her boots. The phone in her purse rang; she pulled it out to discover Wyatt's name across the screen. It took a moment to register because he usually texted.

Shocked and nervous, Charlotte heard her voice crack when she answered, "Hello?"

"Hi, it's me."

"Hi... How are you?" Charlotte trembled as she spoke.

"Well, I got your text...and I think we should talk about it over a milkshake." His voice sounded irresistible.

She laughed timidly. "Okay...and when should we do that?"

"How about right now at Momofuku Milk Bar on 56th? They close in an hour."

"Perfect. It's near my apartment. Be there soon!" Charlotte's heart pounded.

A half an hour later, she sat across from Wyatt stirring a crunchy vanilla cereal shake with a spoon while he slurped his chocolate malt cake shake through a wide straw. Over ten years had passed since their first milkshake date. This time, Wyatt reached across the table and took her hand in his as butterflies fluttered in her stomach.

She spoke with sheer honestly. "I was surprised to get your call because you never responded to my text."

"Well, I didn't see it while I was working. And then I wasn't sure how to answer." Wyatt thought for a second. "I liked you from the moment I met you. The most beautiful creature I've ever discovered shivering in the rain on Hollywood Boulevard at midnight."

Charlotte giggled, smitten by his sense of humor.

He continued, "But you never seemed interested. You were always dating someone or traveling. One time I invited you to my Saint Patrick's Day party with the intention of admitting my feelings—until you showed up with another guy."

"But I didn't think you liked me!" Taken aback, she tried to choose her words carefully. "I mean, I've done some self-reflection lately and I think maybe I'm always in a hurry while you move at a thoughtful pace…" Charlotte was pensive. "Maybe if I was more patient and honest about my feelings for you, our relationship would've been different."

"If I was a drinker, I'd say that you've aged like fine wine. You're even better than when we met." Wyatt smiled.

Charlotte lit up. "But you are a drinker—a milkshake drinker!" She moved from across the table to sit next to him and stare deep into his soulful blue eyes.

"You know, this milkshake thing is just a metaphor," he said as he studied her face carefully, putting his arm around her.

She was puzzled. "A metaphor for what?"

"A metaphor for mixing things up. It's all about the senses, how something looks, feels, and tastes. Everything is layered and then blended together to make the perfect combination *at the right time*."

A year ago, she'd find his sentiments nonsensical. However, after everything she'd endured during the last four seasons, his statement resonated. She was courageously embarking on a new career path and muting her pregnancy obsession with newfound faith that everything would fall into place *at the right time*.

She pondered his comments and realized that some things were simply beyond her control. You can't rush love. There was no way to plan or predict when the right guy would wake up and finally reciprocate affection, but Charlotte had realized that you can be honest with yourself and communicate your feelings to your beloved. Sometimes, no matter how hard you look, the one you're meant to be with is right in front of you.

Wyatt leaned in and gave her a light peck on the lips followed by a deep, passionate kiss. His mouth was cold and tasted like chocolate while hers had hints of vanilla. The more they kissed, the more they melded the flavors together to become one delicious blend. Charlotte buried her head against his chest as they embraced, realizing that they finally found a home in each other.

It was just after midnight when they left Momofuku Milk Bar. Wyatt held the door open while Charlotte stepped into the first snowfall of spring as he reached for her hand and pulled her close for another kiss. Although she didn't accomplish her original goals during the past year, being in Wyatt's arms felt better than anything she'd ever planned. With a twinkle in her eye and new inner warmth, Charlotte basked in the moment, exhilarated by long overdue love and happiness destined to prevail during the next four seasons.

END

Acknowledgments

My heartfelt gratitude to Paul Allen for broadening my perspective on books through countless discussions about literature and memorable bookstore visits. Always a huge source of inspiration, Paul encouraged me to write fiction, and naturally, he was the first person I told when I determined the theme of this novel. I miss him beyond comprehension.

Deepest appreciation and thanks to my mom for her endless patience and support.

Many friends brighten my life, including the fabulous women who contributed their suggestions throughout this process: Alexa Curtis, Rachel Anise, Polina Margasova, Elizabeth Salusbury, Hallie Hart, Mary Piliaris, Alba DeMichael, Jenn Matson, Amanda Morck, Katja Eiblmayr, and Christina Simon—a true pragmatist who is stuck with me.

I'm also indebted to Robert Simon, Joe Singleton, Rene-Pierre Azria, Ann Tanenbaum, Jasmin Rosemberg, Ian McMahon, and Richard Caleel for sharing their expertise and advice.

Thank you to Anthony Ziccardi for thinking outside the box, Madeline Sturgeon, Devon Brown, Allie Woodlee, and the rest of the team at Post Hill Press.

Cheers to all the restaurateurs, franchisors, franchisees, partners, chefs, managers, bartenders, servers, hostesses, hosts, cooks, baristas, bussers, food runners, porters, and diners I've encountered over the years. It takes a village to prepare and serve a restaurant meal. *Buon appetito!*

About the Author

Caroline McBride is the Director of Public Relations for Serafina Restaurant Group. She has spent the past decade marketing, branding, and launching restaurants around the world, as well as consulting for private clients.

McBride earned her B.A. in Political Science at Loyola Marymount University and holds an M.A. in International Relations from the Universiteit van Amsterdam where she studied as a Rotary International Ambassadorial Scholar.

When she's not on the road reading, writing, and trying new restaurants, McBride divides her time between Los Angeles and New York City.

You can visit her online at www.carolinemcbride.com